D1522296

IꝏꞯeId®

ISBN 1-59632-518-6
ISBN 13: 978-1-59632-518-0
THE BITE BEFORE CHRISTMAS
Copyright © 2007 by Loose Id, LLC
Cover Art by April Martinez

Publisher acknowledges the authors and copyright holders of the individual works, as follows:
SIN AND SALVATION
Copyright © December 2006 by Laura Baumbach
A VAMPIRE FOR CHRISTMAS
Copyright © December 2006 by Sedonia Guillone
THE MASTER'S GIFT
Copyright © December 2006 by Kit Tunstall

Printed in the U.S.A. by
Lightning Source, Inc.
1246 Heil Quaker Blvd
La Vergne TN 37086
www.lightningsource.com

Contents

SIN AND SALVATION

Laura Baumbach

The snow fell in huge flakes, each light bit of fluff looking rough as sand but touching his face as if carried on a baby's breath. Ian Flynn couldn't remember seeing snowflakes this big in over three hundred years. During that time, he'd become something of a connoisseur of snowflakes. He favored cold climates that reminded him of his birthplace in northern England, ensuring there would be snow in the winter, especially for Christmas.

If he had to spend the holiday alone -- and he had for over two hundred years despite having a steadfast, beloved lover for all those decades -- he was determined to have the comfort of a white Christmas. This year was no different; it would be a lonely, if white, Christmas.

Ian knew all he had to do was call to Trevor through the strong bond they shared as master and child, lover to lover, friend to friend, and Trevor would come to him, compelled and unable to resist.

But Ian never pulled Trevor away for trivial reasons, especially from Trevor's single-minded, yearly, seasonal mission of hunting down the murderous riffraff and gang members that still haunted the same London streets where Trevor himself had met the end to his own mortal life so long ago. Christmas Eve had a different meaning to Ian and Trevor than to most people.

Trevor celebrated by taking revenge on the same type of men who had murdered him, and Ian spent the season contemplating his greatest sin. Even vampires had ghosts that haunted them and demons that needed excision. Dirty blood soothed Trevor's pain; snowflakes eased Ian's.

"Are you coming in soon, sir? It's a bit chilly and I have almost completed dressing the shrub in the main living room. The lights need your approval before the baubles are hung."

The smooth, cultured tones cut through the cold night air in a neat, precise, clipped voice, but Ian could hear the slight chatter of his manservant's teeth. Sighing, Ian blinked the remaining flakes off his eyelashes.

He glanced over his shoulder at the waiting man and, not for the first time, marveled at Stuart Graves's capacity for understatement. The temperature had been hovering slightly above two degrees for the last week, the "shrub" was a twelve-foot blue spruce with an eight-foot span at the bottom, and the "baubles" were hand-blown, one-of-a-kind antique glass ornaments. Nodding, Ian gave Stuart an exasperated smile.

"I'm sure you've done an outstanding job, like every year, Stuart. Nobody has the eye for color and details that you do."

Ian turned back to watch the flakes fall from the sky, each frozen droplet riding the sharp gusts of frigid air. He tried to lose himself in the warm memories of long ago holidays and happier times. Things would be better in a few days. They always were.

When his hearing told him Stuart hadn't moved, Ian softly added, "Go on back inside before you freeze. I'll follow you in a second. I just wanted to watch it snow for a bit."

Stepping to the vampire's side, Stuart lowered his voice. Clearly uncomfortable, he suggested, "If you're concerned…for his safety, maybe…you should call him home." Hesitant, Stuart glanced up at Ian and caught his gaze. "Just this once."

After a moment, Ian lowered his gaze, then stared up into the falling snow. He didn't need to intimidate Stuart. The man had been his servant and confidant for over twenty years. Ian knew he had lost any real fear of him long ago.

He sighed and studied the cloud-cloaked, inky night sky. He wished he could see the stars. His mother had always told him as a boy that the stars were actually prayers on their way up to heaven and God's ear. He'd believed that if he prayed hard enough and was a good son, his prayers would become stars, too. But that was all in the past. Ian was pretty sure that heaven didn't answer the prayers of demon spawn, even if a little part of him still believed in his mother's tales.

He wondered if it was snowing for Trevor right now. The dirty back streets of London were far away from his cozy, New York City penthouse.

"He can take care of himself."

Stuart didn't move. His voice stayed low, but grew firmer, concern and conviction in each word. "He can't continue to haunt the same alleyway Christmas Eve after Christmas Eve, year after year without running the very probable risk of capture. Not in these modern times, sir."

"He'll be all right." Ian swallowed past the lump in his throat, almost smiling at the thought he could still feel terror after all these years of existence as an undead creature of the night. He could feel terror, and pain and love and concern, too. But mostly tonight, like every other Christmas Eve, he felt guilt and acceptance. "He's very good at this."

"He's being hunted as a serial killer." Surprised by the ring of desperation, Ian turned to study the man's face as Stuart tersely added, "They call him the 'Yuletide Terror.' A madman. They'll hunt him down like one, too."

Ian didn't outwardly flinch, but he felt his eyes narrow and his vision grow yellow-tinged with the first signs of his vampire nature coming forward.

Stuart paid the warning sign no heed. "They almost captured him last year." He stepped one pace closer. Ian let him, taking comfort from the man's concern, if not his words. "This year the London police are sure to be even more prepared."

"I can't interfere." Last year's brush with the police frightened Ian just as much as it did Stuart, but he refused to let it show. He did appreciate Stuart's concern. Not many humans grew to care about vampires the way Stuart cared about Ian and his mate. He sighed and stared off into the night, resigned and unhappy. "I don't have the right."

Fastidiously dusting the fine layer of snow off Ian's broad, firmly-squared shoulders, Stuart let his hand linger a moment on the vampire's arm and gently said, "He doesn't blame you."

Spine curving under the weight of the centuries-long guilt he carried over what he considered to be his greatest sin, Ian slumped under Stuart's comforting touch, gold-tinged eyes staring unseeingly up into the silent heavens and whispered, "*I* blame me."

His voice sounded old and raw, reflecting all the years his age had gathered in the time since his turning. It *was* old and raw, but also strong and primal, leaving no room for argument. He knew Stuart would heed it and as if on cue, the man stepped back, sighing.

"I'll tend to the fire. It will have faded by now." Stuart turned and walked back to the balcony doors, but paused in the open doorway, concern etched into his aging, aristocratic face and dark, caring gaze. "I'll have a goblet of something warm waiting for you when you come in." He shivered, rubbing at his upper arms. "Please, don't stay out here too long." His tone lightened a touch and he briskly added, "The blood will congeal and you'll have to eat it with a spoon. And I'm not staying up to watch that."

With a huffed, halfhearted chuckle, Ian dropped his chin to his chest, nodded, and then turned to face the man.

"I wouldn't want to put you through that, Stuart. I'll be in soon. I'm going to count the stars for a while." He turned back to look up at the sky, snowflakes collecting on his dark lashes and hair, blinding him. He glanced one final time over his shoulder at the waiting man. "Thank you, Stuart." Ian stared at a small snowdrift gathering in one corner of the penthouse patio, suddenly unable to meet Stuart's imploring gaze. "For everything."

Silence was his only answer for a second longer than he thought was reassuring, but then a firm but sad "Yes, sir" banished his fears. Stuart did understand. That was important to Ian. Stuart was the second most important person in his life, a trusted servant, a father figure and a confidante.

The door shut softly behind him and Ian knew Stuart had retreated into the warmth of the apartment. Within moments, the mellow, moody sound of Bing Crosby's "White Christmas" drifted out to him. The phrase "I'll be home for Christmas" reached his ears, and he had to give an ironic chuckle at Stuart's pointed lack of subtlety in songs. Beneath his formal manners and acid-tipped tongue, the man cared very much about him and Trevor. The fact that he would be so brash proved it.

Next to Trevor, Stuart was the only other person Ian had allowed himself to have feeling for. He dreaded the moment when the man would grow infirm with age and die, leaving Ian to face the world and future Christmas Eves on his own again. Loss was the hardest part of being immortal. If he hadn't had Trevor by his side all these years, he would have walked into the sun long ago. Trevor was his salvation.

The desire to have Trevor at his side was nearly overwhelming. Something powerful and compelling told him to search the black, clouded skies, and with a childish sense of hope and anticipation he did, memories of his first meetings with Trevor piling like the snowflakes in the corner of the balcony wall.

* * *

It was three weeks before Christmas and the streets of London were clogged with people, carts, street vendors, and filthy slush. The year would be turning to 1824 with the approaching New Year celebration, but the Christmas season had yet to be played out, and for that Ian Flynn was immeasurably happy.

Despite having been a vampire for over two hundred years, he still took pleasure in the sounds and smells of the season. Even the cold was welcomed, its icy hands bringing a tingle to his sensitive skin and a touch of color to his perpetually pale cheeks.

Even as a creature of the night, his olive skin and dark good looks still hid the outward signs of his demonic affliction from the human world he existed in. Only the slight yellow tinge to his eyes warned of his unearthly nature, but it was only revealed when his need to feed consumed him or his temper outdistanced his practiced hold on his fiery nature.

A sharp gust of December wind battered at Ian's long, heavy cloak and threatened to tear the top hat off his head. He stepped out of the carriage and landed on both feet on the dirty cobblestone lane, the controlled power in his large, square frame evident in every movement. He had been a miller's son, his days spent lifting and hauling sacks of grain and assisting the huge grinding wheel in his father's mill in its grueling job of grinding grain to flour.

Standing six foot three, Ian's shoulders were broad, his back strong and straight, and his legs were thick and long. Brushed back off his handsome face, his brown hair hung past the nape of his neck, its dark mahogany color matching the gold-speckled depths of his keen, mesmerizing eyes. A square jaw and high broad cheekbones completed Ian's solid look and commanding presence. He turned heads, both male and female, wherever he went.

Even the dark of night and the poor torchlight of the gentlemen's parlors and stage halls he frequented couldn't mask his compelling aura. More than one young lass, and lad, had lost more than their virginity to him, but never their life.

In all his decades as one of hell's unnatural children, Ian had never killed while feeding, never taken more than his unsuspecting and usually willing victim could spare, careful to never spawn a child of his own, or bind a thrall to his will. Raised by hardworking, loving parents and being born with a calm, easygoing nature, Ian didn't want a servant *or* a lover who was compelled to stay at his side for reasons outside of true loyalty or love.

To Ian, the curse of the vampire was best unshared past a moment of carnal pleasure and the satisfaction of feeding well from a comely bed partner. Being alone was never a problem for him. He had accepted being lonely as his accursed fate.

Fresh from a heavy sleep induced by a prior evening of fun, frolicking, and feeding, Ian was out to enjoy a night of cultural entertainment and bask in the delights of the theater. He had always enjoyed listening to the tales his mother told to him at night or when the harsh winter storms kept them all barricaded behind their stone walls and thatched roofs.

Once he had found the thrill of the theater, where stories came to life on the bright stage and in the colorful costumes of the players, there was no going back. He attended every theater and playhouse in every town he traveled through. He marveled at the skill and courage of the actors on the stage and their ability to become someone else for an evening, occasionally longing for that same ability to transform him from creature of the night to a fanciful hero in one of the fairy tales acted out when the curtains opened and the lights fell.

Tonight's play was a well-hailed effort by the playwright Richard Brinsley Peake, with an adaptation of Mary Shelley's much-gossiped-about novel *Frankenstein*. It was billed as a romantic drama, but Ian doubted there was anything romantic about it. He was looking forward to seeing if the fictional story of life after death took on a new perspective under the kerosene lamps and costumes. He lived his own version of it every day, giving him sympathy for the monster in the novel. He, too, had been thrust into an unholy afterlife he hadn't asked for nor wanted.

The carriage pulled away and he ascended the steps outside the playhouse, allowing the footman to brush off the sprinkling of snow on his coat as he climbed to the building's entrance. The place was old and only moderately kept up, but the hall was spacious and well lit and the decor bright, neat, and well polished. He handed his hat and cloak off to a young, eager attendant who appeared at his side. He smiled at the young man and flipped a coin into the air, allowing the attendant to catch it and pocket it as he walked away.

"Thank you, sir. It's very good of you, sir." Ian inclined his head toward the boy, and the young man winked and brashly added, "Name's Jules, sir. If you need anything at all, sir. Jules." Jules gave a suggestive smile and then sauntered away to store Ian's things, making sure Ian caught his flirtatious glance.

Ian smiled and kept walking, knowing it had been coin well spent. It assured him good service and no waiting for his cloak at the end of the performance. And if his tastes ran to snacking on lamb later between scenes, he knew he had a willing sheep in hand for the shearing. The young man was crude, but he showed experience and he was obviously willing. Ian supposed Jules found many a wealthy man at the theater who was looking for companionship and willing to pay well for it.

He thought about the feel of a smooth, lithe body under his, and arousal immediately blossomed in his blood. He savored it a moment, tasting it, then shook it off. He was well sated from last evening, and he never took home a partner just for sex. That way led to affection, feelings, longing, and ruin, but then Jules didn't strike him as the type to form emotional commitments that weren't tied to gold coins.

It was just as well. As far as Ian was concerned, beds were no longer for the making of love or sharing of emotions; they were for "eating" in. He'd keep Jules in mind when the play was over.

Caught up in the sudden flow of patrons, Ian let the tide carry him into the hall where he took a seat off to one side. The chair was partially hidden in the shadows of the room, but with a clear view of the stage. His looks and unaccompanied state tended to draw attention in public places. Everyone seemed to have an unattached daughter or niece they wanted to introduce him to. Tonight he simply wanted to watch, not be watched.

Before long, the small orchestra signaled the start of the entertainment and Ian lost himself in the tragedy and farce of Frankenstein's creation. As compelling as the story was for him from a personal viewpoint, the play took on a new attraction when the character of Felix DeLacey walked on stage.

Felix was the son of one of the principal characters, and though not a major part of the production, Ian was instantly taken by the young man playing the role. He was young and beautiful, with luminous blond hair that framed his lean, pale face like a halo, the lamplight glistening through the nearly white strands. He was of average height, slender and lithe, but Ian could see the lines of firm muscle under the tight-fitting breeches and form-fitted vest buttoned over a stark white shirt with billowing sleeves.

When the young man clasped his hands behind his back, the puffy sleeves looked like angel's wings on his back. His voice was throaty and slightly raw, as if his words had been lightly sanded before they were spoken aloud. His diction was crisp, but Ian's vampire hearing detected the undertone of a cockney accent the man tried very hard to hide to lend credence to his role as a gentleman's son. High cheekbones and a tapered, masculine jawline completed the package.

Ian was smitten from the first moment the actor glanced at him and seemed to hold his mesmerized gaze during a pause in the action. Play forgotten, Ian stared at the man through the entire performance, his attraction and need growing through each successive scene. During the first intermission, he signaled an attendant and sent his calling card off to be delivered to the actor, and in the process learned the actor's name was Trevor Sheffield. Entranced, Ian started when the cue caller announced the end of the play.

Walking backstage to the dressing area, Ian was surprised to discover he was nervous about meeting this young man, a mere human a half a foot shorter than he was and easily forty pounds lighter. Yet with all his age, supernatural powers, and strength, he was suddenly nervous as a lad at the thought of being rebuffed by this man. It irritated and thrilled him, making his arousal soar. The air around him nearly crackled with energy. These two feelings, irritation and unbridled desire, Trevor would always instill in him.

He waited by the closed door the attendant had indicated, accepting his cloak and hat from the man moments later. He tipped the man generously and ignored the knowing wink and leering smile the man let slide across his face just before he walked away. Ian inhaled deeply, noticing the man's scent, cataloging it should he have to correct the man's lurid impression for Trevor's sake at a later date and time. Humans always seemed to need to think the worst of their fellow man. Ian supposed it made them feel better about their own lot in life.

As he waited, Jules appeared out of the throng of milling actors, stagehands, and backstage patrons. He rushed headlong at Ian, a smile on his lips and saucy sway to his slim hips that suggested a practiced air of unspoken seduction. Ian had no doubts Jules made his extra income bedding patrons and street cads alike. It was of no matter any more; Jules paled in comparison to Trevor's beauty and grace. Ian had lost interest in anyone else.

He caught Jules's gaze and returned only an unwelcoming, stony stare that made the young man falter in his confident steps. Ten feet away, Jules slowed as Trevor emerged from a curtained-off alcove, traces of the harsh stage makeup still on his neck and cheek. Jules came to an abrupt halt when Trevor stepped between them, locked eyes on Ian, and shyly smiled. Thoughts of Jules faded away, despite that young man's continued, angry presence.

Unable to resist the hesitant twist to Trevor's naturally rose-colored lips, Ian smiled back, feeling the urge to take and claim the man surging through his entire body. He had thought his soul had been destroyed with his turning, but if it had, he knew it had been reborn at this moment. His still heart ached and his stirring groin pulsed with need unlike any he had experienced before. His mouth watered with the scent of him and the thought of this man's taste -- his blood, his seed, even the bead of sweat on his temple -- all called to him. And he had yet to say hello.

"Good evening." Ian walked up to Trevor, towering over him by several inches. His smile widened and he extended his hand to the surprisingly shy man. "Ian Flynn, shameless admirer of your talents."

The young man huffed a nervous sound and flashed Ian a nervous smile, saying, "Evening, sir." Trevor shifted awkwardly from one foot to the other, his uncertain gaze darting between Ian's face and the floor then back again before settling on the vampire's still extended hand. "Oh, sorry, sir, wasn't thinking!" He clasped his hand into Ian's and firmly shook it.

The vampire savored the warmth, barely suppressing the shudder it chased down his spine. Trevor's skin was a combination of rough and soft, his fingertips and lower hand lightly callused, but his palms were soft and smooth. It delighted Ian just to touch it, a sensual caress against his own sensitive flesh. He lingered over the texture before allowing Trevor to reclaim his hand. He noticed the way Trevor immediately rubbed his fingers together, but Ian didn't know if the man was wiping off his touch or trying to re-experience it.

"Why don't you just call me Ian?"

Trevor ran one hand through his blond hair, running the tip of his tongue over his upper lip. "My name's Trevor. Ah, Trevor Sheffield, actor."

"I know that part." They both laughed lightly and Trevor licked at his lip again.

The tongue was pink and wet as it danced over the plump fullness of upper lip. Ian's gaze followed every nervous wiggle and thrust. He wondered what it would feel like dancing over the head of his cock or into his ass. He wanted to taste it and feel it battle against his own before he tamed it and swallowed it whole. He could consume every inch of this man and still need more of him.

The scent of harsh soap and lime invaded his nostrils and he had to push it aside to detect the slightly salty, musky smell of Trevor's body. It reminded him of almonds and chestnuts, slightly bitter and heavy, tempting him.

"So very pleased to make your acquaintance, Trevor." The tang of masculine arousal struck him like a blow as Ian bent nearer to Trevor over the pretext of more intimate conversation, and inhaled, nostrils flaring, cock hard and needy in the confines of his trousers. He shifted his cloak over his arm to hide his response from Trevor's shy glances. He needed to taste his man soon.

"I admired your grace and talent on the stage tonight, though seeing you without the trappings of your profession --" He boldly reached out and wiped a smear of paint from Trevor's blushing cheek with his thumb. "-- enhances my opinion of your attributes, both of the flesh and the mind, even more." He let his touch linger a second longer than publicly acceptable.

Ian let an appreciative smile light his eyes as he studied Trevor's surprised, but pleased, reaction to his compliments.

"I was hoping you'd be free to share a late meal with me." Ian didn't make it a question. He quietly waited, watching desire, uncertainty, excitement, and attraction all battle for dominance on Trevor's expressive face. Ian knew why the man was so well suited for acting. His emotions played freely across his fine-boned face and flowed over his audience, even an audience of one. He could read every thought that crossed Trevor's mind.

Much to Ian's relief, attraction and desire won. Trevor dropped his gaze, pausing before hesitantly confessing, "Don't usually go out this late." A flush of pink bloomed at the top of his high-boned cheeks as he stumbled over an almost whispered explanation. "Got me mum to look after." He licked his upper lip and his voice grew firmer, his own gaze darting longingly over Ian's face and broad, muscular body. "But her sister's come to visit with her for a time." He stood a bit taller and returned Ian's smile. "Warm meal'd be nice. Be honored to join you, sir."

"Ian. I'd like you to call me Ian. An accepted dinner invitation allows us the indulgence of this one, tiny intimacy, don't you think?"

Trevor ducked his head, nervously fingered the edge of his cloak, and then looked Ian in the eye. "Would be all right, I think." He paused then added, "Ian."

Liking the way Trevor's throaty voice and soft cockney accent made his name sound, Ian moved closer and took Trevor's cloak from the man's arm. He held it out and indicated the young man should put it on. Trevor instantly obeyed and Ian enjoyed the feel of his warm, firm body close to his own as he shrugged the cloak over and around Trevor's lean shoulders. Slipping into his own cloak and hat, Ian guided Trevor out the side exit to a line of waiting cabs, not sparing the fuming, dismissed Jules a second glance.

* * *

"Let me take those things for you." Ian hung up his own cloak and hat, then expertly divested Trevor of his soaked outerwear.

The snow and wind had picked up volumes during the time the two of them had spent dining at a posh hotel. The thin fabric of the young man's cloak had not weathered the wet and wind well on the short walk from the hotel to Ian's townhouse flat. Trevor was left chilled and shivering, his shirt collar soaked and his worn but serviceable boots dull and squeaky from icy puddles.

Flinging the offending garment over the back of a chair, Ian guided Trevor through the dim sitting area to stand in front of the flickering hearth.

"I keep the fire banked while I'm out. It makes starting a blaze easier. And besides --" Ian knelt at the grate and began stirring the flames to life, adding more logs and a few lumps of coal to the embers. "-- I like a room bathed in fire light."

"It's romantic." He stood and brushed off his hands, then reached up and grabbed Trevor's shivering arm. "I like romance." Gaze searching Trevor's face for some sign of resistance, he slowly drew the man nearer the fire and his partially open lips. "I like you."

"I...I-I like you, too." Trevor swallowed hard and softly, shyly added, "Immensely."

Trevor came like a moth to the flame, gaze locked on the vampire's intense and questioning stare, attraction and desire easily read on his open face. He moved into Ian's arms, hesitant but willing, uncertainty in his eyes and an awkwardness in his too-rigid stance.

"You're safe. I've got you." Ian wrapped his arms around Trevor and soothed his shivers with long sweeping strokes of his square hands and strong arms down Trevor's back and arms. He tucked the young man in close to his chest, delighted at the press of Trevor's firm arousal that branded his inner thigh.

Trevor gasped at the intimate contact, but Ian merely slid his hand down to Trevor's taut buttocks and gently, but insistently, pulled him closer. Trevor's breathing increased, but so did his hold on Ian's waist.

When the chills tapered off to a fine, occasional shudder, Ian nuzzled at the side of Trevor's neck, inhaling the sweet elixir of his scent and feeling the warm flow of Trevor's blood as it erratically pounded through the artery under Ian's cheek. He could smell the wine they had drunk during dinner on Trevor's skin and in his blood. It was a very good wine that left Trevor talkative and sleepy-eyed, though still quick to flash his shy, twisty smile, a combination Ian had instantly liked on the man.

Dinner had been exhilarating. Trevor's companionship had proved to be both physically arousing and mentally stimulating. While Ian found the young actor to be modest and relatively inexperienced in the ways of the world and its sexual pleasures, he discovered Trevor was well-read, inventive, amusing, and quick-witted. The hour had passed quickly, and Ian knew he needed more than just release and nourishment from Trevor. For the first time in centuries, he began to want more.

He brushed his lips over Trevor's ear and felt him shudder with excitement. He took the reaction as permission to do more and slowly worked his lips over Trevor's neck and cheek to run a line of moist kisses around Trevor's trembling jaw and up to his other ear.

Ian breathed into the shell and nipped at the small lobe before whispering, "You're a beautiful man, Trevor. And as striking as you look by firelight, you feel even better."

He pulled Trevor's ass in tight and ground his own trapped, swollen erection against Trevor's, pleased by the answering jump and urgent answering press of flesh under his restraining hand. "I want to feel your flesh against mine."

He felt Trevor tense, then relax in his arms. He kissed over Trevor's ear, thrusting his tongue into the narrow channel twice before nipping and licking his way down the offered neck and back up to Trevor's now panting, parted mouth. "Want to share the need in my loins, satisfy our desires. Let me do that for you, Trevor. Let me pleasure you like you've never been pleasured before, by man or woman. I'll make you feel things you didn't know you could."

Sliding a hand through Trevor's thick blond hair, Ian coaxed the man's head back and sealed his hungry lips to Trevor's. He devoured the willing mouth, opening his own wider and thrusting his tongue deep into the hot, wet cavern. He bathed the smoothly ridged palette, then stroked over each tooth, memorizing the contours and savoring the flavor of his lover. He teased the sensitive silky skin between lip and gum and drew Trevor's eager tongue into a battle for dominance he quickly won.

Vampire senses buzzing, the smell, sight, and feel of this man invaded every corner of his mind and newly rediscovered soul. Ian struggled briefly to gain control over the rising vampire impulses trying to break free to experience Trevor as well, but centuries of practice kept the ancient monster in chains, much like Mary Shelley's Frankenstein's monster earlier tonight.

Breathless and dazed, Trevor jerked back from the kiss far enough to gasp, "Never met anyone quite like you before, Ian. You make me want to do things I never have."

"There is no one else like me, Trevor." Ian rained a flood of frenzied kisses over Trevor's upturned face, then kissed him hard, whispering into his lover's waiting mouth. "Do those things with me. You'll never regret them. I promise." He licked up Trevor's arched throat and bit gently behind his ear, a spot Ian knew was tender and vulnerable and connected directly to Trevor's cock. He felt the man's shaft jump and surge against his own. He bit down harder, forcing a needy groan and then a whimper out of Trevor.

Voice raspy and full of lustful need, Ian growled. "Good. You agree."

Ian scooped Trevor up into his arms, ignored the throaty yelp of surprise, and strode out of the living area and into an upstairs bedroom. The room was colder than the other one, but the large, lavishly made bed was heaped with duvets and down comforters, and the smoldering fire was only a few logs away from being revived.

Planting Trevor on the edge of the bed, Ian disrobed with an amazing amount of speed and skill, then began working off Trevor's disheveled clothes. If he had any worries that the need to be naked was one-sided, they were banished each time his fingers collided with Trevor's less nimble, shaky hands over a buttonhole or a belt buckle. Within seconds, Ian had Trevor gloriously naked and stretched out full-length on the bed. He slid his own body alongside Trevor's slender, smooth form, letting the silky hairs of his chest tease the sensitive ribcage and underarm of his lover. His hands worked over every inch of flesh he could reach, while his lips and tongue re-explored the depths of Trevor's mouth again.

Moans and groans, dotted with whimpers and stuttered gasps, filled the air, raising the tension between them to higher levels. Trevor was already squirming and whimpering with need, hips thrusting and legs unsure whether to be bent or splayed wide. Ian slid his lower torso between them and Trevor instinctively wrapped his legs around the vampire's hips. The restless squirming became an urgent thrusting of pelvis against unyielding pelvis.

"You need a bit of release so we can make the evening last, my beauty." Ian pushed his muscular body down over Trevor's trim hips and grabbed hold of his waist. He grinned and locked gazes with Trevor's confused, desperate stare, then expertly swallowed Trevor's cock to the root in one stroke.

"Ian!"

Arched off the bed, Trevor nearly bowed in half at the sudden movement, a sharp cry of surprise and amazement twisting his face into a mask of intense pleasure that appeared to border on pain. Ian held on to the slim hips that bucked and heaved under him by pinning Trevor down with the weight of his own solid body on the young man's legs. He lapped and sucked at the swollen shaft in an unrelenting rhythm meant to bring Trevor the most pleasure in the quickest amount of time.

Ian had plans for the entire night, and making Trevor come as often and as hard as physically possible was among them. He intended to experience every inch of this beautiful, shy creature from his satiny, pale skin right down to the taste and smell of the golden strands of hair on his head. But first he thought he'd start with the taste of his cum, the smell of his musky opening, and the sight of Trevor's face, eyes closed in rapture, hair tousled and cheeks flushed with passion, fists tightly entwined in the bed sheets.

Unable to drag his mouth or his eyes away from the man, Ian stared up at Trevor's lusciously sprawled body while he suckled the man's cock. Every hollow corner of his ancient, empty soul was being filled with the essence of the delightful, hesitant being he now possessed body, mind, and hopefully, by morning, heart. He refused to give up this ray of sunshine that had unexpectedly entered his dark existence. In one short evening, this responsive, shy, and tender man had shown Ian he still had a soul buried deep within him. The soul with which Ian intended to capture Trevor's heart, along with his lean, passionate body.

Swallowing Trevor's cock to the base again, Ian worked his throat and sucked hard, one hand moving to fondle and tug the tight, wrinkled sac beneath. As he rolled the sac, he slid one long, thick finger between Trevor's ass cheeks and stroked the tip firmly over the tiny opening to Trevor's body, loving the way the ring of muscle spasmed and puckered under his touch. The exotic and unexpected stimulation seemed to drive Trevor to new heights of excitement and responsiveness, his body writhing under Ian's hold.

The air in the bedroom was cool, but Trevor's body was flushed pink and his cheeks burned red as he arched up and gave a hoarse cry, climaxing into Ian's eager mouth, giving over his seed as well as his liberated passions.

As the last droplet of cum touched his tongue, Ian swiftly moved his lips to the thin strip of flesh between Trevor's thigh and groin and sucked hard on the satin-like skin. Blood rose to the surface over the pounding pulse of the artery buried there, coloring the small circle of flesh a deep crimson. He used the sharp edge of a pointed canine to scratch the blood-filled surface and then feasted on the trickle of blood that oozed out.

The blood was rich and sweet, musky and pure, a sip of heaven on his tongue. Ian's senses reeled and his chest ached as visions of sunlight and blue skies entwined around feelings of joy and immeasurable arousal. Trevor was the taste of blatant lust and sweet victory to Ian. Trevor was bliss. Trevor was his for the taking. His forever. He could taste it, he could feel it, now he needed to proclaim it.

Still riding the crest of his climax, Trevor moaned and instinctively pulled away from the slight pain of the scratch, but Ian coaxed him into submissiveness by alternately massaging the root of his shaft under his sac and exploring the fluttering opening to Trevor's eager body.

Trevor whimpered, his groping hands reaching blindly for Ian, his over-stimulated cock never softening, despite his climax.

Capturing the most recent blood droplets on his tongue, Ian reluctantly moved away from Trevor's groin, abandoning the heady mix of rich, innocent blood and freshly spilled cum. He climbed up over Trevor and settled slightly off to one side so as not to crush his lover.

"Don't know what to do, Ian. Don't know how…"

The wild, uncertain look of desperate need and escalating desire on Trevor's beautiful face made Ian release a throaty, almost demonic rumble to the passionate gasps and moans that filled the room.

"I'll take you there, beauty. Don't worry. I know the way."

He reclaimed Trevor's mouth and this time got as good as he gave. Trevor returned his ravenous attack of lips, tongue, and grasping, groping, stroking hands over flesh and bone. They both appeared lost in the urgent impulse to consume each other whole.

Ian trailed his sensitive fingertips over Trevor's skin, mapping its texture with his callused but gentle hands, tracing the curve of Trevor's trim muscles, the shape of his spine, the swell of his firm, round ass, and the taut cords of his thigh wrapped over Ian's hip. Ian wove a hand through Trevor's hair, marveling at the fine, soft strands that caught the dim firelight and turned themselves into threads of pure gold before his eyes.

The sound of Trevor's heartbeat called to him and the lingering taste of the man invaded his soul. Ian pulled Trevor over on his side along with him as he turned, putting them chest to chest. He pulled Trevor's leg up over his waist and nestled their groins together, cocks aligned head to head and dripping. He engulfed both shafts in one large hand and began a slow stroking up and down, occasionally running his thumb over the heads and under the tip, making sure Trevor got the majority of the stimulation.

Seasoned and older, Ian could maintain an erection for hours, but he was sure Trevor was close again. It was obvious the young man had little experience or practice in bed. Ian liked that, but he planned on changing it, as well.

He worked his hand over the twin shafts of swollen flesh, ignoring the sharp bite of discomfort from Trevor's nails as his writhing lover scratched at his shoulders and chest, his arousal fueled by the combined scents of his own blood mixed with the remaining blood from the small wound he had given Trevor. When he felt Trevor's cock thicken and his balls tighten, Ian released their cocks and slipped his hand lower, finding the entrance to Trevor's quivering body.

"I-I was...so...I need...I --" Trevor's eyes were glazed over with lust, embarrassment burning high in his cheeks as his eyelids shyly fluttered with the obvious uncertainty of how to ask for something he didn't even know he wanted.

"Ssshh. I know." Ian quickly kissed Trevor's lips, then his sweaty brow. "Soon. I'll make you feel even better." He tipped Trevor's chin up so that their gazes met. Ian knew his own heavy-lidded gaze carried the full heat of his desires and he was pleased when Trevor didn't shrink from it. "Trust me?"

A trembled nod and Ian reclaimed Trevor's lips, pulling the man tightly to him, ravishing his mouth, hands everywhere on his slim, tense body until Trevor moaned and whimpered, limp and pliant in his strong arms.

Still devouring his lover, Ian reached across Trevor to a nightstand. He impatiently knocked the lid from a small earthen jar sitting on top and dipped his fingers into the container, coating his fingers with a thick, oily balm that smelt faintly of fish and herbs.

He turned them both slightly on the bed, then tucked Trevor under his side and coaxed his lover's knees apart with his elbow, exposing the rosebud entrance to Trevor's body. His slick fingertips found the fluttering ring of muscle and teased it, stroked it, and cajoled it open.

Trevor jumped, instinctively closing his legs at first; then he splayed them wider, hips thrusting up and in time to the muffled grunts and gasps coming out of his mouth, which Ian simply swallowed down with a kiss.

Tongue moving in a sensual rhythm along with his fingers, Ian rubbed the tip of his middle finger over Trevor's hole, soothing it and inflaming it with each stroke, while his tongue did the same to the soft recesses of Trevor's mouth. He drew Trevor's tongue into his own mouth and sucked on it, bobbing his head in time to the thrusts of his hand. Pinning Trevor's squirming torso to the bed with his own, Ian wrapped his free hand in Trevor's hair to hold him still against his lips and nudged two slick fingers into Trevor's ass.

All movement beneath him froze for a split second; then Trevor pressed down onto his hand, forcing his fingers deeper, the tight muscles clinging and grasping at him. Ian obliged them and slowly explored with his fingers until they could touch the small nub of hidden ecstasy buried inside his naïve lover. Ian was sure Trevor had never been touched this way and reveled in the fact that he would be the first and only man to see the passion and fire in the beautiful man's face when he stroked the virgin nub to life.

He pulled out of the fierce kiss and held Trevor's face inches from his own, gaze locked on the man's face, his intense stare taking in every nuance and flicker of emotion that flashed across the young actor's expression.

To Ian, Trevor looked dazed, his eyes wide and his jerky movements near frantic. He grunted a sound of distress as Ian abruptly ended the kiss, then arched and cried out, panting and gasping when Ian flicked at the virgin nub deep inside him and swirled long, thick fingers over the swollen gland.

"Bollocks!" Trevor cried out, twisting his hips and grinding his ass down on the thick invading digits up his ass.

Ian began slowly pumping his fingers in and out, striking the little sweet spot with each jab, gradually building the rhythm until he had a steady, deep stroke stretching and coaxing Trevor into a state of lust-dazed euphoria.

Impulsively, he bowed his head and licked at one erect nipple on Trevor's chest. Encouraged by the way Trevor grabbed his head and pressed it more tightly to his breast, Ian suckled the tit, biting and tugging it with his teeth until a bead of red blossomed on one side.

The fresh taste of Trevor's essence carried the spice of his arousal and Ian felt dizzy and drunk with the strength of it. He could read Trevor's deepest desires in his blood and Ian was shocked and thrilled to find that he was one of them.

Elated, he removed his fingers from Trevor's opening and wiped them off on his own straining cock, smearing the head with the balm and his own flowing juices. Moving quickly to silence the croaked murmur of discontent from his startled lover, Ian rolled Trevor over on his side again and slipped in close behind him, cock nudging the cheeks of Trevor's ass. He pulled Trevor's leg up and hooked his arm under the knee, then slid his arm high enough to rub his palm over Trevor's taut belly while holding the leg up high to expose Trevor's rosy, wet hole.

"Trust me, Trevor." Ian kissed Trevor's neck and then mouthed the lobe of his ear, whispering, "I'll never hurt you."

Pushing pillows to the floor, he wormed his other arm under Trevor's head, and then dropped his arm down to embrace the young man's torso and pressed Trevor's back to his chest. With little effort, his cock found the slick hole and the head pressed past the now lax guardian ring of nerves and muscle. With one smooth, unending thrust he eased into Trevor, all the while gauging his speed and force by the shudders and moans escaping his partner. Once the length of his shaft was fully encased in Trevor's sweet heat, Ian coaxed Trevor's face to tilt up with his chin.

"I want you, now, tomorrow, forever. I have to have you. Say you'll stay."

Not waiting for an answer, Ian gently kissed the parted, swollen lips again and again until Trevor returned his attention in kind, letting the kiss build their passions to a raging fervor once more.

Satisfied Trevor was fully aroused and ready, his flesh craving fulfillment and his gold-speckled, dark eyes brimming with need and desire, Ian began to move his hips. He thrust deep inside Trevor, then slowly withdrew, over and over again, until his movements morphed into snapping strokes and Trevor's throaty groans turned into blissful cries begging for release.

Ian took Trevor's shaft in his hand. He tugged and pressed the velvety, iron-hard flesh until the young man bucked and heaved, impaled on Ian's swollen, thrusting cock, and cum splattered his hand, filling the room with the tangible scent of unbridled passion.

Ian groaned, losing himself in the bliss of having his shaft milked by the spasming muscles in Trevor's ass, the press and release of hot flesh like a wanton embrace to his soul. Releasing Trevor's mouth, Ian rained rough kisses and sharp nips along Trevor's collarbone, sucking the warm flesh until it glowed a dark pink and bore his teeth marks in multiple places.

Trevor pressed his shoulder hard against Ian's lips, startling the vampire by breathing a husky whisper, begging, "Do it, mark me. I want you to."

The raw request spiked Ian's already burning desire higher and he felt his climax barrel down on him. He slammed his hips forward and plunged deeper into Trevor's tight channel at the same time as his teeth lightly pierced the first few layers of skin on Trevor's shoulder. Having just fed the evening before, Ian wouldn't need blood again for weeks, but he wanted the taste of his lover on his lips as he came. It would make his climax sweeter and more intense, bonding them together on a level others couldn't understand without experiencing. He didn't understand it himself, but he knew it existed. He'd never let it happen since he realized he could control it, but this time, he wanted that bond with Trevor. No one made him feel the way Trevor did.

Cock buried to the root, Ian froze in place, his body spasming, his seed pouring forth into his lover as Trevor's blood flowed into his mouth. Sensations of joy, bliss, fear, shame, want, and even love coursed through him like a hit of lightning, setting him on fire.

His mind reached out and touched Trevor's, capturing the man's essence, learning his keen mind, and invading Trevor's very soul. He felt the soundless cry of surprise and pain from Trevor's soul, and he withdrew slightly, only to be pulled back around as the feeling turned to despair and longing at his sudden retreat. Grabbing the thread of tentative welcome, Ian's essence flowed into Trevor's being, claiming him, washing over his soul and binding it to his own. They would be forever tied until the ravages of old age stole Trevor from him.

He planned to never show Trevor his true nature.

Riding a tide of euphoria like he had never known, Ian emptied himself into Trevor, clasping the man tightly to his chest. His lips released the smooth, warm shoulder, giving up the trickle of heady elixir that was Trevor's life force, and sought out Trevor's warm, willing mouth.

During the kiss, Ian eased out of Trevor's ass and rolled his lover over onto his back. Ian settled his own weight beside and partially on top of Trevor and wrapped the panting, dazed man in his arms. The chill of room began to register again, and Ian pulled up a rumpled duvet from the tangled heap on the foot of the bed and covered them both. Trevor shivered and cuddled closer. Ian tucked both the comforter and his lover to his side.

"Never done that before. I feel...like I can't...can't live without you now. It's so strange."

The words were soft and throaty, raw with a dazed, sleepy quality to them. If Ian had been human, he knew he would have had to strain to hear them. He tilted Trevor's downcast face up to look at him and gently stroked the side of his lover's flushed face with his thumb, reassuring and coaxing. After a moment, gold-flecked brown eyes met his waiting gaze. Ian smiled.

"I want you, too, Trevor. I don't ever want to spend another night without you by my side."

The emotions playing on Trevor's face were the same as when he was considering being Ian's lover -- joy, uncertainty, fear, and desire; this time they were about their future together. The veil of shadow fell over Trevor's beautiful face and panic edged out the joy in his eyes. "I'm scared, Ian. What do we do?"

"Sshh, ssh. I'll handle everything. I'll take care of things, no worry." Ian gently kissed Trevor's mouth and petted his hand down Trevor's side, soothing away any worries and fears. "Sleep, beauty. I have you and nothing will take you from me."

"Promise?" Trevor's eyelids fluttered and fell and his breathing turned shallow. Ian savored the hot puffs of sweet breath that ghosted across his cheek.

"Promise. Now sleep."

Laying his head down on the pillow next to Trevor's, Ian vowed to make this last, make this work, make this be the only moment of pure joy in his long, lonely, pointless existence. They would be one together for whatever years Trevor lived and Ian would make each one a day of love and joy. There was no point to life without love.

And he knew right then, after Trevor passed, he would walk into the sun himself.

* * *

Instead of waiting in the confines of the playhouse among the perfumed ladies and their cigar-smoking escorts, all packed into too small a space for Ian's comfort, the vampire elected to wander outside. The night was filled with the scents of the Christmas season. The enticing aroma of roasted chestnuts mingled with the heavy scent of pine from the fresh boughs that decorated the doors and several carriages that stood waiting for fares.

A light dusting of snow had begun to fall, covering the dirty cobblestone houses with a graceful, white mantle of innocence. Ian turned to watch a group of bundled carolers stop to serenade the playhouse patrons, hoping for a bit of coin or a kind word. Ian gave them both and was rewarded with a fresh chorus of song. The festive trappings and good cheer around him stirred something indefinable in his chest and he wished Trevor were standing with him to enjoy it, too. When the carolers passed on to new territory, so did Ian.

Unnoticed, he naturally gravitated to the gray shadows of the building's edges where lamplight and pedestrians refused to go, seeking solitude to enjoy the sights and sounds before him.

A long, debris-littered alley ran down beside the playhouse. He was no stranger to alleyways. Ian tucked himself around the corner and leaned against the building to wait, his keen hearing picking up the faint sounds of rats scurrying over the uneven cobblestones.

Even with his soul reborn, Ian took comfort in the darkness, enjoyed the cool hands of the shadows that wrapped around him and comforted him from the masses of humans milling around him. He longed to take Trevor away from this town to a more secluded, peaceful place where they could explore the land and each other in more detail. After the holidays maybe he would talk Trevor into exploring the Italian countryside with him.

As Ian watched the Christmas snow fall from the sky in spits and starts, contemplating his blissful future with Trevor, a gang of young street thugs moved down the lane, shouting and nipping between patrons, undoubtedly nicking purses and pockets as they worked their way toward the alleyway. So well hidden was he in the concealing shadows, the young men passed within a few feet of where Ian stood and never noticed him. Ian was used to blending into the night.

One scruffy, carrot-topped young man lagged behind the group, glancing impatiently back out into the street. Two others from their gang still mingled with the departing patrons of the playhouse.

A fellow street grub, short and stocky, with a round face and a festering sore on the point of his chin, broke away from the first two headed down the darkness toward the back of the playhouse. He turned back down the alley to grab the redhead and tugged on his arm, insistent and exasperated.

"Gawd, Mickey, you're lagging 'ahind! We gots work ta get done. Hurry up!"

Mickey's bright gaze shifted from the two out in the street to his companion and back, his movements restless and jerky. He glanced at the retreating back of the two that had already entered the alley, then gave the stocky man an almost desperate, pleading look.

"Know that, Todd. Just thought we should all be together on this." Fidgeting with the hem of his tattered scarf, Mickey shivered in the cold air and glanced at the street again. "Nigel and Pern ain't keeping up!"

From the shadows, Ian focused on Mickey's hammering heartbeat, curiously studying the nervous shift of his shoulders and the uneasy expression on his dirt-streaked face. He wanted to go back inside and snatch his lover from his impromptu celebrations, but some instinct he couldn't ignore kept him still and watchful.

Gripping Mickey's arm, Todd pulled him down the alley. He brushed a layer of snow off his hair and out of his eyes, scoffing, "No never mind 'bout those two. They're keeping the finery busy watching them so as no one's watching us. Come on!"

"Shouldn't it be all six of us? I mean…" Mickey paused, swallowing hard. "…he might fight back." He reluctantly stumbled along, drawn more by Todd's strong arm than his own willpower.

"Don't be daft! He's an *actor!* The poof'll never know what done him in." Todd pulled out a gleaming knife and proudly flashed it in Mickey's face. "It'll be so easy, I could do it meselfs. Wouldn't that be something?"

All of Ian's senses were immediately directed toward the two, the puzzle of what they were up to piquing his curiosity. He expanded his hearing, pushing aside the muffling effects of the snowfall, the cheerful, holiday-inspired chatter outside the playhouse, and the rattle of horse-drawn carriages on cobblestone. He tracked their fading conversation, losing nothing to the sharp wind.

Reaching the end of the alley, Todd and Mickey paused to glance suspiciously at their surroundings, never seeing Ian's tall shadow and hooded, now yellow eyes. Todd yanked

Mickey out in front of him, urging the nervous young man along with a shove to his back. Their movements became more fugitive as they edged off to Ian's left toward the playhouse stage door.

Before they disappeared, a knife suddenly appeared in Mickey's hand as well.

"Then why don't you?" Mickey's hand wavered, his grip on the knife overly tight and shaking. "Do it yourself, I mean."

Ian could read the panic on his thin face and hear it thundering through his blood vessels.

"This one don't feel right, Todd."

"You're crazy, just edgy 'cause it's Christmas Eve, you are. What better night for a bloke to meet his maker than tonight, eh? Kinda religious experience." Todd laughed, a hushed, ugly sound, and slapped Mickey upside of his bowed head. "'Sides, need all of us to be sure it gets done right. Jules's got a rich patron's pockets to pick and this nuisance is in his way."

Ian was stunned, the pieces of the tiny puzzle falling into place.

The sounds of a scuffle grabbed his attention and Todd started. He slapped Mickey's shoulder, forcing him to move faster. "Let's go! Arty and Reg have already got him!" Todd ran down the side alley into the darkness. Mickey skittered behind him, obviously torn between running forward and running backward.

A muffled, garbled shout and the sudden scent of familiar blood galvanized Ian into action. Even with all his vampire speed and agility, it took too long for him to reach the huddled group of filthy street rabble. It had already found its prey.

The four men beat and stabbed at a figure pressed up against one wall of the old playhouse. An occasional flash of pale blond caught in the bright moonlight between the dark heads of ragged caps and dull, dirty hair. As Ian descended on them, the blond head slid out of sight to the filth of the snow-covered ground while the grunting huddle of pounding arms and hunched shoulders finally stepped back.

The scent of Trevor's blood overwhelmed Ian. He logically knew what to expect -- the sounds of the brief struggle, the dull thud of flesh hitting flesh and cries of pain and disbelief all too familiar and brutal to his ears. The sight of his beautiful beloved lying, unmoving, in a bloody heap in a dark, desolate alley like so much human waste was unbearable to the vampire.

Outrage, pain, and horror overtook centuries of control and discipline. Ian let his inner power burst free in a surge of unforgiving rage. He descended on the flailing mass of unsuspecting assailants like the night he existed in, silent, unmerciful and unstoppable, throwing the entire group back with one sweeping blow.

He ended Mickey's startled cry of surprise quickly by breaking his neck. Todd was torn limb from limb, his own wetly gleaming knife finding a new home in his own black heart.

Art and Reg, the first to grab their prey and begin the assault, were less charitably dealt with. Their eyes were torn from their sockets, their grasping arms shattered, and their throats ripped open. Then their writhing, mangled, and broken bodies were thrown against a wall where they dropped to the slushy cobblestone, left in the filth and waste to slowly bleed to death, dinner for the ever-present scavenging rats.

It had taken Ian seconds to turn the alley into a death house, but he was still too late. Free of his assailants. Trevor lay at Ian's feet, unmoving, unnaturally pale in the dim moonlight, a layer of glistening white captured in his hair and eyelashes. Ian could barely hear the stuttering rhythm of his lover's heartbeat and only the movement of snowflakes drifting off his chest signaled the occasional shallow breath. From the street, Ian could hear the faint sound of the joyous carolers as they sang. *While Shepherds Watched* would forever take on a new and dark meaning for Ian.

Dropping to his knees, Ian scooped Trevor into his arms, cradling his lover's rapidly cooling body to his chest. He smoothed Trevor's snow-dampened hair off his face, surprised to see his own hand trembling. It had been so very long since he had experienced genuine terror. Loving Trevor had awakened so many long-forgotten feelings in the vampire. He had been so bewitched by the joy in the good emotions, he had not remembered the agony of the bad until now.

All his dreams and plans of a bright and happy future with his lover until Trevor's natural final days were lived out dissolved and blew away with the cold wind. His reason for continuing in his dark, empty existence was slipping away with each draining pulse of Trevor's wounded heart. Ian's heart felt the same pain; each thrust of the knife had entered his chest as well.

But while Trevor's pain would be brief, like his young life, Ian's pain would be eternal. He couldn't face the specter of life without Trevor in it. He wouldn't. He had waited hundreds of long, lonely years to find his love and now that he had, he wasn't leaving him. This night, this hallowed, blessed eve, they would face judgment in the afterlife as one and die together in this accursed alleyway.

Ian heard Trevor's faint heartbeat flutter and stop. He clutched his lover to him, heart-to-heart, and let out a silent, anguished cry of indescribable pain. Tears streamed down his face as his pain transformed into rage. He held Trevor in a brutal grip, looked down into his lover's beautiful face, quivering fingertips gently tracing the delicate curve of Trevor's eyelids to feel the soft feathery brush of his long lashes one more time against his skin.

A flicker of movement under his touch stilled his hand. He bowed his head and stared at Trevor's pale face, straining to hear his heartbeat again. A faint, barely audible thump-thud touched the edges of his keen senses and Ian's firm vow to end both their lives crumbled to dust.

Ian had never created a new vampire; not in all the years of his existence had he inflicted his curse on another; never had he committed what he considered to be a vampire's greatest sin. Killed, as he had tonight, for protection or revenge, yes, but never to feed and never to damn another to the dark loneliness of vampirism.

But it wouldn't be lonely for Trevor or him if they had each other in the darkness.

When Trevor woke to his new existence and hated Ian for turning him, Ian would destroy them both. It was that simple, and yet, so complex.

A single, shallow breath of air escaped Trevor's lips, ghosting over Ian's face. The fear that it may have been

Trevor's last pulled Ian from his internal debate and let his heart decide the matter.

Panicked, Ian tightly clasped Trevor to him, and sunk his now-extended fangs into the soft, smooth skin of his lover's exposed neck, the move brutal and primal, the wound horrific and deep.

* * *

Nausea rolled through Trevor's stomach and a flash of pain made him jump and gasp. He opened his eyes to the lamplight of Ian's bedroom and a flood of disjointed, horrific memories embroiled him in their chaotic rush, stealing his air and his voice.

He ran his hand over his smooth, hairless chest, noting the coolness of his flesh and the ivory tone of skin. Panic shot down his limbs, exploding in his chest, the sharp stabbing pain of his attackers' weapons suddenly remembered by his body in vivid detail. More detail than he had been aware of at the time of the assault. Enough detail that Trevor knew he should not be lying comfortably in Ian's bed, naked, aware, and unmarked. Enough detail that his hand slid to his left breast and lay there searching for the familiar thump of his own heartbeat.

His chest was still and cold.

As terror rose up in his lifeless heart, but before it could burst out, a hand slid along his arm and his fingers were firmly laced together with larger, blunt ones. Trevor stared at the interwoven hands for a moment, then turned his eyes up to meet Ian's waiting brown ones.

Ian had been lying beside him, still and silent as the dead. As Trevor stared at his lover, a yellow cast gave his warm brown eyes a luminescent glow. Trevor thought he should be frightened or repulsed, but Ian's eyes remained warm and loving, his face open and concerned. Trevor couldn't help but be reassured and beguiled by the small tentative smile on the large man's usually firm mouth. It was the first time he had seen Ian anything but supremely confident in his action.

Trevor wet his dry, cool lips, his gaze searching Ian's face for answers, dreading an explanation, but needing to hear his lover's soft, commanding voice.

"Am I dead, Ian? Are you?" Trevor's gaze flickered around the confines of the luxurious room and soft bedding. "Are we dead, together, in heaven, then?"

He heard his own voice waver. Trevor clamped his jaw shut to keep in the whimper that rose in his throat. Maybe it was the set of Ian's mouth or the odd color of his eyes, but something told him it wasn't going to be that easy.

"Not heaven, my beauty, but not hell, either." Ian squeezed their entwined hands, the touch firm, gentle, and real, anchoring Trevor. "Not as long as we are together."

Despite the stillness in his chest, Trevor didn't feel "dead." Indeed, he felt strangely energized and hyperaware. The threads of the fine linens were like rough twigs under his back and the snowflakes hitting the window sounded as if pebbles were being pelted against the rippled glass.

Suddenly, the light of the smoking lamp was too bright and the weight of the down comforter too heavy. Trevor flung the blanket off his naked body, shielding his eyes from the light with his free hand, panic and confusion fueling his jerky movements.

"Then what am I? What's been done to me? Why am I not dead?" Trevor's voice rose, his eyes burning bright. "I was killed in the alleyway, I know it. I remember the knife in my chest and the slowing of my heart. I know I died!"

He tried to fight his way free from Ian's hold, but the bigger man slipped behind him and pinned Trevor's back to his broad chest. Holding Trevor's arms crossed over his own heaving chest, Ian wrapped his arms around him and gently held him. The feel of Ian's naked flesh against his own sensitive skin was like lying on the finest satin draped tightly over iron. Trevor had never felt so much power and strength in a man before. It was thrilling and frightening all at once. Before tonight, he thought he had known everything about this man.

Trevor gradually stopped tugging and pulling as the urge to flee subsided, with Ian's softly murmured words finally breaking through the haze of terror in his mind.

"Hush, my beauty, sshhh. I'm here. I'll guide you." Ian nuzzled his face into Trevor's hair and breathed warm air against his skin and scalp.

The warmth was sweet and welcome. Trevor pushed his head back into it, allowing Ian to soothe him.

"You'll not face this alone, Trevor. I swear." Ian tightened his embrace. "Never alone."

Calmer, Trevor focused on his body and the demands of his overwrought senses. He felt things more keenly, heard things clearer, and even his sight, always slightly short-sighted, was now crisp. Colors were more vibrant and smells were almost overwhelming if he focused on them. He could hear the mice scurrying through the walls and the snow falling on the window ledge outside the room. He knew he was dead, but he had never felt so alive before.

Trevor slid his hand over his cool, naked abdomen, then ran his other over Ian's marble-hard arm where it held him pinned in place with a gentle but firm embrace. They felt exactly the same. He wasn't as brawny as Ian naturally was, but now, his once pink skin was a shade paler, firmer, and cool, just like Ian's.

"I-I feel strange, Ian. Unnatural." Trevor's whole body shook this time, not just his voice. "I should be dead." He concentrated on what his body and mind were telling him and he grew more confused. "And I'm not."

He clasped Ian's large hands tighter to his left breast and hung on to them like they were his only hope of remaining sane. "My heart doesn't beat and I feel a hunger unlike any I have ever known."

Trevor twisted in Ian's grip so that he could see his lover's face. The yellow cast to Ian's eyes was almost hypnotic. It held his gaze captive, focused on Ian's face. He started for a brief instant when he noticed Ian's eyeteeth looked longer and sharper than they normally did.

A flash of sudden insight, absurd and outlandish, surged through him, an innate, primal knowledge that was a part of him now. His stomach fluttered and his breathing became shallow.

Even instinctively knowing the answer, he had to hear it from Ian. He faltered, then breathlessly asked, "Why am I like this, Ian? What's happened to me?"

Ian buried his face in Trevor's hair and gasped into the blond strands, voice ragged and possessive, a raw hunger to them Trevor had never heard before. It made his cock stir and his blood race even as he fought back a tinge of horror.

"I couldn't lose you."

Trevor's voice caught in his throat. He partially turned in Ian's embrace to face him. He watched as guilt and stubborn defiance battled for dominance on Ian's face, neither winning, but both inexplicably touching Trevor's heart.

"You did this to me?"

It was only a whisper, but Ian flinched as if shouted at. His eyes pleaded with Trevor for understanding, but his voice was as strong and unyielding as his continued grip on Trevor's body.

"You were dying in my arms." He took a deep breath. His voice wavered slightly. "I couldn't lose you." The light in Ian's eyes burned brighter. One hand caressed Trevor's shoulders, back, belly and beyond, soothing, begging, arousing Trevor with its bold touch. "Please forgive me. I couldn't lose you or I'd lose myself, as well."

Looking into Trevor's eyes, Ian softly vowed, "We were as one before this, and now that's true more so than ever. We are inseparable for all time." He swallowed hard, guilt winning over confidence for a moment. "If you choose to stay with me."

His gaze darted over Trevor's face, obviously seeking some sort of clue to Trevor's thoughts. As much as the new, overwhelming voice in Trevor's head screamed for him to accept and indulge in this unnatural existence, a tiny part of his old self resisted, frightened and unsure of this shadowy future. His Christian upbringing was well ingrained, defiant even in the face of the dark, insurmountable changes Trevor knew his body and world had undergone.

A sharp stab of pain rippled through his mouth. Trevor felt the budding, elongated points of new fangs emerge from his upper jaws, the razor-fine edge of one slicing his own lip as he grimaced in surprise. He smeared the blood away with his fingers, but the smell pulled a dark thirst up from deep inside him.

It coursed through his body like boiling water, scalding his senses and heightening them. His arousal stood tall and aching, pressed against Ian's hard abdomen. He felt powerful and raw, sinfully base and suddenly tainted. Air left his lungs and his throat constricted with fear as the need to be free crashed in on him.

"At what cost, Ian? My soul?" Trevor struggled against Ian's hold, repulsion and terror temporarily overpowering his desire to be at Ian's side. He grunted and twisted in Ian's grip, but the larger, stronger man couldn't be budged. "Am I one of the accursed undead, a servant of the devil now?"

"Do you think I am? Did you fall in love with a devil, Trevor? An evil man?"

"No." A mere whisper of sound, Trevor licked his lips and answered Ian again, this time with more conviction, and more uncertainty. "No, you're not, Ian. You're not."

"We are shunned by the light, and all things holy, but that doesn't make us Satan's minions. We need to feed from other living creatures just as we did before, but we need not kill to do it. We need not harm or damage, take a life or change a life, if we choose not to do so. I have been in this form for hundreds of years and I have not killed a single being in the quest for nourishment."

Ian brushed the tousled hair from Trevor's hopeful face and reverently rubbed a callused thumb over the fine line of his lover's cheekbone and down his jaw. "I can teach you. Show you how."

He slid his hand to Trevor's hair and worked his fingers over the scalp beneath them, relaxing and calming Trevor's skittishness with just his touch. "I do not murder for food and neither will you." Tightening his grip, Ian lightly shook Trevor's head, then pressed their foreheads together and quietly vowed, "I'll see us both perish before I'll let that happen."

The hold on his arms lessened as Ian's hands found other places on Trevor's now unresisting body to touch and hold. Desire surged again, forcing aside the fear. Trevor whimpered and arched into Ian's hands, hungry for his touch.

"What are we, Ian?" Trevor's arms wound around his lover's neck, clinging to Ian's powerful shoulders, fingers digging into them. His tear-filled gaze searched his lover's face for answers and reassurance. "What will others call us now?"

"Others?" Ian kissed Trevor's mouth, the brief caress of lips chaste and fleeting, less than Trevor wanted, but almost more than he could stand. Ian's answer ghosted over his face. "Others will call us demons." Ian said the word in a detached, nonjudgmental way, as if he had just called them carpenters. It oddly reassured Trevor.

"What name do we give ourselves?"

"The ancient one." Once again Ian kissed him, light and teasing, a taste of things to come. "The one belonging to the first of our kind, the true masters of the dark." This time he breathed the word into Trevor's mouth, warming his lips and setting his darkened soul on fire with its heated, airy caress. "*Vampyre*."

Ian pronounced it with the lilt of his native northern accent, giving the word a sensual, powerful sound that vibrated through to Trevor's very core. His cock jerked and his blood raced faster through his veins. He arched and ground his erection against Ian's bare flesh, wanting release from at least one of his hungers.

A gust of icy wind rattled the window, its mighty swirls of air carrying the faint sound of carolers up to them. Both glanced at the frost-edged panes that separated them from the rest of the world, a sudden reminder of the masses of humanity they had left behind.

Trevor lowered his gaze, a pang of guilt striking through him, as he remembered what night this still was. He shrugged, uncomfortable with his own thoughts, and darted a beseeching look at Ian. His cockney accent became prominent, strong and thick, as it always did when he felt deeply about something. "Seems blasphemous for this to happen on Christmas Eve, don't it? Mean, it's a holy day, and all."

Shaking his head, Ian stroked Trevor's side, long, firm caresses that calmed his mental turmoil and excited the rest of his body. Trevor knew he could never face this new existence without Ian at his side. No one did the things this lover did with just the mere touch of his hand. His words were even more soothing to Trevor, each word passionate and strong.

"It's the perfect time, Trevor. The night of the Savior's birth is exactly right for the night of *my* savior's birth. It couldn't be more perfect. Salvation comes in many forms, Trevor, and you're *mine*. Without you, I would gladly perish."

Ian swooped down and kissed Trevor passionately. Lips sealed together, he rolled them so that Ian was on top.

"You have just fears, beauty --" He kissed Trevor's eyelids and lips softly between words. "-- but let me show you some of the pleasures of your new life." He lifted Trevor's arm, holding the soft inner arm against his cheek. Ian ran his lips and fangs down the delicate flesh, wrist to elbow, slicing a shallow furrow. When the blood welled rich and full from the wound, he followed the red trail back up Trevor's arm, licking and sucking the bright red flow off the skin to Trevor's wrist.

Trevor gasped at the burning pain that came with the wound, but his hips bucked and he squirmed with need, as a bolt of arousal shot through his veins and rocketed to his cock. His shaft was hard and full, trapped between them, poking uselessly at Ian's stomach, a smear of his own pre-cum lubricating the patch of flesh he rubbed against.

His gasp was captured by Ian's lips again and swallowed as Ian invaded his mouth, exploring and bathing his entire being with his power. The weight of Ian's body was solid and firm, iron hard, his skin luxuriously silky. The hair on his chest was darker than on his head, but fine and thick under Trevor's palms. Trevor's fingers blindly searched until they found the taut buds of nipples. He flicked and rubbed at them, loving the way his efforts fanned Ian's passion higher.

A strange hunger mixed with his lust. It rolled through Trevor until he couldn't control the impulse to bite at Ian's lips, his newly emerged fangs tender, but sharp. A droplet of blood touched his tongue and the hunger exploded in his gut like oil thrown on a fire.

He lunged upward trying to gain a better biting hold on Ian. An unearthly power rippled through him, and he twisted and fought to find the nourishment he needed, but he was no match for Ian's ancient strength. Trevor bucked and jerked, but his wrists were calmly pinned to the mattress over his head and his bucking hips held firmly in place by the vampire's weight.

Flinging his head from side to side, Trevor growled out his frustration inches from Ian's calm face. "I need!"

He didn't recognize his own voice, the tone raw and dangerous. It shocked him and he dropped his head back on the pillow and stared up at his lover. "I-I…need…" He was at a loss to verbalize exactly what it was he *did* need. "Ian?" He heard the pleading tone to his own voice. Tears welled in his eyes as they searched Ian's face for some kind of understanding.

"Hush, beauty. I know, I know." Still holding Trevor's wrist tightly, Ian moved their hands so he could gently brush Trevor's cheek with his thumb, artfully avoiding teeth as Trevor twisted and strained against him. "The taste of my blood has awakened the first hunger in you."

He pressed Trevor's head into the feather pillow, forehead pressed to forehead, and whispered, the sound faint and breathy, but easily heard by another vampire's ears. "This will be the strongest of the urges to feed. After this is properly sated, I'll teach you how to control it, hide it, turn it to your advantage." He teasingly nipped the tip of Trevor's nose, easily avoiding Trevor's unrelenting, eager fangs. "You're an intelligent man; you'll do well."

Thwarted, Trevor settled back, emotions in turmoil, but still aroused and oddly thrilled by Ian's restraining hold and powerful presence. Hopeful, he locked gazes with Ian. "I won't have to kill?"

As soon as he said the word, the urge to destroy something living flashed through him and he panicked. Frantic with fear and confusion, he cried out. "Ian! I feel like I could <u>kill</u>!" Trevor renewed his struggle for a moment while Ian hurried to patiently calm him again. "I'll kill, I *will!*'

"You won't! I swear it." He shook Trevor until the young vampire's teeth clattered and his hair flew into his eyes. Trevor gasped and shuddered, then calmed, a sob escaping his lips with his words.

"Never?"

Ian pushed the stray blond strands off Trevor's face with his chin and gently said, "Not to feed."

The brush of Ian's beard stubble blazed along his skin and relief flowed in Trevor's veins. He believed Ian with all his being, dark and unfamiliar as it was to him now. Ian was still his anchor in life, the past one and this new, shadow-filled, stormy one. He was its originator and Trevor's only source of guidance and understanding, as well as his one true love. He put his trust in Ian, despite the vampire being the reason for his distress and predicament. Ian had done it for love, Trevor knew that.

The hold on his wrists loosened and Trevor turned questioning eyes on his lover as Ian firmly tilted Trevor's face up to meet his steely gaze. "But maybe for self-protection, if you have to." Trevor blinked rapidly to keep the panic at bay and Ian gently added, "but never for nourishment, never because of starvation. I swear it."

"Cross your heart and hope to --" Trevor huffed a tiny, embarrassed chuckle and averted his gaze. "Guess that doesn't mean too much now, eh?"

Letting out a loud laugh, Ian tilted Trevor's face back to meet his stare. He smiled, seductive and teasing. Heated gazes locked together, Ian licked across Trevor's mouth, then sucked on his lower lip, tugging it before letting it slip away, wet and slick, to whisper, "How about we make it a blood oath?"

The hunger rose again.

Without moving from on top of Trevor, Ian seductively tilted his head to one side, exposing his throat. Trevor instinctively lunged, driven by a new, indefinable need to taste the vampire's rich, aged blood a second time. His fangs pierced Ian's flesh, making a soft pop as they penetrated.

New and inexperienced, Trevor made to brutally shake his head and widen the wounds, but a massive, firm fist clamped onto his hair and held him still, preventing him from inflicting more damage than necessary.

"That's my beauty. Bold and fierce. You'll learn to use finesse over time. For now just slay the hunger." Ian gasped and pressed Trevor's mouth more tightly against his neck, a moan of pleasure rumbling from deep inside his throat. "Feast from me."

The blood rolled over Trevor's tongue, thick and silky smooth like liquid satin. It tasted of berries, hickory, and lime, rich and intoxicating. Flashes of emotions washed through him, love, lust, desire, and guilt, and it was some time before he realized they were Ian's feelings, not his. The realization he was sharing his lover's most intimate emotions made them all the more intense. Trevor's ever-present arousal slowly began to overwhelm his ebbing hunger for blood. Now his body craved to be satisfied in other ways.

As if Ian was aware of the change in Trevor's needs, the grip on Trevor's hair lessened and he was able to pull back. As Ian broke away, Trevor smeared the last droplets of Ian's blood from the healing wounds over his lips.

Ian's face appeared inches from his own. They locked yellow gazes for a brief, intense moment, then Ian's tongue darted out and began to lick the blood from Trevor's ruby red lips, slowly and thoroughly. Each languid lap of wet muscle was erotic and arousing to Trevor, his lips hypersensitive and his sexual need beyond explosive.

Ian's hips began to move in concert with his attentions to Trevor's mouth, sliding their cocks together in a delicious dance. The licks turned to sucking kisses as Ian worked his lips from Trevor's mouth, over his cheek, down his neck and across his chest.

He raised one of Trevor's arms and slowly worked his kisses up the inner aspect, grazing the soft flesh with his fangs, never breaking the skin but leaving a trail of teeth marks in his wake. When he reached Trevor's wrist, Ian suckled at the pulse point, teasing it, until Trevor was squirming with need and anticipation.

"Ian! Please!"

"Not yet, beauty." Ian dropped Trevor's arm and returned his attention to Trevor's mouth while his hands slid under Trevor's ass and kneaded the firm globes of flesh, spreading them.

His fingers were in constant motion, edging their way closer and closer until they touched the puckered entrance to Trevor's body. Once there, Ian began to stroke and rub at the tight ring of muscle, relenting only when it fluttered and relaxed under his fingertips.

Trevor groaned and arched his hips, then pushed down on the blunt fingertip pressing into his ass. The need to be filled, to have more than just a touch raced through him and Trevor bucked his lower half, spreading his legs wide and wrapping them high around Ian's waist.

"More. Want more." Trevor twisted and tossed his head and shoulders, pinned in place, exposed and open, at Ian's loving mercy, desperate to feel Ian inside of him.

Ian's cock rubbed at his balls and the blunt head of the vampire's shaft replaced his finger. He reached for Trevor's abandoned arm, licking over the smooth flesh as he inched his cock into the tight, fluttering opening.

Moaning at the thrill of the familiar, delightful burn and pressure of the large shaft, Trevor met each small thrust of Ian's hips with one of his own, trying to pull Ian's cock in deeper and faster.

The sensation of Ian's veined and bulging cock sliding against his channel walls, spreading his asshole wider with each inch that was buried in him, made Trevor gasp and moan, his thoughts jumbled as the room spun.

Making love as a hyperaware vampire was different than before, more intense, more exotic, and more satisfying. He felt every emotion Ian felt and understood his desires and needs like never before. Trevor knew why Ian had not been able to face the future without him and he understood the decision to bring him across to the dark. He knew Ian would willingly die without him. Ian's love for him was that strong.

He nearly screamed when Ian's slow, tiny thrusts unexpectedly turned into faster, smoother, longer strokes that rubbed slickly along his channel and bumped relentlessly over his prostate with each pass. His climax built way too soon and too fast. Trevor wanted this to go on forever.

Making love with Ian had been amazing and wondrous before this, but now it was indescribable. They seemed linked on a level that transcended the rest of the world's existence. Blood lust and vampirism be damned, Trevor wanted a lifetime of this and Ian.

His climax teetered on the edge, waiting for one last touch or sensation to push him over the brink. Trevor's frustration mounted and his body cried out for release as the sensation intensified but no relief came. Trevor's pleading gaze locked on Ian's lust-filled stare.

Never pulling away his gaze, Ian drew Trevor's wrist to his lips and kissed the soft vulnerable inner strip of pale flesh. He thrust hard and deep once, biting into the wrist at the same time, cock buried to the root, and lusting gaze riveted on Trevor's face.

Trevor screamed, his body spasming, and then came, the burn of the hard thrust and the sheer ecstasy of the bite too much to bear together. It was exactly what he needed to fall over the razor-sharp edge he had been teetering on. His climax was explosive. His skin sizzled and his senses reeled. Sweat broke out over his body and his mind became dazed and clouded. His cock jerked and erupted, coating his abdomen and Ian's chest, the scent of the cum intoxicating.

Flesh was pressed to his lips and Trevor opened his eyes. He grabbed onto Ian's arm and licked over the same spot on his lover's wrist that Ian had feasted at on his own body. He felt Ian grip his hip in a bruising hold and then arch, plunging deep into his ass and staying there. Trevor understood his lover's desire and bit into Ian's wrist, losing himself in the joy and pleasure he found in Ian's blood.

A roar of triumph shook the walls and Ian's hips thrust in rapid, staccato rhythm, the vampire emptying his load deep inside of Trevor. When he was spent, Ian withdrew and collapsed in a heap beside Trevor, panting. He turned on the mattress to give Trevor a sated smile.

Trevor met Ian's sultry gaze with one of his own and leisurely licked the last trickle of blood from Ian's arm as his lover watched. The look of feral want that sparked in Ian's eyes fueled his own arousal to stir again. He felt his cock burst to life when Ian returned the gesture and began to lick and suckle the open wounds of Trevor's wrist, too.

Ian leaned over Trevor, bringing the wrist up with him. He alternated between kissing Trevor's lips and sucking on his wrist, occasionally licking a droplet of his own blood off Trevor's lips as well.

"Now do you believe me, beauty?" Ian's hand wandered to Trevor's rising cock and lightly stroked it.

Gasping softly, Trevor arched his hips. "Not sure I'm a hundred percent convinced." Trevor shoved his straining shaft into Ian's playful hand and turned a hot, sultry stare on his lover and breathlessly asked, "Can you explain it to me again?"

* * *

Ian stared at the night sky, lost in the memories of his and Trevor's first Christmas. It had been the only Christmas Eve the two of them had spent together. They had kept their oath and Trevor had never killed for food, but he had used his vampire skills and abilities to kill for revenge.

As much as Ian wanted Trevor with him for this one night, he never interfered. In all his centuries as a vampire, he considered turning Trevor to be his greatest sin. His own guilt kept him silent about his lover's absences, but modern times and police methods were making Trevor's yearly haunt more and more dangerous.

Ian noticed a small patch of sky where the clouds had parted. His breath caught when one star caught his eyes, its brilliant light twinkling solitary and bright through the falling snowflakes.

He couldn't resist. Even if heaven didn't listen to a demon's prayers, that didn't mean he couldn't say one. Maybe the star would understand and carry it to the heavens anyway.

Fixing his gaze on the tiny pinpoint of light, obvious to the cold and snow, Ian pictured his love in his mind and softly spoke to the still night air.

"*Please take care of him and protect him from harm.*"

The only prayer that came to mind was an ancient Irish poem he thought fit their situation in an oddly perfect way, although he was pretty sure the creator hadn't been talking about the undead when it was written.

"*Do not stand at my grave and weep,*
I am not there...I do not sleep.

I am the thousand winds that blow...

I am the diamond glints on snow..."

Pausing to remember all the words, Ian took a deep breath. The snow silently drifted around, clinging to his eyelashes, hair, and clothing. Trevor filled his thoughts and his senses. He knew it was all of his lover he would be able to have this night and he cherished each one of the memories, holding them close to his heart, childishly hoping his Christmas prayer would be carried in the star's light.

* * *

Christmas Eve was only one day away and the streets were jammed with shoppers, carolers, hooligans, and school kids. Even late into the evening, the London streets were overrun with people window shopping, coming home from work, and just out enjoying the festive holiday season. A smattering of pickpockets and petty thieves wandered among the strollers, but every corner seemed to have two police bobbies stationed on it.

Even the alleyways, dirty and foreboding places on the best of days, now wore a thin cloak of clean, glittering snow, a rarity for London. But despite their illusion of purity, they were still the playground of the disreputable and immoral, traveled by the city's most undesirables.

Here was where Trevor came to re-enact his last night on earth as a mortal. It was his chance to alter the outcome, to pay back his attackers and to soothe his conscience.

And his conscience needed to be soothed. His guilt over enjoying his present life, loving an existence that enabled him to spend all eternity with the one man who made his every moment on earth worth the price he had paid for the gift. His guilt over loving Ian more than he hated his unholy existence as a dark creature banished to the night for all time. Love of a greater power could not transcend his love for Ian. For that, he paid tribute every anniversary of the Savior's birth and his own rebirth.

Trevor leisurely strolled past a small side alley that he knew led to a maze of dozens of other poorly lit, filthy back streets between the stores and workshops that populated this seedier section of town. He waited until the tall police officer a few feet away was looking in the other direction, then moved silently into the alley. He was swiftly swallowed by the shadows of the closely packed buildings.

Following the faint but familiar sounds of a scuffle he had heard from the mouth of the alley, Trevor sidled down the dark pathway, back pressed to the cold damp brick walls, feet soundless as only a vampire's could be. It took only three turns to put him in the heart of the confrontation.

In the light of the single bare bulb hanging from a warehouse iron rod twenty feet up the side of the building to his right, he could see four men entwined a battle of fists and bats. The occasional glitter of metal shone in the dim light as arms and legs twisted around each other and under bodies so rapidly, Trevor wasn't sure who was battling whom.

Not that it mattered to him. In these secluded paths where the underbelly of society basked in the grime, anyone here had nothing but evil on their mind and they deserved whatever happened to them. He felt no pity for any of them and knew he would grant them no mercy.

Trevor cocked his head, listening, to be sure there wasn't anyone else in the nearby alleys or shadowed doorways to witness his actions or creep up on him, whether they be more scum or a wandering policeman. A faint fluttering heartbeat that didn't belong to the group of men in front of him touched his hearing, but it was too fast to be a man's. He shrugged it off as a stray cat and turned his attention to the business at hand.

Allowing the change to happen, Trevor ran his tongue delicately over his fangs as they descended in his mouth, and marveled at how clear his vision became despite the sudden yellow tint to it.

Soundlessly, he swooped down on the men as three of them forced the fourth to the ground and they all rolled around in the gray slush of the alley floor, grunting and swearing. Trevor found it telling that no one called out for help, reinforcing his conviction that none of the men were innocent bystanders.

Baring his teeth and gleefully anticipating the fight, Trevor swooped down on the most aggressive man in the huddle of flying arms and weapons. He snapped the man's neck with a satisfying crunch that only his hearing could detect. He tossed the useless body aside and grabbed a second attacker, the remaining men still unaware of his presence.

The blood lust rose and Trevor battled it down, refusing to feed fully from the likes of this human trash. He did allow them to feel the terror and pain of his vengeful power during the last moment of their lives. He was forced to make it faster than he would have liked, needing to dispatch them quickly before the ever-vigilant police force was alerted to his presence.

By the time he had coldly finished off the top three assailants, his face was contorted in rage and covered in the blood. Moonlight had broken through the clouded night sky and he could see his pale hands shine with an almost luminescent quality. Trevor imagined his face and blond hair looked much the same in the eerie light, unearthly and bright.

The final brawler was sprawled in a heap, wet and gritty from the alley's debris and slush, alive, but nearly senseless from the blows he'd received. Trevor felt no compassion for him. He was no better than the others, just unfortunate enough to be on the wrong side of the numbers. Reaching down to grasp the shirtfront of the man, Trevor paused, body bathed in a ray of moonlight, his fist wrapped in the man's torn, bloodied shirt. His mouth was open, fangs ready to deliver one more round of dark, symbolic justice, when a tiny sound scratched at the edges of his hearing, drawing his attention.

His head snapped up and his keen eyes picked out a small figure near a barred cellar window, jammed into the small shadows of the brick-patterned overhang. As he watched, frozen in place by the presence of an unexpected witness, a young girl crawled out into the moonlight and slowly approached him.

She was just as tattered and grimy as the men, her dark curls tangled and matted, and her soiled clothing inadequate for the season.

Trevor knew he was a terrifying sight, bloodied and fanged, eyes bright yellow and pale skin glowing, but the child slowly walked closer to him, eyes wide and a look of awe on her lean, dirt-smudged face.

"Are you an angel?" She looked and sounded about eight years old, but her sad eyes told of decades beyond that.

"You look like an angel. One of those avenger angels the minister talks about. From the big church daddy takes me to sometimes." She reached for Trevor with one shaking, tiny hand, but halted as the man in Trevor's grip stirred and moaned. "Daddy?"

The man groaned again and slumped. Wordlessly, Trevor let him fall from his grasp, gaze still riveted to the child's tear-streaked face and dark, expressive eyes.

"Thank you for saving my daddy." She gave Trevor a solemn nod and knelt down in the alley slime, gently cradling the man's head in her barely-there lap. Stunned, Trevor let her. "Daddy said we needed to stay away from all the policemen so they wouldn't take me away, but it's awfully dangerous back here."

"I'll be sure to thank you when I say my prayers tonight." She didn't try to shake his hand, but he knew she thought about it by the way her gaze danced over his bloody fists. "My name's Becca. What's yours?"

Trevor stared at her and thought about what to tell her. He decided the less she knew, the better for her. "Gabriel."

He glanced around at the seedy street and was suddenly overwhelmed by the desolate scene of a homeless child and father fighting off villains and leeches for what little they owned. He had miscalculated his victim for the first time in all his years of seeking vengeance. It unsettled him, made his response harsh and clipped.

"You going to sleep here? In the alleys?"

He softened his voice at the child's fearful, startled expression. "This how you're spending Christmas?" Glancing over his shoulder to make sure they were still alone and unheard, Trevor gestured at the gloom surrounding them, his gaze lingering on the bodies of the dead men. "What kinda holiday is this for a little bit like you, eh?"

"It doesn't matter where you spend Christmas as long as you're with someone you love, Gabriel. Daddy says so."

Her words ate at Trevor's heart and he thought about Ian, alone and far away. He knew where he should truly be on this night. But revenge was so hard to let go of.

Becca rubbed the blood off her father's forehead with the cuff of her thin jacket, gaze still locked on Trevor's face. The man was slowly coming around. He hadn't suffered any serious damage that Trevor could see, and his heart sounded strong and regular.

Rage fading, he allowed the change to slip away, self-consciously rubbing the blood off his hands onto his pant legs. "Don't you want presents? Warm food? A safe place to sleep?"

"Uh-huh. I'll get some." She sounded amazingly convinced, considering her present circumstances.

"And just how do you know that, niblet?" Trevor almost laughed at her innocence. It had been so long since he had been exposed to a child's simple, pure reasoning.

Becca looked over her shoulder at the cellar window where she had been hiding, then looked up at Trevor, awe back in her gaze. "Before, when they were fighting? Before you came?"

Uncertain, Trevor nodded to encourage her when she appeared to expect an answer from him.

"I prayed for someone to come and help." She shrugged and a small, solemn smile creased her red-cheeked face. "And then you were here. A Christmas angel." She patted her father's cheek. "And then the bad men were…" She glanced at the nearby corpses from the corner of her eye and quickly looked down at her hands. "…gone."

Becca turned a bright stare on Trevor. "I know prayers get answered now." She leaned into Trevor's personal space and whispered, "I know I'm not supposed to pray for 'things,' but I'm going to ask for a Christmas dinner and a warmer coat for daddy."

The child looked Trevor over from head to toe and then glanced curiously behind him. "Nobody should be alone on Christmas." Reaching out, Becca slipped her hand into one of Trevor's and hesitantly invited, "You can spend it with us if you don't have to go back to heaven right away."

Something sharp lanced through Trevor's chest, and a strange pressure expanded under his ribcage, making it hard for him to draw a breath. His tightly held desire for revenge suddenly dissolved away into the cold night air, leaving the taste of burnt ashes on his lips where traces of the dead men's blood still lingered.

There was someplace he needed to be, someone he needed to be with, this Christmas Eve and every night after that. Someone who loved him despite his selfish, foolhardy quest for unobtainable justice.

Trevor looked at Becca's open, trusting face, her injured father who had only been trying to protect her, and her outstretched hand. He slipped his own hand into hers, marveling at the strength in the tiny fingers that curled around his.

The sound of footsteps hastened his decision, a faint conversation between two bobbies carrying clearly on the crisp night air. He fished in his pants pocket with his free hand as he shook his head at Becca.

"Thanks anyway, but I can't stay, sweetpea." He disengaged his hand and replaced it with a roll of bills. "There's a bit to help get your da fixed up and buy him that coat and such. There enough to keep the coppers from nicking you away from him, too." He stood and darted a glance at the still empty alleyway, waiting to be sure that Becca wouldn't be left prey to some new menace.

"Do you have to go?"

He leaned down, tapped Becca on the nose with a clean knuckle, and winked. "Heaven's waiting for me. Gotta go."

Two officers came into view as they rounded a corner one building away. Trevor leapt into the air, grabbed the fire escape ladder overhead, and scaled the side of the warehouse in under two seconds. He was long gone before the bobbies' eyesight picked him out of the shadows. Shouts and whistles filled the night.

* * *

The single bright star glittered and pulsed, its brilliant light stark against the black sky, surrounded by the feathery gray wisps of slow moving snow clouds.

Ian stared at the star, snowflakes catching in his long, dark eyelashes. The captured snowflakes glistened, distorting his vision as it melted into his eyes. He blinked the moisture away, uncomfortably aware that some of the wetness escaping his eyes wasn't only melted snow.

For the first time in a very long while, Ian let down his guard and allowed his love, loneliness, and the nagging anxiety over Trevor's uncertain safety have free rein. He'd never let anyone else see it, but even a being as self-confident and controlled as he was had doubts and fears. Tonight, these seemed especially strong. He sighed and picked up on the verse where he had left off, speaking softly to the waiting starlight.

"*I am the sunlight on ripened grain...*

I am the gentle autumn rain.

When you waken in the morning rush

I am the swift uplifting rush..."

Pausing for breath, Ian started and turned when another voice took up the poem and finished it for him.

"*Of gentle birds in circling flight...*

I am the soft star that shines at night.

Do not stand at my grave and cry --

I am not there...I did not die..."

Silhouetted by the cheerful Christmas lights and decorations Stuart had hung in the living room, Trevor stood in the open doorway to the patio. The sight took Ian's breath away. His chest ached and his stomach fluttered. Trevor was home.

"I'm sort of glad not to be buried in some cold, wet grave with a load of dirt sitting on my chest." Trevor slowly walked out onto the patio and stood in front of Ian just out of arm's reach. "*I did not die.*" He sniffed and glanced away, then met Ian's expectant gaze. "Kinda glad of that."

The mellow tunes of Nat King Cole drifted on the stream of warm air that escaped the apartment and muted light filtered out from behind Trevor. It shimmered in the pale strands of his blond hair while the crisp, clean snow that still clung to his clothing glimmered in the starlight. He was bathed in the combined rays, front and back, and the effect was glorious. There was a slight pink to his cheeks, marking him as well fed, and a shy smile on his lips. To Ian, he looked like an angel with a burnished halo.

"You're home." Ian swallowed hard and resisted the urge to grab Trevor and drag him into a crushing embrace. He took in a deep breath to steady the flutter in his chest.

"Back early, aren't you?" The thought that Trevor had returned for some darker reason than wanting to be with Ian on Christmas darted across Ian's mind and made him uncharacteristically hesitant.

"Running late, actually." Trevor scuffed his toe in the snow then locked gazes with Ian's uncertain stare. He took another step closer, entering Ian's personal space. He slowly edged forward, closing the gap between them until their bodies brushed.

"Met a Christmas angel last night. Little bitty one named Becca." He ran his hands up the front of Ian's chest, and then slipped his fingers under the edges of Ian's open collar to rub at the carotid pulse points on the vampire's sensitive neck.

"A Christmas angel?" Ian stood very still so as not to dislodge Trevor's tenuous hold. He couldn't keep a skeptical smile from tugging at his lips. "Named Becca."

"Uh huh. A real, live angel. Too skinny, but a sweet bit of fluff." Trevor smirked at Ian's expression, but Ian could tell Trevor was uneasy, maybe even nervous about Ian's reaction to him being home. "She told me Christmas was to be spent with someone you loved."

"Smart bit of fluff." Ian shifted closer and let his hands find the man's slender hips. There was a skittishness in Trevor's approach that made Ian cautious. Instead of pulling Trevor to him, he swayed his own body forward and let their groins touch.

"She was that." Trevor's hands traced the curve of Ian's jaw, his thumbs brushing lightly over Ian's parted lips. His gaze followed his fingertips, then bounced up to meet Ian's appraising stare. "Smarter than me, apparently." Trevor sighed and moistened his bottom lip before admitting, "As bad as it was, she was where she belonged and I wasn't." Trevor pressed his length against Ian.

Ian's arousal burst to life and he felt Trevor's body answer in kind, but he stopped himself from pushing the moment. Instead, he smiled down at Trevor's upturned face and studied his uncertain expression for clues to what his lover was thinking. He saw lust and attraction in Trevor's eyes, along with a new mix of embarrassment and guilt. Puzzled, Ian moved one hand to the small of Trevor's back and massaged the tense muscles there.

"You're sure about being here? After all these decades, you're suddenly done handing out punishment? You're ready to stay with me instead?"

Trevor wordlessly nodded, but the embarrassment in his eyes grew.

Ian cradled Trevor's face between his hands and softly kissed his lips before drawing back. His tone was soft but the look in his eyes was steely. "Why now, Trevor?"

"Realized I was punishing you right along with the thugs that did me in. Didn't mean to, but I was." He dropped his gaze for several seconds. "Might've even meant to. A little."

His own buried guilt surfaced, and Ian felt a rush of forgiveness and understanding wash over him. He'd never known Trevor harbored any guilt over that fateful night. He hadn't objected to Trevor's Christmas activities because he felt he deserved to be punished just as much as Trevor obviously had.

When Ian gently raised Trevor's chin, the starlight glistened in the twin streams of wetness trailing down his face. Snowflakes stuck to the moisture and instantly melted. Ian brushed the tears and flakes away with his thumbs then moved them to brush over Trevor's mouth.

"And now, beauty?"

Trevor leaned into Ian's caress and closed his eyes, his hips slowly grinding against Ian's thigh and cock, a tremulous sigh escaping his lips. "Don't want revenge anymore."

Ian kissed each closed eyelid, first one side then the next, and then back again. "What do you want?" He kissed his way down the side of Trevor's face and nuzzled his neck.

"You. Just you. Best gift I ever got. You and me forever." Trevor craned his head to one side, encouraging Ian to explore further. "You and me on Christmas Eve, just like the first one."

"You remember that one, do you?" Ian nipped the thin skin between neck and shoulder, then licked off the resulting ooze of blood.

Trevor gasped and pressed Ian's face closer. "Can't forget one of the best nights I ever had. You made me go blind for a while that night."

"Blind? Really?" Preening, Ian smirked with delight at the revelation.

Trevor smacked Ian's broad shoulder, unimpressed when the solid bulk didn't budge. "Big-headed bastard, aren't you now! Should never have told you!"

Ian laughed and wiggled his eyebrows at his lover. "Maybe we could try for mute this time." He grabbed Trevor and wrestled him into a crushing embrace, kissing and exploring his lover's mouth and neck until Trevor was breathless and squirming in his arms. His cock was hard and ready, but Ian wanted this to be a seduction unlike any Trevor could remember before this.

An unexpected, overly loud, and dramatic clearing of a dry throat momentarily broke them apart. Still entwined in each other's arms, both vampires glanced guiltily toward the source of the untimely interruption.

"I was going to bring out the mistletoe to set the mood, but I see it isn't necessary." Tossing the festive twig and berries in the air, Stuart turned on his heel and headed back into the apartment, droning tonelessly, "Possibly you would like to tie it around Master Trevor's waist instead?"

Ian instinctively lunged for the object, snatching it out of the air in mid-arc as it sailed overhead. He looked at the mistletoe and then arched one eyebrow at Trevor. He pulled Trevor close and held it up over their heads.

Trevor reached up and slowly pulled Ian's hand back down, mistletoe included. He softly kissed his lover's mouth, breathing his words into Ian's parted lips. "I like Stuart's idea better."

A wicked glint in his eyes, Ian grinned and dropped to his knees. This was going to be a very merry Christmas, indeed.

~ * ~

Laura Baumbach

Laura Baumbach has written fan fiction, short stories, novellas, novels and screenplays. Her first published book was a collection of erotic horror short stories entitled *Demon Spawn: Tales from Demon Under Glass*. Published in March of 2004 by Sybaritic Press, it was the winner of the 2004 DIY awards for best of fan fiction, as well as two SCREWZ awards and two SIZZLER awards. God's Work, a short story from this collection has been nominated for a Huggie Award. She contributed three stories to a second anthology published in March of 2005, *Demon Spawn2*.

A number of her short erotic stories have been published in several on-line e-zines. Her short erotica story, *A Bit of Rough*, nominated for a Fruity Award in 2005, evolved into her first gay erotic romance novel of the same name, published in October of 2005 by Sybaritic Press.

Working in several genres, she is also the author of *The Flight of the Sparrows*, an action/adventure thriller, and three screenplays, *Details of the Hunt, Heartless* and *Second Soul*. She is currently working on another contemporary gay romance novel with a thriller element, *Mexican Heat*, set in the steamy tropics.

For more information check out her site at: http://www.arkwolf.com/LauraBaumbach.

* * *

A VAMPIRE FOR CHRISTMAS

CHRISTMAS

Sedonia Guillone

Chapter One

New York, December 23

"If you want to see your sister alive, you'll bring me St. Cyr's head." Noiret took a drag on his cigarette, his smug gaze never leaving Jesse's face. The vampire exhaled, grinning through the cloud of smoke. "On a silver platter would be nice." He continued watching Jesse, eyes glittering and took a sip of dark crimson blood from the wineglass before him. Around him, the flashing lights of his dance club reflected off his pale skin and hair.

Jesse stared at him, hatred simmering in his very being. God only knew what the fucking bastard had done to Hannah. Through the psychic link Jesse had with his sister, she constantly reassured him that Noiret hadn't touched her, but Jesse knew Noiret was toying with both of them, the typical cat and mouse game the sadistic brand of vampires liked to play when manipulating their victims. Hannah was strong, with the iron physical strength all immortals possessed, but she wasn't strong enough to get away from a pod of vampires alone.

In the background, the sinuous, driving beat of dance music vibrated through his chest, aggravating his already pounding heart. "Why me, Noiret? There are scores of vampire slayers out there. I haven't slain for centuries." Not since a Coeur Eternel, vampires whose heart still beat and only fed in the act of mercy killing, humanely put Sondra out of her misery during the American Revolution.

The beautiful woman he'd loved with his heart and soul was bleeding slowly and painfully to death when the CE found her. Instead, her last moments of life were pleasurable and she was able to pass on without all the agony that accompanied a bayonet wound in the gut. Jesse had seen the dark figure hulking over Sondra's dying form and had raised his stake with both hands about to plunge it into the vampire's back, right where the heart was. However, Sondra's sighs of pleasure and the blissful expression that replaced her agony had caused Jesse to freeze. In that moment, when he'd understood the mercy the CE had imparted to Sondra, he'd never touched another vampire, Coeur Eternel, eternal heart, or Sans Ame, without a soul. Not with the intent to murder, anyway.

"The answer is simple, Harmon." Noiret set down his glass and took another leisurely puff on his cigarette. "Because you were once the best."

Jesse gritted his teeth. Noiret did not possess one redeeming quality, something even the worst of vampires had. This fucker came the closest to pure evil Jesse had ever met. And he'd met some bad ones, as was inevitable when you were an immortal who'd inhabited this godforsaken planet since the Roman Empire.

A lock of Noiret's platinum hair came loose from its tie. The woman fawning over him from behind his chair reached forward with a long red fingernail and pushed it back for him. Noiret grasped her hand and scraped one fang across her palm. She cried out and tried to yank her hand back, but Noiret held her wrist hard and swiped his tongue across the broken skin.

He spent a moment feasting on the cut and finally looked back up at Jesse, his pupils dilated and glowing with bloodlust. Jesse was glad not to have the heightened senses of a vampire, for he would have had to smell the scent of blood that no doubt filled the space around Noiret's corner table. Being empathic was bad enough most of the time. The woman's pain and distress already echoed through him. She'd thought getting involved with Noiret would be orgasmic and life-enhancing. She was about to learn otherwise, the poor creature.

"Why do you want St. Cyr dead?" Jesse didn't know St. Cyr and didn't care to. He also hated taking this time for questions while Hannah was in Noiret's clutches, but the more he knew about the situation, the better chance he had of, perhaps, finding Noiret's weak spots. Every vampire, like every human and every immortal, had at least one. If he was going to get Hannah away from Noiret, he needed all the help he could get.

Noiret's eyes narrowed, the glow of lust in the fathomless irises intensifying. "Not that it's any of your fucking business, but he once killed someone very special to me. Murdered her. Drank every drop of her blood, until she was gone." The vampire stared at him as if to drive his passionate hatred straight into Jesse's soul.

Vengeance. *Great.* Hannah's life was in Noiret's filthy hands because of a vendetta. Vampire vendettas were always hideous.

Jesse studied Noiret's expression another moment before his empathic senses kicked in. Something was off here. Vampires never hired out for vengeance killings, preferring to do the work themselves. Jesse knew he risked Noiret's wrath by asking the question hovering on his lips, but his intuition told him the information could be valuable. He crossed his arms in front of him. His body was warm in its black leather jacket, but he didn't care. He wasn't going to be in this hellhole of a club much longer. He was going to be out hunting down St. Cyr. "Why not kill him yourself?"

A frisson of anger slithered through Noiret's eyes, the irises returned to their ice blue color. His unshaven upper lip curled. "You think to humiliate me, Harmon. But *I'm* the one holding your sister's lush body for myself."

Jesse's hands curled into fists. He wanted nothing more than to drive the knife in his belt through the vile creature's heart, but to even try was suicide. And would cost Hannah her life.

"If you must know, I want him humiliated. If I or another vampire were to kill him, it's a fair fight. However, if he were to die at the hands of an immortal, well, there's no honor in *that.*"

Jesse watched Noiret's face, waiting for the reverberations from the vampire's being to give him the truth of Noiret's essence. Even the soulless ones could be read.

For several moments, nothing happened. Jesse's chest tightened for fear that his empathy was failing him. But no. In the next moment, the curls of heat penetrated his mind. The knowledge rose. He struggled to keep a straight face.

Noiret feared St. Cyr.

Hmm...

Jesse sighed, realizing it didn't matter. Fear or not, Hannah was Noiret's prisoner. Jesse's beautiful sister was all he had left in the world. Immortals were scattered across the globe. They weren't clannish by nature like vamps. Immortals mistrusted each other and remained isolated. They weren't like the immortals portrayed in that popular film in the sense they had to kill each other off. It was more like the reality that immortality was damned painful and immortals couldn't bear the sight of one another, agonizing reminders of their never ending fate. Miraculously, Hannah was different. She adored her brother. It was mutual. They cherished each other, kept each other company. Losing her would leave him completely alone for eternity. Not to mention that her death at Noiret's hands would make medieval torture a desirable alternative.

"Where will I find St. Cyr?"

Noiret grinned, his eyes lighting with his obvious hunger for St. Cyr's head. "Boston. Beacon Hill."

"How will I know him?"

"Tall, blond, with a nice deep scar on one cheek. A gift from me a few hundred years ago."

Strange. Vampires didn't scar. At least not the Sans Ame. Christ! Was St. Cyr a Coeur Eternel? Damnit, the very kind he'd especially sworn never to kill. He thought of Hannah, of what she could suffer at Noiret's hands. And fangs. Resolve pounded through him. Fuck it. For Hannah, he'd kill anyone. He nodded.

"I want him by New Year's, Harmon. Or...well...you know."

Jesse's blood chilled. "Fucking bastard," he muttered.

Noiret's grin deepened. "Yes, I am, aren't I?"

Before Jesse lost it completely, he turned. The sooner he left this club, the better.

"Oh, Harmon."

Jesse stopped, gritted his teeth again. But he didn't turn around.

Noiret chuckled. "Merry Christmas."

Chapter Two

Boston, December 24

Christian smelled death as soon as he entered his patient's hospital room. The heart of the man in the bed still beat, but the asphyxia he'd suffered in his suicide attempt had killed his brain.

A nurse entered the room behind Christian, the soft whoosh of her scrubs crashing in his ears. After nearly a thousand years of life, he'd never quite gotten used to the heightened senses of a vampire. Perhaps that came with wishing you could get your soul back.

The craving to feed rose from deep within his belly. He glanced at the nurse, a Coeur Eternel named Bettina, who'd been placed in Mass General by Darelle Mimieux, the priestess of the CE's sect headquartered in Paris.

Bettina nodded to him, silently giving him the go ahead. Her own desire to feed showed in the soft glow in her eyes, but the CE's warned against conspicuous behavior. Two of them in one hospital room, feeding, could attract too much attention should someone walk in unexpectedly. "Call me if you need assistance, Dr. Cullen," she said, using his assumed name, the name he'd adopted back in medical school.

"Thank you, Bettina."

She nodded and slipped from the room, leaving him to feed.

Even though Christian wasn't completely one of them, the CE's had shown only sympathy to his plight and allotted him a fair share of mercy feedings. Darelle had warned him that mercy feedings would not get him his soul back as he wished, but she understood that his conscience ached and tried to help him. She'd shown great forgiveness to Christian St. Cyr, whose mixed ancestry of Coeur Eternel and Sans Ame had caused him to feed for pleasure so often that the repentant side of his being was tormented nearly beyond repair. Not even the absence of a heart beating in his chest had dampened their compassion for and acceptance of him.

With the door safely closed, Christian turned to the dying man. He reached out, pushing back a lock of the young man's blond hair. He'd been handsome and Christian wondered what had made him so unhappy as to want to end his own life. This wasn't the first botched suicide attempt that Christian had needed to put to rest, but the fact that a living being had felt such depth of despair rocked Christian deep inside, as if it were the first.

Even though the young man's brain was already dead, the CE's felt that a mercy killing for such a soul could still help them. The soul was bigger than the body, they said, a reality Christian already knew. Dying from an act of compassion could still help the soul when it took its next embodiment, hopefully one that would find a better life and more happiness than the last.

The scent of blood moving through the man's veins stirred Christian's hunger again. The desire churned, radiating through his entire body, bringing with it a sexual rush he needed to satisfy. He leaned over, driven by the pale supple flesh of the man's throat, the tiny pulse moving underneath, weak yet throbbing with just enough life to entice him.

Christian tenderly swiped his tongue across the spot he was to bite. The drag of his taste buds across the sweet flesh caused his fangs to ache. Curling back his lips, he pushed, piercing the flesh with as little force as possible.

The man made no sound, but inside, where his soul was trapped, Christian could almost hear the sigh of pleasure, the orgasmic tightening throughout his body that he himself had experienced centuries ago under his sire's fangs.

Slipping his fangs out, Christian closed his lips over the puncture marks and suckled, drawing the coppery liquid into his mouth. It pooled deliciously on his tongue and slipped down his throat, the muscle contracting with each swallow.

Sip by sip, he drank, until the sound of the man's beating heart ceased and Christian felt him at peace. Taking a deep breath, Christian stood up, licking the residue of blood off his lips. He pulled a tissue out of the box on the bedside table and wiped his mouth, stuffing the tissue into the pocket of his white coat.

Leaving the room he passed the nurses' station and nodded to Bettina. She nodded back, the signal that she would take the necessary steps to ensure that the man's passing did not look at all suspicious. The CE's understood all too well that even though the suffering they eased was appreciated by those who were suffering, the rest of the world wouldn't see it that way and their existence would be threatened.

He glanced at the clock on the wall. His shift was over. He was free to go home. Heaviness settled over him as it did each night. What was he going home to? An empty brownstone whose loneliness echoed off the hardwood floors and white walls? The Christmas tree blinking multi-colored lights in the corner of the vast living room only reminded him that he was alone. Yet, he could never resist putting one up every year. Hope, perhaps.

Christian changed out of his doctor's coat and bundled up to go outside. It was two in the morning and the trains weren't running at this hour, so he chose to walk the distance from Mass General to Beacon Hill where he lived.

What the hell. What else did he have to do? When one was alone for eternity, a solitary walk on a winter's night before Christmas Eve could do a body good. Even if the body didn't have a soul.

* * *

Alone on the empty street corner, Jesse rubbed his gloved hands together, then chafed them up his arms, stomping around to keep warm. One more shitty thing about being immortal. Unlike vamps whose sense of heat and cold was muted, immortals felt the changes of temperature almost like any normal human. He should have dressed for the season, but he'd been in too big a rush to concern himself with warmth.

His breath puffed into the winter air, illumined by the streetlamp. He checked his watch. Almost three in the morning. Where the hell was St. Cyr? According to the reconnaissance Jesse had done since getting to Boston, the vampire was working as a physician in Mass General and finished his shift at two a.m.

He double-checked his information, scribbled on a piece of paper. Yeah, this was the right address, a high-end neighborhood, one of the oldest and fanciest in Boston, with beautiful brownstone houses in quiet rows. A swanky neighborhood such as this one befitted a vampire who'd had God knows how many centuries to gather wealth. So why was St. Cyr working as an M.D.? Certainly not for the cash.

Jesse shook himself. It did no good to speculate about St. Cyr. Doing so only made him more...human, for lack of a better word. Harder to kill that way. Even in Jesse's heyday as an eager vampire slayer, he'd had to not think of the personal lives of his targets, even those of the vilest characters. Maybe that characteristic of his had pointed to the fact that all along he hadn't really had the heart of a killer.

That didn't matter now. Heart or no heart, Hannah's life was in his hands.

The worst part was he couldn't possibly know if this plan would work. He had to be cautious. Vampires were by nature intelligent and suspicious. They also had a high degree of empathic ability. Granted it was limited to the ones with whom they'd established a link through feeding, not free-for-all like Jesse's, but the ability was still there.

Feeling restless, Jesse went halfway down the block, making sure the hit he'd hired was all set. The guy in the car waved to him. Jesse signaled for him to wait a bit longer. He could only pray his plan worked. As soon as he saw St. Cyr, he'd signal to the driver of the car, the guy would pass, put a couple of bullets into Jesse, and when St. Cyr went to assist him, Jesse would pull his knife out and plunge it into St. Cyr's chest. It wasn't a stake, but an immortal's slaying knife, if placed in just the right spot, would serve to incapacitate the vampire enough to let Jesse finish him off and get his head. Jesse couldn't help feeling his plan was half-assed, but he didn't have the luxury of time.

The sound of footsteps caused him to turn. Someone was coming down the sidewalk. Jesse made his way back up to the spot where he'd been waiting and pretended to be a passerby. He glanced at the figure drawing closer. Tall. Broad-shouldered. So far fitting the description. A little closer and Jesse caught the glint of golden hair, soft and full, like a lion's mane, under the street lamp. The kind of hair he'd always found sexy...

A little closer and the man's face came into view. There it was, the gash-like scar on the cheek. Noiret's "gift." Jesse was face to face with his quarry.

St. Cyr.

Jesse's gaze connected with the vampire's. He couldn't see the color of St. Cyr's eyes in the dim lamplight, but he noticed their fathomless depth of emotion. He gave the signal to his hired hit before he lost his nerve.

The engine, which had been idling, gunned to life and pealed away from the curb. Jesse kept walking as the tires squealed past him and the shots rang out, pumping lead into his body.

It had been centuries since he'd had bullets pound through his flesh and he was unprepared for the impact. His body spun out of control as the bullets sprayed his body, embedding themselves deep inside him. The pain was unlike any he'd ever known.

The last thing he felt was the hard strike of his buckled knees hitting the pavement. He keeled over, utterly powerless. Then the world went black.

Chapter Three

Christian spun around, the sound of screeching tires and the acrid smell of gunpowder assaulting his senses. The echoes of the shots reverberated through the freezing still air, punctuated by a dog's barking and lights going on in windows facing the street.

He bounded to the fallen man, who, just a moment before, had caught Christian's eye with his Roman good looks.

Christian knelt down and peered into the man's face. Surprisingly, the dark eyes were still open, though mostly the whites showed, the irises rolled back. His lips were parted, breath panting. By all accounts, he should be dead. No one survived such a shower of lead.

The man let out a couple of choked coughs. His eyelids closed, his breath rasped. Strong as he was to still be at all alive, he was certainly dying.

A siren rang in the distance. Christian looked around. Lights in apartment windows were flicking on and in another moment, the street would no longer be quiet. He needed to move quickly.

Sliding his gloved hands under the man's body, Christian lifted him up carefully, turned and sprang, gliding, weightless, to the roof of his building. Here, he could have privacy to put the man out of his misery.

Christian set the dying man gently onto his back on the graveled roof. He pulled off his gloves, his heightened sight distinguishing the dark stains of crimson on the sleeves of his coat. He put his fingertips to the pulse on the man's neck. The tiny beat throbbed slowly, at the same sluggish rate as the pulse of the man in the hospital earlier. He sensed this man's life ebbing away.

The siren drew closer, coming to a stop by the spot where the shooting had been. Christian ignored it, giving his complete attention to the man lying before him. The metallic scent of blood curled into his nostrils, teasing, rousing his hunger even though he'd just fed. He pulled open the man's coat and gently tugged down the turtleneck collar of his black shirt.

Curling up his lips, he bent over and sank his incisors into the soft flesh on the side of the man's throat. Pulling them out, he suckled blood from the punctures, his own body throbbing with arousal. The man's skin had a feral, musky scent that spoke to Christian, deep inside. The salty sweet taste of his flesh mixed with his blood sang through Christian's body. He drank deeply, inhaling the man's sweet essence along with his blood. He was a good soul, Christian sensed, someone Christian could have loved.

The man's heartbeat, loud in Christian's ears, slowed to a dying crawl and halted.

Christian imbibed one last drop of blood and sat up, swiping his lips with the heel of his hand. He knelt beside the still body, staring down at the tranquil face, now more visible by moonlight. Christian's ethereal heart ached, unable to house all the emotion and appreciation of the man's physical beauty it felt. The man had a high forehead across which a small lock of dark hair had fallen. The eyebrows gracefully arched over dark thick fringes of lashes. His cheekbones planed down to beautifully sculpted lips and a cleft chin. The lightest shade of stubble growth covered his jaw and upper lip, giving him a rugged appearance.

Christian marveled at the beauty of his form, the likes of which he hadn't seen since the days of Roman soldiers. Not that there weren't handsome men in the world. There certainly were, but this man had something...something Christian couldn't identify, that mystified him and made him ache that he'd never know him.

Before he knew what he was doing, Christian reached out and tenderly passed his hand over the man's forehead and hair, caressing as if to comfort him.

Sudden movement caught Christian's eye. What the...? Is that what he thought it was? The eyelashes fluttering? He drew back his hand, staring. The pouty bottom lip worked slightly, followed by the whoosh of an intake of breath.

Christian gasped. No! He hadn't brought this man across, had he? He'd vowed centuries ago, when the CE's had taken him in as one of them, that he would not sire ever again. He'd only sired a couple of times before that, regretting each one. Death had always seemed preferable to a soulless existence, and he hated damning another to that fate, no matter whether the person desired it or not.

Christian's heart sank. The man was undoubtedly coming back to life and Christian didn't bother to check for a pulse. The life that showed itself now was certainly that of the undead.

Dammit! As magnificent as this man was and as much as he'd stirred Christian's desire to mate, Christian had broken his sacred vow. He'd fed from this man and rendered him immortal, doomed to bloodlust. Christian was responsible for him now. For eternity.

Tenderly, he slipped his hands underneath the limp body, now pulsing again with weak life. Lifting him up, Christian carried him gently through the roof entrance, into the house, to his bedroom.

He set his new charge carefully onto the rug in front of the fireplace and went to build a fire. The glow of flames and cozy warmth would ease his charge's shock at waking and finding himself a vampire. The transition, of course, was gradual, but the man would no doubt be experiencing physical illness as his insides regenerated.

Christian built the fire, something he hadn't done in a long time even though he kept the flue and chimney clean and ready, then turned his attention to the man lying on the rug. The soft glimmering of flames illumined the man's features, making him appear god-like, showing off the olive tone of his skin. The dark fans of his eyelashes still rested on his tanned cheeks and his breathing had grown stronger, steadier, as life -- such as it was -- infused him.

Christian gently pulled open the man's black leather coat, noting that the garment, though sleek and attractive, was lighter than the season demanded. Underneath, he wore no sweater, only a black turtleneck, now in blood-soaked tatters from the shower of bullets. Christian went for a pair of scissors and carefully cut the shirt open, revealing the man's torso. The firelight danced off the mass of damaged flesh and crusts of drying blood. The bullets had burrowed deep into the man's body, no doubt piercing internal organs. However, even as Christian watched, the skin was healing, the bullet wounds sealing up, slowly expelling the mounds of lead like a film rewinding in slow motion.

For nearly an hour, Christian watched the man's body heal. When the process had almost finished, Christian collected the bullets, dropped them into the fire and went down to the kitchen to pour a glass of cow's blood for his protégé. Doubtless, he'd awaken with great hunger and thirst for blood, as was always the case. Christian brought the glass back upstairs, set it on the bedside table and crouched back down by his charge, his breath catching when he looked at him.

The flesh of the man's torso had completely healed, revealing two round hard hillocks of chest muscle topped with smooth, cinnamon-colored nipples. A sprinkling of soft raven hair covered the muscles, then tapered to a sleek trail down the center of his flat hard stomach. His waist was lean and sculpted, the belly button deep and inviting for the swivel of the tip of Christian's tongue. He was magnificent, this creature, the sight of his olive-toned flesh ending where his jeans covered it.

Christian stared down at his still unconscious protégé, his conscience unable to distinguish between affection and lust churning within him. Chris hadn't had a lover in several years, when the strain of wanting to feed during sex overwhelmed him and made abstinence the less conscience-wracking course.

The man's chest rose and fell steadily now, the hairs on his flesh glinting in the firelight with each inhalation. Suddenly, his eyes opened, the heavy fringes of lashes parting to reveal dark liquid eyes, huge and fathomless.

Chris returned the unblinking gaze, which alternately seduced and surprised him. His protégé's pupils weren't dilated at all with the glow of the undead, nor did they shine with the hunger of blood lust. Chris frowned. Something was different here...off. Or, perhaps, Chris was merely out of practice at siring. Remembering the waiting goblet of blood, he retrieved it and knelt down.

"Are you thirsty?"

The man stared up at him, his dark luminous eyes not appearing to comprehend. In spite of that, he gave a tiny nod of his head.

"I thought as much." Chris slipped a large hand into his patient's coal-black hair, sleekly soft against his fingertips, and cradled the man's head, lifting it the tiniest bit. Chris put the goblet of blood to the man's lips and tilted it until some of the crimson liquid slipped into his mouth.

The man swallowed, then immediately choked, sputtering the blood out of his mouth as if it were acid. The blood ran down his chin, onto his neck.

Chris frowned again and set the goblet aside. He used the man's tattered shirt to wipe the scarlet liquid gently off his skin. "I'm sorry," he murmured, "Perhaps I gave you too much."

The man was staring up at him, his chest heaving, the liquid depths of his eyes showing panic. The expression touched off Chris's own despair. What had he done? In the name of ending the man's suffering, he'd turned this man into something he obviously didn't want to be.

Tenderly, Chris lowered the man's head back down to the rug and slipped his fingers out of the thick hair. Sorrow burned in Chris's throat and chest for the poor, magnificent man…vampire…lying before him.

His protégé's softly arched lips were working. A hoarse scraping sound came from his throat. He was obviously trying to speak. "Wa…wa…" He fell silent, speech clearly difficult.

Chris furrowed his brow, trying to understand what his charge needed. He lifted the goblet up to offer another try at sipping, but the man recoiled with the lift of his chin, eyeing the cup as if it contained the vilest substance imaginable. "No blood?" Chris asked.

He shook his head. "Wa…wat…"

"Water?"

The stranger nodded with surprising swiftness for someone in his condition.

Chris stared at him another moment, then rose and went to the bathroom. He dumped the unwanted blood down the sink, rinsed the cup and filled it from the tap. Returning to his charge, he knelt down, cradling the thick head of raven hair gently and lifting it again. This time, when he tilted the goblet to the man's lips, the liquid was swiftly sucked down in greedy gulps. The water itself seemed to restore the man's strength to some degree and he continued to take long, heavy swallows until the water was gone.

When he'd finished, Christian lowered his head to the carpet. "Do you need more water?"

His...protégé -- or was he his protégé? -- shook his head, still breathing heavily.

Christian set the cup aside and studied the now living breathing man who'd closed his eyes again, seeming to rest from the exertion of drinking.

* * *

Jesse heaved a deep breath. Fuck. Fuck. *Fuck.* Something had gone terribly wrong. The bullets shouldn't have affected him this deeply. Since when had he developed a weakness for lead? He'd never considered that could happen, but it had. He'd known of other immortals developing such weaknesses. If he'd communicated a bit more with other immortals over the centuries, perhaps he would have known sooner.

Too late now.

Even in the haze of his wounded state, he understood that St. Cyr had fed on him and now believed him to be a vampire.

If he's not a vampire, what is he?

Jesse's eyes shot open. The voice had spoken strongly in his mind. Not his own voice. Not his own thoughts. He looked at the large blond vampire hovering over him, the firelight reflecting off his pale skin and deep blue eyes. The sight momentarily captured him. His gaze went to the scar on St. Cyr's high-boned cheek. Not even the reddish jagged scar detracted from the vampire's rugged, masculine Norse Viking beauty.

Strangely, the way he lingered on St. Cyr's face caused a spot on his neck to tingle, reminding Jesse of the pleasure his body had experienced when the vampire had bitten him and suckled his blood. With the first touch of St. Cyr's lips on Jesse's neck, Jesse's entire body shuddered deliciously, as if every nerve ending had exploded in orgasm. Though his skin had no doubt already healed, the ghostly memory of the feeding remained.

Perhaps he's immortal.

Shit! St. Cyr again! The feeding had connected them. Jesse's rejection of the blood had raised St. Cyr's suspicions. It would only get worse when he found Jesse's knife in the belt at his back. He had to kill St. Cyr as soon as he had his strength and get the hell out of here with St. Cyr's head.

Can you hear me?

Jesse's breath caught. St. Cyr was addressing him directly now. He couldn't let on that there was a mind link between them. The difference between the mind links of vampires and that of immortals was that immortals had greater lateral access to thoughts and feelings. Vampires' psychic connections were limited to telepathic communication only. Thank God for small miracles.

Jesse stared up at St. Cyr, as if there were no connection. He watched the corners of St. Cyr's beautifully shaped masculine lips curve downward. He waited for the vampire to speak again.

St. Cyr remained quiet. He reached out a large hand and smoothed back Jesse's hair. The vampire had a surprisingly gentle touch. His bite had been tender as well, so careful about how deeply he pushed his incisors into Jesse's skin.

"You should rest now," St. Cyr told him. His voice had a pleasing tone, deep and resonant. The vampire's loneliness emanated from him and Jesse felt the emotion in his touch. He continued to caress Jesse's hair, causing Jesse's traitorous body to tingle and relax. Jesse's eyelids shuttered rapidly with the pleasure of the touch. In centuries of life, he hadn't felt another one quite like St. Cyr's. Gentle, soothing. Kind and…erotic, all at once.

Jesse's cock stirred in his jeans. If he hadn't been so enervated from the bullet wounds, he would have reached up and pulled St. Cyr down on top of him. His exhaustion was the only thing that stopped him.

Well, that and the fact that he was here to kill St. Cyr.

Jesse prayed that in a few hours he'd have the strength to carry out the task before St. Cyr discovered their connection. And he would figure it out. It was inevitable. They were linked for eternity now. Or until Jesse got the vampire's head.

That is, if Jesse could bring himself to slay someone whose psyche was now deeply entwined with his own.

Fucking shit. Being immortal not only sucked much of the time, now it was a downright curse.

Jesse opened his eyes again and looked up at St. Cyr, panic rising deep inside as exhaustion overtook him again. He thought of the knife in his belt, concealed only by his body lying on top of it. All St. Cyr had to do was slip his hand underneath him and find it. The vampire's innate intelligence and suspicion would help him put the truth together, if he hadn't already begun to.

Damn this fucking lead to hell! The weakness the substance had produced in his body exceeded his own healing powers. His skin was no longer broken and his body had expelled the bullets. However, this latent weakness of his left him unable to rise and finish what he'd begun. By all appearances, he wouldn't be killing St. Cyr anytime soon. Especially with his eyelids growing sooo...heavy.

Must...not...sleep. Jesse thrashed his head back and forth, struggling to keep his eyes open. He was losing the battle. The lead had done something inside him, prolonging his complete healing. If he tried to kill St. Cyr now, the vampire would easily overpower him and kill *him*. He needed his full strength in order to go against a vampire, no matter how compassionate the vamp seemed to be.

Compassion wouldn't win out over survival, to be sure.

Losing the battle against his illness, Jesse released a long shuddering breath and surrendered to the call of sleep.

Chapter Four

Chris watched the man sleep. The dark-haired god, for that was how he appeared to Chris, had seemed to fight the sleepiness that overcame him, but then succumbed. He needed a bath desperately to wash away the encrusted blood covering his healed body, but he'd obviously been too tired, so Chris had simply watched him lose the fight against his exhaustion.

Fine. If he'd healed in one hour from a shower of bullet wounds, most likely, he'd be ready for a bath when he awoke.

In the meantime, Chris was content to gaze on him, to watch the dance of the firelight on his skin and hair and to imagine what those voluptuous Roman lips would taste like. *What manner of man is he?* The question in his mind made Chris smile, as it was phrased in the Elizabethan English of centuries ago he'd loved so much.

The man wasn't a vampire. That much was certain. A vampire would have sucked down the goblet of blood before even realizing what the substance was. Scent alone would have roused his hunger to a pitch. Chris, remembering his own moments of awakening as a vampire, had responded precisely that way to his first whiff of blood.

That left two choices. Werewolf or immortal. Chris reached for one of the man's hands and gently lifted it, examining it in the firelight. He searched for the telltale crook'd thumb that weyres had while in human form. This man's thumb was perfectly shaped, as were all his fingers, the digits sensuously thick and rugged, made for stroking and caressing a lover.

Sooo…his Roman god was an immortal.

Chris sighed his relief, even as his insides tingled. He hadn't sired the man into a vampire. Praise God. And…well…though vampire-immortal pairings were exceedingly rare because the two groups were often at odds and always suspicious of each other, the few brief affairs Chris had had with immortals had always been the most delicious he'd ever known. The blood of immortals regenerated, just as this one's had, enabling the vampire to feed on his partner whenever it was desired without the risk of death. And then, if the two were to fall in love, death would never separate them. Christian sighed. A long time ago, he'd run from his last lover, hating his own desire to feed for pleasure. Now, sitting here, gazing on this beautiful Roman immortal, long-slumbering desires for a mate resurged, making Chris ache.

In any case, he was letting his hopeful imagination get away from him. What were the chances that this particular immortal was available for such a mutually enjoyable pairing? They had literally been passing each other in the night when a car had sped by, the driver shooting the immortal full of bullets.

Wait a second. A tiny warning voice…a niggling, intelligent voice borne of centuries of existence began to speak deep in Chris's mind. In his memory, he ran through the incident over and over, wondering each time at the extraordinary timing of the shooter.

Perhaps it wasn't so extraordinary. Perhaps the bullets had been meant for him? Lead wouldn't have killed him but it would have incapacitated him long enough for someone to…

Christ. Chris had collected enemies over the centuries. However, none of those enemies was an immortal, not even among the few with whom he'd gotten romantically involved. No bitterness between himself and any weyre as well. He'd always lived peaceably with his fellow kith. That left vampires.

Hmm…A vampire who hated him, who would send an immortal to do his work for him. There was only one he knew of that cowardly. That low. Only one vampire with a vendetta for him still existed on this earth who would try to blindside an enemy.

Noiret.

Chris stared down at the sleeping immortal, his mind slowly but surely putting the pieces together. He, himself, like Noiret, was a powerful vampire, being very old and sired by Valmont Lascaux, *the* oldest vampire in existence. If the immortal had simply tried to attack him on the street, Chris would have had an equal chance of killing his opponent. No. The bullets had been meant for the immortal who'd staged the shooting, somehow knowing Chris would take him in and make himself vulnerable in the act of nursing the wounded immortal back to health.

It all made perfect sense.

However, obviously, something had gone seriously wrong. If it hadn't, the immortal would have been able to attack Chris as soon as his wounds healed. Perhaps the bullets had rendered more damage than the immortal had meant them to. Immortals did, Chris knew, develop weaknesses to certain substances over time. Perhaps this Roman had a weakness to lead.

Which meant that Chris's intended killer was still ill and at the mercy of his own quarry. Unless he was faking, feigning serious illness until Chris no longer had any doubts or suspicions. Any immortal worth the knife he carried would understand the thought processes of a vampire.

A knife. Of course!

Carefully, Chris slipped his hand under the sleeping man's back, his fingertips coming immediately into contact with the hard steel of a blade. Immortals had their own brand of knife, especially those immortals who were vampire hunters. Immortals' slaying knives were weapons strong enough to end the life of any kith.

A vampire slayer. Which this immortal apparently was if Noiret had hired him.

Christian worked the knife out of the immortal's belt and slid it out from underneath him. He held the blade up to the light, watching the glow of flames glint off the polished steel. The blade was long enough and sharp enough to impale a vampire, no matter how powerful, and bring about his or her dissolution.

Christian sighed, his hopes of having found a lover cruelly dashed. He gazed down at the beautiful Roman asleep on the carpet as he came to terms with what must happen next.

Of course, there was only one thing he could do now.

* * *

Jesse, where are you? Are you all right? Jesse!

Hannah's voice sounded, louder and louder, rousing Jesse from sleep.

His eyes were closed, his body heavy and immoveable. *Hannah, he hasn't touched you, has he?*

No. But he's threatened to. Soon. Where are you, Jesse?

I'm where I'm supposed to be. I'll come soon. I'll have the vampire's head and I'll get you free. I promise.

Oh, Jesse, please be careful. I couldn't bear it if something happened to you.

It won't, Hannah. I promise.

Jesse opened his eyes. His body felt stiff and sore. He went to stretch and found he couldn't move at all. Heavy weight pressed into his wrists and ankles. He tried to move again and couldn't.

Suddenly, reality slammed in on him. His hands and feet were bound, his limbs spread-eagled. The softness of a bed cushioned his weight, pillows under his head. Four posters, dark wood, heavy, like those found in a lord's castle, loomed up around him. Firelight danced in the hearth, the same fireplace he remembered from the last time he was conscious. Only now, as his awareness grew, he realized he wore not a stitch of clothing, his naked, prone body covered by a sheet.

He blinked several times, realizing he wasn't alone. A second weight pressed into the mattress beside him. Jesse tilted his head and saw...him. St. Cyr. The blond vampire, himself fully clothed, his button down shirt opened enough to reveal most of his broad chest with its soft mat of golden hair, sat close beside him, staring down into his eyes.

However, that in itself wasn't enough to alarm Jesse. What stirred his fear and caused him to tug at his bonds, however vainly, was the fact that St. Cyr held Jesse's slaying knife, the shiny blade pointed directly at Jesse's heart.

Chapter Five

Jesse remained silent, his weakened body unable to tug free of the bonds. He glanced up at the shackles, not needing to guess at their substance. Lead, of course. He sneered inwardly at himself, at how truly half-assed his plan had been, not to test himself first and make certain he could withstand lead. He'd seen other immortals develop weaknesses to certain metals, but having lived a basically peaceful existence since giving up slaying, he'd not bothered to keep himself up to date on his own weaknesses.

St. Cyr must have figured things out while Jesse slept and had chosen the shackles with that in mind.

Now Jesse was fucked. Without a kiss.

St. Cyr cleared his throat. "I suppose it would be useless to ask who sent you here to kill me." His voice floated softly in the air, surprisingly free of menace. "Seeing as I already know."

Jesse didn't respond. Having his own knife pointed a few inches from his chest made him a bit extra cautious.

The vampire sighed. He turned the blade over as if fascinated by it. "Beautiful craftsmanship," he murmured. "The immortal craftsmen are the last true artisans left in the world, I'm afraid."

Jesse watched him, every nerve in his weak body tensed, trembling. Was St. Cyr toying with him? Tormenting him in his last moments? Vampires often did like to bat their prey around psychologically before moving in for the kill. And yet, with his empathic abilities still intact, Jesse didn't get the sense that St. Cyr was playing a game. The sound in his voice was too...hurt.

Well, seeing as Jesse had come to kill him, such a response was understandable. But, then again, wouldn't St. Cyr be more angry? Ready to kill Jesse to protect himself? What was the vampire waiting for if he wasn't tormenting Jesse before killing him?

A moment more passed and Jesse understood. His empathic understanding flooded in unimpeded. St. Cyr's tone conveyed more than hurt. The vampire felt betrayed. Let down. When Jesse had revived, the vampire had hoped for a mate, only to learn that his potential mate was really there to kill him. In spite of the situation, Jesse sympathized with St. Cyr. He, himself, knew only too well the feeling of betrayal, having lived through it so many times himself over the centuries. He experienced another flash of sympathy, an emotion that could have been stronger in him if Hannah's life weren't hanging on St. Cyr's head.

St. Cyr examined the knife a moment longer and leaned over, setting the weapon gently down on the bedside table.

Jesse heaved a deep sigh, the relief flowing in such a rush through him that he couldn't suppress the sound he made.

The vampire looked down at him, his blue eyes smoldering in the strangest way. "I know *why* Noiret sent you," he said, his tone still free of anger. He folded his arms across that broad chest. "The only thing I haven't figured out is why he sent *you*. I know there's a reason. Noiret has a perverse taste for drama and torment. He must have something you want. Something important." St. Cyr tilted his blond head, the movement causing the firelight to glint off the thick golden tresses. "Or maybe...someone."

Jesse continued to watch him, the sound of his own heartbeat crashing in his ears. The knowledge that he was completely at St. Cyr's mercy gripped him with the same agony as if he'd been forced to drink lead. Whatever the vampire wished to do to him, he could. As long as Jesse's strength was at all hindered, he didn't have a chance. As strong as immortals were, vampires were stronger.

Unless...well, St. Cyr was a Coeur Eternel. That possibility existed. From his experience of CE's Jesse knew that compassion was a force within them they couldn't control, as strong in their very makeup as the hunger to feed.

Of course. He'd forgotten completely about that. The scar in St. Cyr's cheek wouldn't be there unless he was a CE. Perhaps if he'd simply insinuated himself with St. Cyr to begin with, he could have explained his plight to him and gained him as an ally. Then, the two of them could have joined together and freed Hannah.

Of course, there was no guarantee of any of that. Even *if* such a plan had worked with St. Cyr, there was no guessing Noiret's reaction when Jesse showed up again without St. Cyr's head on a platter. Jesse knew one thing for certain was:

you didn't fuck around with a really old vampire. At least not if you expected to live.

All considerations and could-have-beens aside, he was in a no-win situation, no matter what. In all reality, the truth was the only hope he had. "Noiret has my sister," he murmured. His throat was horribly dry and scratchy and the sound came out as more of a croak.

St. Cyr leaned over, poured a glass of water and held it to Jesse's lips. Gently, he tilted the cup, his other large hand cradling the back of Jesse's head, letting just enough water slide into Jesse's mouth without choking him before pulling back.

Jesse swallowed, panting as the cool wetness coated his parched throat. In spite of his own condition, Jesse felt how gently the vampire was handling him and his suspicion that St. Cyr was a Coeur Eternel grew.

The flame of hope intensified. If he could feel St. Cyr's chest, feel the thump of a heartbeat under his hand, he'd know. A CE would help him, would not be able to deny him aid once he knew. However, there was one problem -- Jesse's hands were bound and he could not simply come out and ask St. Cyr what manner of vampire he was. If he wasn't one of the compassionate ones, there was a frightening chance he'd take horrible advantage of Jesse's vulnerability.

St. Cyr fed him sips of water until he nodded. The vampire set the glass down, lowered Jesse's head to the pillow and continued to gaze at him. "What's your sister's name?"

Jesse ran his tongue across his lips, catching excess droplets of water before he spoke. "Hannah," he answered softly.

Chris suppressed the shiver of desire that rippled through his body at the small movement of the immortal's tongue. This was no time for lust. He had a larger problem at hand.

A wave of potent, searing emotion for the immortal was cresting inside him, preparing to break and flood him. From the way the immortal had answered the question, the love between him and his sister was unmistakable. Just as doubtless was the danger his sister actually was in as Noiret's prisoner. No doubt, now that the immortal's plan to kill him for Noiret had backfired, he was using sympathy as a ploy. Noiret certainly had informed this man that Chris was at least part CE, and even if he hadn't, the scar was a clue, providing that the man lying naked before him knew enough about vampires to make the distinction. That would be all the knowledge he'd need to use Chris's compassion for his own ends.

It didn't even matter whether or not the immortal was using him, subtly seducing him for his own desperate purposes. Chris could do nothing to stop the wave of love cresting inside him. From the moment he'd turned on the sidewalk and seen the fallen man, his body shot full of bullets, Chris had felt for him. Then, after having fed on him, bonding the man to him intimately, the compassion had only grown. Not even finding the knife and figuring out the immortal's true purpose had stopped the burgeoning emotion. Mix that sympathy with Chris's potent loneliness, his desire for the beautiful Roman immortal, and his deep-seated hunger for a mate, and the combination was lethal. Intoxicating.

In other words, Chris was a goner. His for the taking. The only thing Chris needed to do was ensure that the immortal didn't kill him before he understood this.

Chris fought back the urge to reach out and touch the immortal's face. "And what is your name?" he asked softly.

The immortal swallowed hard, his Adam's apple sliding in his throat, touching off Christian's desire to lean down and put his lips to the supple skin just under the man's unshaven jaw. The man's scent, distinguishable to Christian through the dried blood still covering the man's magnificent torso, rose to his nostrils, a heady musk that made Chris feel almost drunk.

"Jesse."

No surprise there that the man would be named for the father of King David. "Jesse," he repeated, hearing a dreamy quality in his own voice. "You already know mine, I presume."

Jesse nodded. "St. Cyr."

"I'd prefer if you called me Christian, or Chris, strange as it may seem, considering I have you bound."

Jesse didn't answer. He just continued to stare up at him, obviously afraid the vampire would kill him at any moment.

Chris sighed. "I think the best thing to do right now is for you to have a shower and something to eat. We can deal with our situation after that. Is that agreeable to you?"

Jesse nodded. The thought of hot water and food called to his stricken senses. He realized that St. Cyr...Christian...didn't understand what had happened to his physical strength and believed Jesse still capable of killing him. Best if he believed that. God only knew how the vampire would use such knowledge if he turned out to be a Sans Ame. All Jesse could do now was try to get St. Cyr as an ally. And the best way to do that, he realized, was to give him what St. Cyr seemed to desire in the first place.

The thought sent a thrill of heat straight into Jesse's groin. Truth was, he could stand some of that for himself. It had been a long time since he'd been with anyone and he, too, had often known the gnawing desire for a real mate, someone you knew would be there, a steady burning flame in the constant shifting of time.

St. Cyr rose from the bed and began undoing the bonds around Jesse's ankles. The vampire's fingertips dappled lightly against Jesse's skin, warming him as he unwound the heavy ropes that held the lead shackles. He then produced a key from his pocket and undid the manacles. The lack of metal against Jesse's skin was glorious and he moved his feet around, relishing the freedom. He realized soon, however, when St. Cyr re-pocketed the key and undid the bonds chaining Jesse's arms that he wasn't going to remove the lead around his wrists.

Instead, St. Cyr gently lowered Jesse's hands in front of him and chained him in the front, leaving him handcuffed. "Can you sit up?" he asked, still holding the line of rope bound to the chain.

Jesse tested his muscles, feeling quite a bit restored after his lengthy sleep, though nowhere near where he needed to be. He nodded, preparing to rise to his feet. There was no sense in trying to rush. He was of no use to Hannah if he fucked up even more and got himself killed. His gaze remained on St. Cyr's chest. He needed just a few seconds to feel the vampire's chest. A heart beating within would tell him his course.

"All right." St. Cyr's large hands planted firmly but incredibly gently on Jesse's upper arms. The warm touch softened Jesse inside, almost causing tears to flood his eyes. He blinked back the salty sting and jerked his concentration onto his only mission: to get a hand onto St. Cyr's chest.

"Ready?"

Jesse nodded again and slid his bottom toward the edge of the soft mattress, the soles of his feet settling firmly on the luxurious Oriental carpet.

St. Cyr's hold tightened a bit on his arms and Jesse wished the touch weren't setting off the beginnings of an erection. He was naked and the vampire would see it immediately.

Jesse pushed off, his weight absorbed by St. Cyr's strong hands. His legs were unsteady, weak, not only from having been filled full of lead, but from the lead shackles against his wrists, bound together in front of him.

Then he realized this was his moment.

St. Cyr took a step back, encouraging him to walk. Jess took a small step and wobbled. He brought his bound hands up, one palm landing on the left pectoral muscle of St. Cyr's chest. The muscle twitched under his hand, warm and alive, the golden chest hairs softly caressing. The pad of his pinkie finger grazed St. Cyr's nipple. The smooth bud tightened in response.

St. Cyr's brow furrowed. He peered into Jesse's eyes "Are you all right?" he asked, huskiness tingeing his voice.

Jesse's heart lurched, certain for one terrifying moment that the vampire knew what he was about. He used every ounce of warrior's discipline he possessed to keep up his façade. "Yes. I…just need a moment."

To his relief, St. Cyr nodded, the lines of concern in his face relaxing. "Take your time."

The scent of the vampire's skin and hair, a musk as intoxicating as incense filled Jesse's nostrils. The vampire's rugged, sensual essence seeped into every pore of Jesse's body against his will. He closed his eyes, forcing his attention to rest solely on the chest under his hand. Several seconds had passed with no heartbeat. Several more passed and the flesh of Jesse's palm met only with the vibrant hard muscle. Nothing underneath that could qualify as a heartbeat.

Fuck.

St. Cyr was a soulless one. A desire-feeder. The kindness he was showing could only be an act, a subtle ploy to torment Jesse in his helpless state. The vampire had fed from him, creating a deep bond between them that could never be broken. Even though Jesse was already immortal and would not change in constitution, he and St. Cyr belonged to each other.

Not that this meant St. Cyr was obligated to help him. It didn't work that way.

"Are you ready to continue?" St. Cyr's voice broke Jesse's tormented musings.

Jesse's shoulders sagged and he looked down, straining to remain squarely on his feet. "Yes."

Without another word, the vampire maneuvered to Jesse's side, his hip grazing Jesse's bare groin. Jesse gritted his teeth as his cock hardened, the shaft filling rapidly, rising into its upward curve. Jesse felt St. Cyr pause, the vampire's gaze trained Jesse's erection, which now jutted mercilessly from his body, telling St. Cyr without words what Jesse wanted.

St. Cyr had the grace not to comment and put a supporting arm around Jesse's shoulders, half-carrying him the short distance to the bathroom.

The room reminded Jesse of Roman baths, a place he hadn't seen in many centuries. St. Cyr had exquisite taste in the way he'd obviously had custom marbles and stone installed, along with a shower large enough to fit five large men with two showerheads and gold fixtures. At the same time, the decadence of the décor belied the vampire's humble mannerisms. The furnishings of the bedroom, though luxurious, were far more understated. The bathroom, on the other hand, oozed with the desire for sex and wet hot bodies plastered against each other, the scent of oils and soaps permeating the air.

In spite of his roiling emotions, Jesse bit back a groan of want. His cock, still fully hard, tingled.

St. Cyr's rugged face lit with a smile. "I can see you like this room. I know it's quite a contrast to the bedroom, but I've always believed the bath is the most important room of the house." His tone sounded almost apologetic. "However, that aside, the shower is perfect for you because there's a place to sit down." He opened the large glass door and indicated the cool marble interior of the shower where a marble bench of sorts, wide enough for a man to lie down on, ran the length of the back wall.

The vampire's blue-eyed gaze fell to Jesse's wrists and his smile faded. "I can see that the shackles are hurting you." A deep sigh caused his chest to rise and fall enticingly under the white shirt he wore.

Jesse's heart quickened. Was it possible St. Cyr...Christian...was truly kind? In that moment, glad for his empathic ability to discern the vampire's real motives, his long-abused faith in love experienced a flutter of hope. "In truth, they do chafe a bit."

A pained look marred St. Cyr's handsome features. One large hand went to the pocket with the key. "Please forgive me." He produced the key and worked open the manacles, letting them fall from Jesse's wrists.

The rush of air against his liberated skin was glorious and Jesse moved his hands around, relishing the freedom from lead. At the same time, an ache tugged his heart. How bitterly ironic that the vampire...that...Christian...should apologize for having shackled a man who'd come to murder him. "Nothing to forgive," Jesse mumbled. "You...had good reason." His own voice sounded strange to his ears, infused with an emotion he'd reserved only for Hannah...and one other time for Sondra.

Damn! For the first time in hundreds of years, he heard tenderness seep into his voice. True tenderness. As much as his soul screamed out in protest, he had to admit to himself he'd met its missing half.

Christian let the manacles fall to the fluffy rug, which absorbed the sound of the metal's clinking. His gaze rested on Jesse's face, obviously continuing the graceful act of ignoring Jesse's now throbbing hard on. "I suppose if you're going to kill me, weak or not, a few chains won't stop you."

Jesse stared back at him, helplessly trapped in the war between overwhelming desire for Christian and the need to fulfill his mission. With his heart careening into love, his body aching mercilessly for this vampire's touch, and his sister's life hanging by a thread, what the hell was he going to do? "No, it won't stop me." The words slipped out before he realized what he was saying. A sharp twinge of guilt stabbed him for letting Christian believe he still intended to kill him.

Christian reached out, and before Jesse knew what was happening, took one of Jesse's irritated wrists between his own large hands. Gently, in soft rubbing motions, Christian chafed the flesh, bringing back the circulation, his healing touch easing the discomfort the lead had caused.

Against his will, Jesse's eyes fluttered closed. He could no longer suppress the groan that now vibrated deep in his throat.

"That feels good, I take it?" Christian's voice had fallen several notches, its smooth tenor broken with a slight rasp.

Jesse nodded, unable to speak. Christian's touch rippled through his whole body, almost feeling as if the vampire's palm were lightly skating up and down the length of his erection.

"Good. I hate to think that I harmed you." Christian's voice oozed regret. He released that hand and picked up the other one, giving it the same tender caressing treatment. His blue eyes glowed, a sheen of desire coating their azure depths. He paused with Jesse's hand flat between his palms, looking as if he wanted to turn Jesse's hand over and kiss the wrist.

He didn't. Wordlessly, Christian released Jesse's hand and reached into the shower, turning the gold faucet. After several moments, steam began to billow through the open shower door. Christian gently leaned Jesse against the glass wall, steadied him and began to work open the buttons on his own shirt.

Jesse froze, his body pulsing with heated need. "What are you doing?" he breathed.

The blue of Christian's eyes blazed. "Well, I'm going in with you. If you're still injured, you'll need help getting washed off."

Chapter Six

Jesse watched Christian remove his clothing. The vampire slid the white shirt off, revealing his broad chest in all its glory, his tawny nipples already tight with his obvious arousal. Jesse's gaze traveled from the heavier thatch of golden hair between his large pectoral muscles to the dark smooth trail it funneled into down his stomach. He tried not to look too obvious as the vampire unbuckled his trousers and let them slide down the strong columns of muscled legs, more golden hairs glinting off the sloping thighs and calves.

Christian, too, was erect, the veined reddish shaft of his cock thick and heavy, the lobes of the circumcised head taut and smooth. He turned slightly as he stepped out of his fallen trousers and tugged off his socks, giving Jesse an eyeful of the full ruddy sac below his cock and the nest of dark golden hair around the whole beautiful package. Christian's pale round buttocks flexed with tensed power, as did the sleek, chiseled muscles of his back, the upper portion partially hidden by his long wheat-colored hair.

Jesse swallowed hard. He knew a fellow warrior when he saw one, and Christian had obviously spent much time in this occupation before having been sired. No other way could he have developed such a god-like physique.

Christian straightened and stilled, evidently caught by the appreciation that must have showed in Jesse's gaze. His softly sculpted lips, dusky pink, quirked. The glint of gold stubble on his upper lips and jaw only heightened the supple, erotic curve of those lips. "Thank you," he breathed, "but your admiration is only a mirror for what you are."

Jesse didn't know how to respond. Even "thank you" was difficult to say. He'd spent so long on his own, staying away from other living beings, both kith, kin and human, that he felt completely divided. Part of him was soaking up Christian's kindness and reveling in the potent erotic attraction between them. The other part of him remembered a world devoid of any other trustworthy companion than his sister. The two parts warred with each other even as his erection tightened painfully under Christian's heated gaze.

For the moment, the erotic, love-starved part was winning.

Christian's hands closed gently on Jesse's upper arms again and for a brief, blood-warming moment, Jesse thought the vampire was going to kiss him. He realized with a stab of disappointment that he was wrong.

Christian gently drew him away from the support of the wall and guided him into the decadently enormous shower to the bench along the wall. The vampire lowered Jesse onto the seat, the marble already warm from the hot water and steam, and positioned him with his back against the wall.

The vampire then reached for the showerhead, detached it and lowered the force of the spray before gently turning it onto Jesse's hair and body.

In spite of the arousal coursing through every nerve ending, Jesse closed his eyes and let his body sag against the tiles, the massage of the water dappling his skin in the most pleasant way. The rinsing made him feel renewed and when he opened his eyes a tiny bit, he saw the dried blood washing off his skin, running into the drain in the center.

Jesse's eye fell on the magnificent vampire standing before him. He watched droplets of water stream off Christian's muscles, beading from the tiny nipples on his chest. His blond hair had darkened, on his head, chest, on his legs, and around his thick cock, plastered to his pale skin, emphasizing the bulges of muscle. Those same muscles flexed with his movements as he replaced the showerhead and reached for a bottle of shampoo.

The scent of heated sandalwood filled the shower as Christian squeezed out the content of the bottle into one large hand. He set the bottle down, rubbed his palms together and then took a step closer to Jesse. Christian's cock, still erect, hovered that much closer to Jesse's face.

Jesse stared, his entire being trapped in an erotic haze. Christian's large fingers worked Jesse's hair and scalp, making a lather with the richly scented shampoo. Jesse's body went languid with the delicious massage. Christian's cock bobbed lightly with the movements of his body as he shampooed Jesse's hair, his hands gently tilting Jesse's head back so that the soap wouldn't go into his eyes.

"Close your eyes, Jesse." The vampire's smooth voice made his entire body tingle.

Jesse obeyed and heard the showerhead being detached again, followed by the gentle stream of water on his head, rinsing the suds from Jesse's hair.

"Your hair is magnificent," Christian said, smoothing Jesse's wet hair back as he rinsed out the shampoo. Jesse opened his eyes again and watched as Christian replaced the showerhead and reached for a washcloth.

Jesse's body hummed in anticipation of the next part of his bath and he almost forgot to respond to the praise. "Thanks," he murmured.

Christian poured the contents of another bottle into the wet washcloth. This time the scent of something spicy, like cloves and frankincense diffused into the steamy air. In the next moment, Christian knelt on the marble floor directly in front of Jesse, his blue eyes glowing with a mixture of amusement and dusky need. "You're welcome." He leaned his brawny torso over Jesse, the hand holding the washcloth coming toward him.

Jesse sucked in a breath at the heated invasion of masculine energy. His cock twitched and tightened beyond pain. His balls practically vibrated from the vampire's closeness.

The wet soapy cloth landed gently on his throat. Christian swished it around, reaching up behind Jesse's ears and swiping the back of his neck. Their gazes locked. Christian paused, the energy humming between them practically palpable in its force. Christian visibly gathered himself and stayed where he was, running the cloth down to Jesse's chest.

In swirling motions, Christian wiped over each shoulder, gently lifting Jesse's arms, one at a time, to wash his armpits.

Jesse's erection strained, wanting nothing more than Christian's hand wrapped around it, bringing him release. Or better yet, his mouth. His lips, too, tingled wildly, wanting only kisses, instinctively craving the light scrape of those incisors against his skin.

Christian trailed the cloth down the center of Jesse's chest to his belly, stopping at his navel. The vampire's gaze rested on Jesse's straining cock, the skin of which registered the heat of Christian's breath. When Christian finally lifted his eyes to Jesse's, the blue pools glowed with hunger. "You're free to tell me to stop," he rasped.

The husky voice sent shimmers of heat through Jesse's body. His gaze fell on Christian's broad chest, the soft hair over the iron muscles plastered down from the water. Water beaded on Christian's collarbone, making Jesse itch to lick it off.

"Don't stop. Please." Jesse watched him, his eyelids heavy, his chest heaving.

Christian nodded, his own gaze almost disappearing under his hooded eyes. Water beaded off his nose and lips and chin as he moved the cloth lower, past Jesse's navel, into his pubic hair.

Jesse groaned. His body sagged languidly against the marble wall. He was completely helpless under the mind-blowingly erotic rasp of the wet, soapy cloth where it sloshed against the base of his cock.

Christian's other hand came out, the thick, strong fingers wrapping lightly around the base. The contact made Jesse thrust his hips upward, wanting more, needing release. Christian lifted the shaft and wiped the washcloth around Jesse's balls, anointing them with a reverent touch.

Jesse's eyes began to flutter closed, but he forced them to remain open, wanting to watch what Christian was doing to him. He rolled his hips upward, giving the vampire more access to his bottom, his effort immediately rewarded with the slide of the warm soapy cloth past his balls, toward his tight, wanting hole.

Christian paused on the little space of flesh between his balls and ass, rasping the cloth in tiny movements over the sensitive skin. Each tiny movement sent sparks of heat through Jesse's balls, straight up into his shaft. His wet hands gripped the edge of the marble bench, his fingers pressing into the stone, bracing himself as he absorbed the onslaught of pleasure.

Christian moved the cloth in a torturously slow trail toward Jesse's ass, the material teasing the exposed undersides of his buttocks, brushing the sensitive skin just enough to make him moan. "Please...Christian." His plea came out in a panting groan and his fevered gaze caught the flash of a mischievous grin on the vampire's lips.

"Whatever you desire, *mon amour*." Christian slid the cloth directly down to Jesse's throbbing hole, teasing the puckered opening with several more gentle swipes.

Jesse hissed in pleasure, then heard the wet cloth hit the shower floor, the material touch replaced with the heated probe of fingertips on his bare flesh. He responded by pulling his legs back further, wanting Christian's fingers deep inside him.

He didn't have to wait long. The soap had made his opening slippery and one thick finger pushed its way in with a searing jolt of pleasure.

Instinctively, Jesse threw his head back, his mouth open, panting.

Christian pulsed his finger in slow slick motions, stretching Jesse open, coaxing from him his complete surrender.

"Yes," Jesse rasped, feeling the pressure build swiftly in his cock.

Christian's thumb caressed Jesse's perineum while his finger moved in Jesse's hole. In the next moment, the moist warmth of Christian's mouth engulfed Jesse's cock.

Jesse's eyes flew open to see the blond water-darkened head bobbing up and down. Those soft lips slid in a fevered rhythmic motion up and down Jesse's aching shaft, the vampire's hot tongue sliding over his veins and muscle while Christian's fingers worked Jesse's bottom, overwhelming him with bliss.

Jesse watched Christian's mouth slide up to the head of his cock, then plunge back down again, taking him almost to the base. The suction pulled a groan from Jesse's throat each time, and he squeezed his eyes shut again, all his consciousness trapped by the hot suction on his cock and the delicious pressure in his ass.

Christian pulled back, sucking hard, sliding down again, obviously taking care not to scrape Jesse's cock with his incisors. The glide of Christian's hot tongue on the sensitive skin brought Jesse closer to the edge...closer....closer...the pressure building, aided by the tiny sparks of heat from Christian's skilled fingers.

Christian sucked. Jesse exploded, his cum squirting in hot jolts into Christian's mouth. Christian's throat muscles worked visibly as he swallowed, taking Jesse's essence into his own body, not letting Jesse's cock slip from his mouth until he'd sucked down the last drop.

Christian's palm caught Jesse's softening, relieved cock and brought it gently to rest against his upper thigh. That hand slid over Jesse hip and upward, until he'd reached Jesse's shoulder and rested, as his blue gaze rested on Jesse's face.

Jesse stared back at him, unable to speak right away. The spirals of pleasure still whispered through his body. He'd received pleasure and given pleasure many times over the centuries, but never before had he felt so worshiped, so adored in the act.

One thing was absolutely unmistakable. Christian loved him.

Years of lonely torment broke Jesse open and he pushed his back away from the wall, reaching for Christian. His hands closed on the vampire's brawny shoulders, the wet muscles quivering from his touch.

Christian's lips parted, his eyes widening at Jesse's unexpected advance. He moved closer, leaning into him, one hand coming to rest on Jesse's cheek.

Jesse stared at him, lost in the tenderness in Christian's eyes. *You really did bring me back to life.* The words rose in his mind before he remembered their mind link.

"So did you," Christian murmured. His other hand laced into Jesse's wet hair, the large palm cradling the back of his head as his other hand slipped down Jesse's chest, across his upper arm, around his back.

Jesse sighed, the tiny sound captured by the sudden press of Christian's lips onto his. The vampire was gentle, tenderly prodding the seam of Jesse's lips with the tip of his tongue. Jesse parted for the moist warm invasion of Christian's spicy flavor filling his taste buds. He weakened languidly in the vampire's embrace, falling backward to the support of the marble wall, bringing Christian with him, their mouths pressed together, tongues mated.

Their wet chests fused together, the warm skin melded from the dampness. Jesse parted his legs and Christian's muscled body slipped between them, his hard cock sliding against Jesse's with a soul-searing glide of pleasure.

Jesse's hands slipped from Christian's shoulders, fingertips skating over his wet collarbone, up his throat to cup his cheeks, drawing their faces closer together. Their kiss deepened with the movement, Jesse's tongue sliding against Christian's, the tip exploring the smooth ridges of his palate and teeth, returning to the lightly rough moistness of his lover's tongue.

Jesse pulled his mouth away. "Please, let me pleasure you in return."

Christian's gaze smoldered and his lips were swollen from their kiss. He reached up, pushing Jesse's wet hair back. "Not yet," he murmured. "You still need food and a bit more rest."

Without another word, Christian stood up, his thick hard cock still straining from lack of release. He turned off the shower and then gently helped Jesse to his feet. He opened the shower door and pulled a towel from the bar, opening it up and drying Jesse's back.

Jesse felt so much tenderness in the way Christian ministered to him that he knew, then and there, the thought of killing his new lover made Jesse want to die himself. How the hell would he save Hannah now?

Christian turned Jesse around and dried his front, wiping ever so carefully around his groin, swiping the fluffy towel across his buttocks and down into the crevice.

Jesse balanced himself with a hand on Christian's strong shoulder. Just touching the muscle like that, feeling it flex, knowing it flexed because Christian was drying him off, was enough to make Jesse realize he loved Christian, too.

He looked down, his cheeks burning wildly. "Thank you," he murmured through his suddenly tight jaw. Words of love did not fall as easily from him as his praise for Christian's physical beauty had earlier.

Christian stopped drying him and straightened, looking down into his eyes. Love swirled and churned in the blue depths. "You're welcome." After a moment's pause, he brushed several fingertips across Jesse's cheek. "Are you up to a shave before getting back into bed?"

Jesse nodded. Truthfully, after the shower and what Christian had done to him *in* the shower, he was feeling more restored with each passing minute.

Christian sat him down on a small stool and prepared shaving things. Jesse watched Christian give his own cheeks and jaw a quick shave and then let Christian do the same to him. He was fast beginning to love the way Christian touched him, realizing how empty his existence had been without these simple small acts of tenderness.

When he'd finished, Christian led him back into the bedroom and helped him into bed. With a gentle hand on his back, Christian laid him against the pillows. "You rest now. There's a restaurant on Beacon Street. I'll go get you something there, seeing as I don't keep food on hand." He smiled and pulled the heavy covers up over Jesse's naked body, tucking the soft down comforter around him.

Jesse looked up at him, his body still tingling and relaxed from the hot shower, the scrubbing and from Christian's mouth massage. The musky tang of Christian's personal flavor lingered in his own mouth, a sweet reminder of what they'd done together. A potent wave of guilt blindsided him. "Christian...I came here to kill you and yet..." He struggled to say the words that were so painful. "I don't understand how you can be so kind."

Christian leaned over him, gentle fingertips skimming along his cheek, leaving soft heat in their trail. "Food first and then answers, all right? No one has to kill, I promise."

A pang gripped Jesse. He wished Christian didn't have to leave him even for a few minutes. All these centuries alone, except for Hannah, the gnawing ache for love had plagued him...until now.

Christian must have read his thoughts, judging by the sympathy radiating from his blue eyes. The pad of his thumb moved back and forth on Jesse's cheek, a comforting gesture full of tenderness. "I won't be long. You must eat. Perhaps food will undo some of the physical harm you suffered." Softly he slanted his lips over Jesse's, tasting him slowly. The tip of his tongue nudged the seam, stealing inside to linger against his tongue.

Jesse reached up, slipping a hand into Christian's damp hair. The sensation was like golden silk against his callused flesh. In spite of his exhaustion and hunger, Jesse's cock stirred again, wanting another loving, heated release. He parted his lips wider, sliding his tongue harder against

Christian's. He almost groaned his disappointment when Christian pulled away.

His golden lover smiled down at him, blue eyes now smoldering. "More of that later, too," he murmured. "I promise."

As Jesse's hand slipped from Christian's hair, Christian caught his wrist. He turned Jesse's hand over and pressed his lips into the tender flesh. Jesse drew in a heated breath at the feeling of Christian's tongue flickering lightly against his wrist.

All too soon, Christian lifted his lips away and brought Jesse's hand to rest on the covers. "I'd better go now, before I can't leave."

Jesse nodded, still in a daze from the mere touch of Christian's kiss, both on his lips and on his wrist. He watched Christian turn and walk from the room.

Chapter Seven

Jesse sat back against the pillows after having practically inhaled the meal Christian had brought for him, a beautiful spread of scrambled eggs, fried potatoes, sausage, bacon, muffins, coffee and juice. Admittedly, Christian had been correct; the large meal went a long way toward restoring more of his strength that the lead had stolen from him.

Christian removed the bed tray and took his seat again at the edge of the mattress.

Jesse stared up at him, bewitched by Christian's sheer physical beauty. The firelight danced off the vampire's pale skin and golden hair, and caused the blue in his eyes to glow. Even the jagged scar on his cheek only added to his rugged magnificence and Jesse wished he could have seen Christian in earlier times, clad in armor, his muscled legs showing beneath his tunic, his brawny arm wielding a sword.

"Thank you again, Chris." He started at his own use of a nickname. Hannah was the only other being he'd ever given a nickname.

The endearment obviously pleased his lover, who picked up Jesse's hand and held it against the smooth plane of his cheek, softer from having been shaved after their shower.

The guilt Jesse had felt before now resurfaced. He remembered that Chris had not answered his question of earlier.

Chris sighed. "Yes, I remember that I haven't answered your question," he said softly. "You were wondering why I'm being so loving with you when you really came here to kill me."

Jesse's heart lurched. His thought must have activated their mind link. He nodded.

Chris pressed a small kiss onto Jesse's hand, then lowered it, holding it between both his hands on his lap. "The answer is simple, Jesse. I fell in love with you." He glanced away, toward the fire and then back, his blue eyes sheepish. "Well, that's mostly why. You had me spellbound from the first moment, even before I fed on you. Even if I weren't Coeur Eternel --"

Jesse shot up to a seated position, his heart suddenly racing. "You're a CE?"

Chris's brow furrowed. "Yes, is that a problem?"

He shook his head. "No...not at all. It's just that...well, I suspected it because of the scar, but when I touched your chest there was no heartbeat."

Chris sighed again. "No, there wouldn't be. I'm what you could call a half-breed, I suppose."

Jesse blinked, his mind confused. "You mean, half human and half CE?"

"No. Half CE, half Sans Ame."

"I've never heard of that. How...uh...how?"

Chris's bow-shaped lips curved in a smile. "It's rare, but it does happen. I was sired by Valmont Lascaux, the world's oldest vampire. More powerful even than Noiret. I was a Viking, raiding the Normans in Britain. Apparently, Lascaux at the time was acting as a Norman lord and it was his estate I attacked. Several of his knights ambushed me, stabbed me and then captured me. I was in too much pain at the time to realize that Lascaux was there, preventing his men from doing me in. Instead, he had them put me in his barn on a bed of straw." He sighed. "There I was, bleeding to death when Lascaux knelt over me.

"In spite of the fact I was so weak from loss of blood, I still remember how it felt, that initial piercing in my neck, the pleasure of the feeding. It wasn't until after that I blacked out. When I finally came to I didn't realize what I was yet. I still felt my heart beating, yet my wounds were all healed and I craved blood. Lascaux was there, the first face I saw. He realized that I had retained my heart in the ethereal sheath of my body."

Jesse frowned. "Ethereal?"

Chris nodded. "Yes. It means that *I* can still feel and hear it beat, but it's not made of flesh as with other CE's." He chuckled softly. "Not many know this, but many centuries ago during his travels, Lascaux came upon a Buddhist monk in a cave in the mountains of Tibet, meditating. He fed off the monk and sired him, as was Lascaux's wont to do. But when the monk re-awoke, he'd retained his heart and soul, and was only able to feed as an act of mercy to a person who was dying a painful death. Perhaps because of all the monk's years of meditation and prayer, Lascaux could only affect him so much. In any case, that monk was the first Coeur Eternel. And there are those of us, who, for whatever reason, fall somewhere in the middle." Chris shrugged. "Hey, life is complex for humans, why not for immortal creatures as well?"

Jesse's jaw dropped and it took a moment before he could respond. "I never knew about the origin of the CE's."

Chris's smile deepened. "Yes. That was one of Lascaux's great foils, siring vampires who retained their heart and souls. For centuries, if a vampire, including Lascaux, sired a CE, their natures kept them apart, isolated. But recent events have brought about a new era of relations between the two strains of vampires."

Jesse found himself fascinated by Chris's narrative. He, himself, had spent so many centuries wandering about, isolated from most other people that the existence of a world of beings came rushing upon him. His new, potent interest in life, he realized, was the effect of falling in love. "What recent events are these?"

Chris gazed at him a moment, then took a deep breath. "Well, Lascaux became mortal recently out of love for the CE priestess, Darelle, whom he sired almost seven hundred years ago during the bubonic plague." His expression darkened. "The Soldiers, a group of rabid slayers, captured Lascaux, tortured him for centuries in the catacombs of his own estate, trying to lure Darelle there and then kill them both. Lascaux cut off his mind link with her and with all of us so we wouldn't know what was happening and risk death to save him. After centuries of this, he became mortal and would have died. The Soldiers finally contacted Darelle themselves and told her what was happening to her sire. She went to him and brought him back across. After that, they were able to fend off the attackers."

Chris paused before continuing, a soft look stealing into his blue eyes. "I must admit that I've never relished being a vampire. Even so, I'm glad to have been sired by Lascaux. He is as loyal, caring and protective of his protégés as he is selfish, decadent and stubborn." Chris looked briefly down at their joined hands.

The sorrow in Chris's voice and then the pride and admiration with which he spoke of his sire, sent a stab of jealousy through Jesse's chest.

Chris's dark look turned in his direction and the blue eyes widened, lit with understanding. "Jesse, Lascaux and I were never lovers. As soon as I woke up in that barn, realizing I was alive when I should have been dead, I panicked. The bloodlust churning in my body was frightening beyond anything I'd ever known. Lascaux gave me a wineskin full of blood. I sucked down every last drop only because my body demanded it of me. And then I ran from him." Chris gave a humorless chuckle. "I feel sorry for Lascaux. Apparently, he's frightened off many a young protégé who is any part Coeur Eternel."

Chris looked at Jesse, his eyes smoldering again with desire. "But even as time passed and I grew accustomed more or less to my fate, and even as I was able to forge a friendship with Lascaux, I never wanted to be his lover." He looked down. "No one has ever had the effect on me you have, Jesse. That is the absolute truth."

Jesse heard the sincerity in his lover's voice and words and his jealousy subsided. He relaxed against the pillows again. His hand still rested in Chris's hands and his lover's thumb brushed across the soft flesh of his palm. The tiny movement was at once tender and erotic and stirred Jesse's yearning for Chris's large, hard body against his. In mere seconds, Jesse's cock stirred and began to harden, pushing against the blanket that covered it.

Chris's gaze darted to the spot where Jesse's erection tented the bedding. His eyes darkened with an immediate sheen of lust and he released Jesse's to undo the buttons of his shirt. In mere seconds, Chris had the article slipping off his broad shoulders and down his brawny arms to the floor.

The glint of firelight off Chris's golden chest hair and pale-skinned muscles made Jesse's mouth water and his growing erection strained against the coverlet. Chris slipped off the bed to his feet, stepping out of his boots. Jesse watched Chris's hands as they went to unbuckle his belt, slowly, torturously working open the leather, the teasing pace continuing as he undid the button and let the zipper of his fly down, one tiny click at a time.

Jesse licked his lips, his gaze riveted to the juncture where Chris's trousers were slowly falling open, giving him a hint of his dark blond pubic hair. The swollen head of his lover's shaft appeared, then the whole cock, the reddish-veined skin stretched taut over the muscle.

The trousers slid past Chris's hips, revealing all of him. The shadowy firelight in the bedroom cast an alluring glow over every inch of his muscled warrior's body. With a seductive grin curving the planes of his cheeks, the beautiful vampire pulled back the covers and climbed onto the mattress, sliding the length of his body against Jesse's.

Their cocks met in a silky glide of skin against skin, their chests rubbing together. The soft rasp of Chris's chest hair grazed Jesse's nipples, causing them to tingle and pebble.

Chris settled his torso against Jesse's, slanting his mouth over Jesse's in one single motion. The air filled with their combined murmurs and the erotic suction of their lips and tongues meeting and tasting each other. Chris nudged Jesse's legs apart with his knee, and Jesse gladly opened to him, hooking his legs around the vampire's slim, delectable hips as Chris fitted his body between them.

In spite of everything that had led up to their meeting, Jesse loved him now, and his surrender to Chris, though fast and hard, felt like the most natural thing that could ever be, as if he'd been made especially for Chris and no one else.

Chris must have sensed Jesse's complete surrender for he lifted his mouth from their kiss and gazed down into Jesse's eyes, his own blue depths smoldering with the ethereal light that came from the hunger to feed. His masculine lip curled back, revealing his incisors. The sight should have frightened Jesse, but instead, made every inch of his body burn for his lover's possession.

The vampire's chest rose and fell in a wild rhythm against him, and his lover's cock pushed firmly against his ass. "Jesse." His voice was tight, strained, conveying his inner battle, his struggle not to give in to his desire to feed for pleasure. "I swore I wouldn't…feed. Not…for pleasure."

"Take me," Jesse breathed, his palms pressing with urgency into the iron brawn of Chris's back. The warm masculine skin under his fingertips quivered and a raw, delicious smell, more potent than sandalwood and wine permeated the air, the primal musk of sex emanating from their entwined bodies.

A feral groan vibrated deep in Chris's throat, obviously inspired by Jesse's complete submission to his lover's needs.

"All of me, Chris," he prodded, that spot on his neck aching for the pierce of Chris's fangs. "Don't fight it."

"Jesse, I mustn't --"

"I want you to. It's all right if you love me."

Chris smoothed back Jesse's hair tenderly, the thrum of tension in his large strong body palpable. "You mean that, don't you?"

Jesse nodded, the desire pulsating through him making him unable to say more.

"I won't hurt you, I promise."

Jesse's throat, tight with emotion, made speech difficult. "I know."

Christian slanted his lips over Jesse's, swiping a brief kiss across them. He leaned over and reached for the small vial of scented oil he'd rubbed into Jesse's skin after the shower. Pulling the tiny cork, he poured the jar's contents into his palm. Replacing the bottle on the bedside table, the vampire reached down, sought out Jesse's ass, and smeared the oil over his tiny hole.

Around and around in tiny circles, he worked the oil into Jesse's sensitive passage. One large finger penetrated Jesse's opening, pushing deep inside.

Jesse threw his head back and moaned at the delicious invasion of thick fingers pushing him open, rubbing in and out, preparing him for their joining. The inner massage caused his whole bottom to tingle madly, shoots of heat slithering down his thighs and up into his belly.

Chris's fingertips brushed Jesse's balls, over and over, nearly sending him over the edge. He felt his lover shift slightly and anoint his cock with the remaining oil. That same hand then slid up Jesse's stomach, a slow, teasing trail that moved to his chest, sliding sensuously over each tight nipple. The slick oil made Chris's touch glide smoothly over the tiny buds, causing them to tighten more and send shoots of ecstasy through Jesse's chest and down in an invisible trail of fire to his cock and ass.

"Now, please," he begged in a tight voice, desperate to feel Chris's thick hardness inside him. His clutched at the bunching muscles of Chris's back to emphasize his hunger.

Jesse's plea roused Chris to a pitch. The sound reverberated in his fangs, which now ached to the point of acute pain. He brushed several fingertips across the supple underside of Jesse's jaw, preparing to feed. He shifted his body the tiniest bit, covering Jesse more. The movement brought the head of his cock right up against the tight oiled hole he sought.

Jesse moaned and grasped at his back, his body shifting underneath Chris's so that the taut lobed cap of Chris's cock penetrated him.

Chris sucked in a breath, holding himself back from sinking his fangs mercilessly into Jesse's neck. He bent down and swiped the tip of his tongue across the salty soft skin where he would feed, his hands covering Jesse's smoothly muscled shoulders. Jesse's musky scent filled Chris's being, driving him nearly mad with want.

Chris pushed his cock in deeper, the friction of Jesse's tight passage engulfing him with delicious heat. Chris groaned, his fangs pulsating, the pain icy hot. He thrust once more into Jesse's delicious ass, driving his oiled cock all the way in until their bodies touched.

Jesse released a long low moan, his head tilted back, his full, soft lips parted. His legs were wide apart, the soles of his feet resting lightly on Chris's ass. *Sweet heaven*, Chris had known intense pleasure in his life, great passion, but nothing quite like this, nothing that had ever engulfed him so completely.

In an even rhythm, Chris withdrew his cock until he'd nearly receded all the way and then drove it in again, impaling himself to the hilt in Jesse's tight channel. Chris paused, swiped his tongue across Jesse's parted lips and then gave several quick, sharp thrusts, wildly pleased when Jesse gasped with each one.

Chris shifted the angle of his body, withdrew and plunged again. The pleasure cry from his lover underneath him echoed through the bedroom. Hovering on the brink, Chris bent his head to Jesse's throat, licked the supple skin again and bit down, a gentle thrust of his incisors that pierced the skin.

Jesse flinched, yet the low moan he uttered as Christian's fangs slid in belied any pain Jesse might have experienced. Jesse's supple flesh throbbed slightly under Chris's lips as he withdrew the incisors and placed his lips tenderly over the tiny punctures. Jesse's coppery blood slid into his mouth, warm and sweet, better than any nectar he could want.

The rhythm of Chris's suckling fell into sync with the glide of his cock in and out of his lover's passage, tight and slippery. Chris's stomach muscles massaged Jesse's cock from the front and he could feel Jesse's body tensing underneath him, his lover's climax building rapidly.

Jesse's fingertips clutched Chris's back, digging in as his body tightened. Jesse groaned, his seed erupting, milky hot spurts pooling on his stomach between them. Jesse's anus clenched, creating even more friction and Chris careened toward his own climax. Tiny spasms, like miniature orgasms, flared in Chris's fangs. The slide of blood down Chris's throat, combined with the slide of his cock in and out of his lover, caused the buildup of pressure to explode.

Chris's climax shuttered through his entire body. One last hard thrust into Jesse and he came, the weight of his body pressing Jesse into the mattress while he filled his lover's passage with his seed.

Jesse's arms closed around him. Jesse's head remained tilted back, eyes shut. Chris collapsed lightly, pressing Jesse deeply into the soft bedding. Chris lifted his face long enough to seal the punctures on Jesse's neck with gentle swipes of his tongue.

In seconds, Jesse's regenerative powers healed the skin over completely, and Chris rested his cheek against Jesse's damp shoulder, his still-hard cock remaining buried deep inside Jesse's ass.

Jesse breathed heavily, his legs wrapped around Chris's hips. The gentle warm pressure on Chris's sides made him smile as he breathed in Jesse's scent. Mmm, there was no feeling in the entire universe as potent as finding one's soul mate.

As quickly as the bliss had coursed through him, so did the fear of loss. Chris froze, remembering why he'd found

Jesse in the first place. Not that Jesse would kill him now. Would he? With an ache, Chris realized the question hung over him. After all, Jesse's sister was still in Noiret's clutches and Noiret was a sadistic fuck. Even if Jesse loved Chris, Jesse must still be desperate to save his sister's life.

Chris lifted his face from Jesse's shoulder and shifted his weight so that he could look down, his hands pressed into the mattress, his arms bridging his lover's lithe, sculpted torso. His cock, now mostly soft, slipped from Jesse's passage, leaving a sudden empty feeling.

Jesse stared up at him from under his thick lashes. Those deep brown pools made Chris fall in love with him more deeply every second that passed. "What is it?" Jesse's voice was a whisper. "What's the matter?"

Chris shook his head, and heaved a sigh. "Nothing, really. It's just that…well…I wanted to tell you that I'll willingly give my life to save your sister."

Chapter Eight

Jesse shot up, pushing Chris onto his side with the force of his movement. He stared down into the vampire's blue eyes, panic rising in icy heat through his chest. "What the hell are you saying?" His hand came out, landing on Chris's hard shoulder, his fingers digging into the muscle with renewed strength. Up until this moment, part of him had remained ready to kill Chris if he had to. That declaration wiped away Jesse's last shred of murderous resolve. He couldn't let Chris die, not now, not when he'd finally found his great love.

There *had* to be another way.

Chris's large hand covered his and he levered up so that his torso pressed close to Jesse's. His breath pulsed warmly onto Jesse's cheek. "Jesse, what you said and did just now was the nicest that anyone has ever said or done to me." His voice radiated a blend of sadness and tender sweetness.

Jesse heaved a deep sigh. Perhaps Chris had been even lonelier than he all these centuries. Jesse looked down, his cheeks burning. "I just can't…" he murmured, struggling for the words to express what was deepest inside him, the kinds of things he'd only ever said to one other person, his beloved Sondra. "I can't let you…die. I'll find a way to get her back."

Fingertips on Jesse's cheek bid him look up with gentle pressure. He met the riveting blue of his lover's gaze. "Jesse, I didn't say that I was *going* to die."

"But you --"

Chris grinned, a sexy grin that turned up one side of his sensual lips. "Give me a little credit, would you? Yes, Noiret is a formidable enemy and one I've spent much of eternity trying to avoid. But there are ways to deal with him that don't include my having to die." He continued to stare into Jesse's eyes, his grin fading. "You know I'll help you. I would have done it no matter what, even before I fed on you and bound us together. You don't have to give him what he's demanding. And you *don't* have to face him alone." The blue of Chris's eyes darkened to a rich cobalt. "You don't have to do anything alone anymore if you choose not to."

Jesse stared at him. Disbelief stabbed him to the core. Was it possible that the help he'd needed had been there the whole time? Could one being love another that much…that is, someone who wasn't bound to him by the bonds of birth? In the course of Jesse's existence, the world didn't work that way.

Jesse sagged back against the pillows, saturated with sudden, horrible guilt. Reaching up, he raked a hand through his hair. "It's not that simple, Chris. I can't let you risk yourself. This is my problem. I'll solve it." He looked at Chris who had opened his mouth to answer and quieted him with a gesture. "Do you know how Hannah got herself into Noiret's clutches?"

Chris shook his head.

Jesse paused, heaving another deep sigh. Her capture had, perhaps, been avoidable had she heeded her brother's repeated warnings to stay out of certain places. "She won him in one of those underground gambling dens."

Chris's golden eyebrows rose. "The ones where the players gamble for live prizes?"

Jesse nodded, his shoulders drooping. Those dens were incredibly risky and only for the toughest and strongest, especially because all manner of beings frequented them. They weren't closed off to anyone, mortal, immortal, vampire or weyre. The combinations could often prove lethal, but the thrill-seeking could also be irresistible, especially for immortals and other kith with nothing but time on their hands. "Yes, those. Apparently, Noiret had followed her and maneuvered himself into her game, making certain she won him as her prize."

Chris's handsome face darkened and he looked down, a pensive air closing around him. "Hmm, that's rough. I'm going to have to call in help for this one."

Energy zinged through Jesse's body. Had he heard correctly? "Chris, I..." He looked down, covering his face with his hands. "I'm moved that you want to help me, really. But I already told you to stay out of this. It's my problem. I couldn't live with myself if anything happened to you."

Strong gentle hands pried his fingers away from his eyes, leaving him open. As he'd done earlier, Chris turned his dark look onto Jesse. "And how do you propose to do that?"

Jesse remained silent. Truly, he knew that he didn't have a chance on his own, and he didn't know anyone else on the face of the earth, besides the vampire in front of him, who would help him. Since his stabilization into immortality, he hadn't exactly spent his existence gaining allies and friends.

Chris chuckled without mirth. "That's what I thought." He cupped Jesse's cheek. "Let's face it. You, my love, are up shit's creek without a paddle." Several soft pats on his cheek and Chris lowered his hand, his intense blue gaze still boring into Jesse's. "I'm afraid you're going to have to let someone help you, the one thing you've not wanted to do in…well…how many thousands of years?"

Jesse looked down, feeling like an asshole. "A couple." When he dared to look back up, his lover's eyes twinkled. Great, Chris was amused by his humiliation.

Chris looked at him tenderly. "As I was saying, you're going to have to accept help and shut up about it."

Jesse looked at him. "I can't shut up, Chris. I can't bear the thought of…" He couldn't finish his sentence. "It's two of us, a semi-weakened immortal and a Coeur Eternel who can't kill except for mercy, against Noiret and his goons. The odds are pretty bad."

Chris grinned. "*Half* Coeur Eternel." He brushed fingertips across Jesse's cheek. "So the odds are not as bad as you think. Also, some of us don't have the same difficulty asking for help."

Jesse furrowed his brow. "What do you mean?"

Chris reclined on the mattress, one brawny arm reaching up to pull Jesse alongside him. Molding Jesse's back to his front, he pulled Jesse close, his hand splayed across Jesse's chest.

Jesse closed his eyes, his body coming alive from the press of Chris's cock into the crevice of his ass and the warm touch on his chest, one fingertip brushing his nipple. Behind him, Christian's breath warmed the nape of his neck and soft lips nuzzled the skin there, washing away all thoughts.

"Mmm, you're delicious," Chris murmured, his smooth voice saturated with contentment.

In spite of his tension, Jesse chuckled. "You would know."

Chris's soft laughter vibrated against Jesse's skin. "Yes, I would."

Jesse picked up the large hand on his chest and held it to his lips, the tip of his tongue brushing one knuckle followed by the soft pres of a kiss. "You taste pretty damn good yourself."

Chris sighed again and snuggled closer, his hand resting in Jesse's.

Jesse had closed his eyes and opened them when a burning question pressed on his mind. "You know, I just realized I haven't yet asked you why Noiret wants you dead."

"Mm, that's right. You haven't. I suppose he told you that I once murdered someone he loved. Fed on her until her life was completely drained, is that right?"

"Yes, he did say that." But truthfully, Jesse couldn't imagine now that Chris could possibly have done that.

"He lied, of course." Chris shifted against him, his cock sliding deliciously between Jesse's buttocks, although the tone of Chris's voice showed that he hadn't meant the movement to be deliberately erotic. "Noiret was the one who drained her blood. I tried to get her away from him. He's stronger than I am."

Jesse frowned. "So...why?"

"Why does he really want me dead?"

"Yes. I can't imagine you did anything to him to make him hate you."

Chris sighed deeply, his chest pressing heavily to Jesse's back. "I did do something."

"You did?"

Chris nodded, his hair brushing Jesse's skin. "I existed."

Jesse stilled. "What do you mean? Just because you exist he wants you dead?"

"That's all the reason Noiret needs."

A sudden rush of bile invaded Jesse's gut. Even in his most rambunctious slaying days, he always had a reason to kill other than the simple desire to take another's life. Justice, for one. And he'd never killed anyone weaker than himself who couldn't fight back.

"I know, *mon amour*, it's brutal. All the more reason we need love in the world, not more hate."

Jesse's breath pumped faster and he felt slightly dizzy from the fear of losing Chris and the helplessness of not being able to rescue his sister.

"Jesse, we're going to get your sister back. I give you my word."

Jesse sighed. *We and which army?*

"No army. Lascaux, myself, and whomever he brings with him."

Jesse stiffened. He'd forgotten that Chris mentioned something about asking for help. The concept was so alien to him; he'd dismissed the statement as soon as it was made. Now, reminded again of his mind link with his new lover, it hit him. "Lascaux? He's coming here?"

Chris pressed another small kiss into the back of Jesse's neck. "*Oui, mon amour.* He's already on his way. A sire, unless he's a complete bastard, will always answer a distress call from a protégé. He'll be here by tomorrow, late afternoon."

A heated curl of jealousy snaked through Jesse, in spite of Chris's earlier assurances. Maybe Chris and Lascaux were never lovers, yet here the other vampire was coming from God knows where to help his protégé. Obviously there was still a strong bond there. Knowing the bond between himself and his lover, he hated the thought that Chris had such a deep connection to Lascaux, who'd sired him.

"Jesse, I love you. In time, you'll come to know how true that is." Chris's voice held a degree of tenderness in it that Jesse had never imagined existed. His words and voice soothed the jealousy away.

Jesse kissed the vampire's hand again, his lips lingering on Chris's skin. "Chris...I...love you."

"I know. Don't ever feel jealous of Lascaux. I honor him only as my sire. *You* I adore. He's coming here to help us. The only way to fight a vampire as old and powerful as Noiret is with a vampire even older and more powerful."

* * *

Jesse rolled over, the lack of Chris's warm body pressed close to him forcing him awake. He blinked several times, the heavy canopy of the bed above him coming into focus. Pale winter sunlight made a rectangle of light on the hardwood floor and a section of the Oriental rug and a fire crackled in the large hearth across from the bed.

Slowly Jesse sat up, his glance falling on the bedside table where his knife still lay. The fact that Chris had left it there showed the trust and faith he'd placed in his new lover. No, Jesse hadn't tried to kill him again.

Jesse's heart warmed in his chest. As able as he'd ever been to deny the reality of love, he couldn't now when Chris had placed that trust in him. Regardless of the fact that Chris was stronger than he, Jesse could still give him a fair fight if he decided to try.

The warmth in his heart morphed into an ache. He wished Chris were here in bed with him, waiting for him to awaken. Where had he gone? To get food? Was Lascaux here already and Chris had gone to welcome him? He hated to think of that. The jealousy was still there, a product of having gone so long without love. His trust and faith were fragile, like seedlings just sprouted from the earth. Anything could trample them.

Realizing his physical strength had nearly completely returned, he sat up, determined to look for Chris. He swung to a sitting position, his feet touching the floor, and tested his limbs, stretching and then flexing his muscles. Damn, it felt good not to be so friggin' weak. As much as he'd come to enjoy his physician's care...

Hmm, maybe Chris had had to go to the hospital. After all, Chris did work as a doctor, strange as the thought was.

Jesse turned his head to stretch the muscles in his neck. As he did so, his eye fell on something on the rug in front of the fire. It looked like a tray, covered with a large white cloth.

Jesse stared at it. Could it be breakfast? Maybe Chris had left it for him before going to wherever he was now.

Still naked, Jesse slipped off the bed to his feet, standing a moment to steady himself before trying to walk. Aside from a light rush of blood to his head, he was fine. Chris had nursed him back to complete health. He crossed the short distance from the bed to the space by the fire. The flames dancing in the hearth warmed him as he drew close and knelt by the tray.

Reaching out, he grasped a corner of the cloth and dragged it off. When he saw what was there, his blood froze. He scrambled back, a yell ripping from his throat, his gaze frozen on Chris's head, the eyes staring lifeless, blood covering the jagged broken skin where someone had cut it from his body.

Chapter Nine

Chris nearly dropped the tray of food he'd prepared for Jesse. Jesse's bloodcurdling shout had echoed through the entire house. He set down the tray and bounded out of the kitchen and up the stairs, nearly skidding into the bedroom. He scanned the room for Jesse, but his lover was nowhere to be seen.

Chris's gaze fell on the mold he'd made earlier that morning while Jesse slept. The drop cloth lay in a heap next to it and immediately he understood what had happened. Fuck! He'd only meant to be gone a minute. It figured Jesse would have woken up and seen it in the two minutes Chris had been gone from the room.

He turned and saw that Jesse's knife was also missing from the bedside table. Poor Jesse. He thought someone had stolen in and murdered his lover while he slept.

Jess, I'm here. Alive. That was a mold I made for you to give to Noiret. I shouldn't have left it there like that. I'm sorry, mon amour. That said through their mind link, Chris stood quietly and waited.

Chris? Is that really you? If you're an imposter, I'll fucking gut you.

Chris stifled a chuckle. He felt Jesse's grief at thinking his lover dead. Sorrow at his carelessness intermingled with the sweetness of realizing someone cared about him so much. *I swear it's me, Jess. I was getting you something to eat. I did a stupid thing.*

Pause. *Where the hell am I? This place is huge.*

Chris chuckled out loud now. He yanked his velour bathrobe from the back of the door and went out into the hallway. *Describe what you see.*

I went down a back staircase. It's friggin' dark in here.

Chris went down the stairs to the living room. *Stay where you are. I'm coming for you.* He crossed the large, airy room, warmed by the lights twinkling on the large ribbon-and-light-decorated Scotch pine in the corner, and headed for the obsolete servants' staircase in the hallway. In a tiny alcove off the hall, he opened a door, revealing Jesse, standing there in all his glorious nudity, staring at him, his knife gripped in one hand.

Chris had to force himself not to stare at the smooth olive skin hugging the terrain of lithe muscles as he held the robe out for Jesse. Remorse gripped him again. "Jesse, I'm so sorry."

Jesse blinked, the pupils of his large dark eyes shrinking from the intrusion of light. He stepped forward, pushing one arm into the sleeve of the robe. "Your hair." His voice held both wonder and disappointment.

With his hands on Jesse's arms, Chris turned him gently, taking the knife from his hand and helping him into the robe. Jesse was pliant under his touch, obviously relieved his lover hadn't been murdered. Chris closed the robe, loosely belting it. When he'd finished, one hand went to his closely shorn scalp. He'd needed to cut off his hair for the fake head. Apparently, he'd done a good job, and in record time. "It'll grow back," he murmured, reaching for Jesse and pulling him gently into an embrace.

Jesse's lips pressed into the crook of his neck, his hands resting lightly on Chris's back, over his baggy shirt. "I thought I'd lost you." Jesse's breath was warm on Chris's skin.

"Please forgive me," Chris said in a near-whisper. Finally he released Jesse and began to lead him toward the living room. "I'd only meant to be gone for a minute to bring you your food. I was going to show you the mold then."

"It's all right."

Chris led Jesse to the sofa in the living room, a wide, deep piece of furniture with plenty of cushions and pillows. He arranged Jesse amidst the pillows and then built a fire in that hearth. Leaving him alone again only long enough to retrieve the tray of food, he served it to him and then sat next to him when he'd finished eating, cuddling him close. They had a little bit of time until Lascaux arrived and Chris wanted to make the most of it.

Jesse leaned forward to set down his coffee cup. When he leaned back, the belt of the robe had come loose and the sides of the robe fell open a bit, revealing a large portion of Jesse's leanly sculpted chest. Chris leaned into him, brushing their lips together, one hand reaching under the robe and lightly caressing his lover's chest, the silky dusting of ebony hair brushing pleasantly against his fingertips.

Jesse moaned softly into his mouth and responded to the caresses with the slide of his tongue against Chris's. Chris could taste Jesse's musky flavor mingled with the coffee he'd drunk. Softly, he pulled his mouth from their kiss and looked into Jesse's heavy-lidded gaze. "You're all recovered now? I mean, from the lead?"

Jesse nodded, his full lips slightly parted, his lips glistening from their kisses. "Yes, and from the shock of seeing that head." His tone was light, communicating to Chris that he shouldn't feel guilty.

Jesse's hand came up and caressed the bristle of what had just hours before been a mane of golden hair. "Your hair…was so beautiful."

Chris brushed a soft kiss across Jesse's lips and grinned at him. "I promise you it'll grow back, *mon amour.* Hair and nails never stop growing, even on a vamp." His insides lit up when Jesse smiled. His Roman lover had the most captivating smile he'd ever seen, more intoxicating because of the contrast between his smile and his usual heavy, dark expression of burden.

"It would be okay even if it didn't," Jesse said. "You're magnificent either way." He sat back slightly, the robe coming loose with the small movement, revealing his beautiful torso. A strange look came into his eyes, the dark irises brimming with what looked like emotional pain and sorrow. "Chris." His voice came out in a hoarse whisper.

The sound rippled through Chris's chest, touching him deep inside. "What is it, Jess?"

A sheepish look stole into those magnificent eyes, large and sweet and softly dark, like a doe's eyes. *I...I...mustn't ever...lose you.*

He'd spoken through their mind link, as if a heartfelt confession were more easily made without sound.

Chris looked at him, his insides leaping. There was no other appropriate inner response to such a confession of love. Except for...

He reached out, pulling Jesse to him. The robe slipped off almost completely, stopped only by Chris's hands on Jesse's arms. He caught a flash of Jesse's rising erection, jutting in a delicious curve from his leanly muscled body, the plump head stretching from its sheath. Next he saw Jesse's full lips and captured them.

Jesse sighed and surrendered, his chest sinking against Christian's, the friction massaging Chris's nipples through his soft white shirt. His hands slipped around to Jesse's back, the lithe muscles warm and flexing under his hands.

Jesse returned his kisses with open-mouthed fervor, suckling Chris's tongue, his hands on Chris's cheeks, cupping them reverently. Passion uncoiled in the delicious slide of his tongue against his lover's.

Chris slid his hand down the hard, delicious muscles of his lover's back, coming to rest on one firm, round buttock.

Jesse moaned softly into his mouth and shifted closer, his hard cock brushing the front of Chris's trousers.

Chris inched his fingers over Jesse's ass, heading toward the crevice between the two firm globes.

Jesse moaned again, rubbing his throbbing erection against Chris's front, the movements growing more demanding, hungrier.

Christian, my dear, I hope you're decent. I'm almost to your front door.

Chris's hand froze. Lascaux. Gently he pulled his mouth from Jesse's and slid his hand away from the enticing body. He reached for the robe and held it up.

Jesse frowned. His chest was heaving from arousal. "What's the matter?"

Chris managed a smile, his body still coursing with heat despite the interruption. "Nothing, Jess. I just don't want you to be naked when Lascaux gets here."

Jesse fathomless eyes widened under their heavy fringes of dark lashes. "He's here?"

Chris nodded, holding the robe so Jesse could slip his arms into the sleeves. He closed it up in front, mournful at having to cover Jesse's incredible body. "Yes. He informed me just now."

Jesse nodded, looking down. "Your mind link."

Chris heard the tinge of jealous worry in his lover's voice. The sound made his heart squeeze and he reached out to cup Jesse's cheek. "Yes, every protégé has one with his sire. It's unavoidable." He brushed his thumb across the smooth cheek still soft from having been shaved. "I love you, Jesse."

Jesse's gaze shot up. Relief flooded those enchanting eyes. *I love you, too.* He looked at Chris a moment longer, then moved off his lap, his hands going to the belt of the robe to tighten it.

Just then, the doorbell rang.

* * *

Jesse watched Chris open the door, trapped between terror and fascination. There was something about meeting the vampire who'd sired his soul mate that compelled him.

Chris opened the front door, revealing three figures, all male. Though they were strangers to him, Jesse knew Lascaux in an instant. He'd never seen the vampire before, but the absolute masculinity that radiated from Chris's sire was unmistakable. Swarthy skin, raven hair swept back off a high forehead, piercing eyes and aristocratic Semitic features characterized the world's first vampire, his radiant beauty enhanced by the sleek black clothing he wore.

Lascaux's obsidian gaze lit on his protégé and the piercing quality of his dark eyes softened noticeably. "Chris," he said, his voice surprisingly soft. He held out a large masculine hand.

Jesse watched Chris accept the handshake, noticing Lascaux's forbearance with him. Lascaux struck Jesse as someone who kissed or hugged those whom he loved, but in this case, he seemed respectfully distant.

"It's wonderful to see you, Valmont." The tone of mutual respect and admiration reflected in Chris's voice. "Thank you for coming on such short notice."

A smile curved Lascaux's masculine lips. He ended the handshake and reached up, giving Chris's cheek a couple of affectionate pats. "As long as I'm not locked in a dungeon, I'll be there for you."

Chris's eyes went momentarily stricken and Jesse remembered the story he'd relayed earlier about Lascaux's centuries'-long imprisonment and torture in his own home. Guilt assailed Jesse for having ever been a slayer, in spite of the fact that his targets had not been...upright, like the vampires he was meeting now.

Chris ushered Lascaux and his companions out of the cold and into the foyer, offering to take their coats.

Jesse remained standing where he was by the fire, overcome with sudden, painful timidity. After all, he'd originally come to Chris with the intention of killing him. No doubt, Chris's sire would have something to say about that.

The eyes of all three guests turned on him in that moment and his heart thumped. Lascaux moved toward him, flanked by his companions. The other two men, though not as commanding in presence as Lascaux, were no less gorgeous. One had ebony hair cut close to the scalp and startlingly blue almond shaped eyes, accentuated by high smooth cheekbones and full lips. He looked Russian, while the third man, blond and green eyed with tumbling curls surrounding his face, an unusual combination of pretty and rugged, appeared Nordic like his own lover.

Lascaux came to stand in front of Jesse, his eyes remaining softer, less piercing. The other two men, presumably vampires, stood close behind him, also studying him.

"Chris has already told me who you are." A hand, also surprisingly gentle, came to rest on his shoulder, sending heat radiating into his shoulder. Immediately Jesse could see how Lascaux could at once terrify and enchant someone.

"Don't worry about the reason you're here to begin with. Chris has already pleaded your case and you come up innocent."

Jesse could barely suppress his sigh of relief.

"I hope you're fully recovered because we must get going as soon as you are."

Jesse stared at him a moment, blinking. In a mere few days, his world had gone from solitary and loveless to having found his soul mate and along with him, several other beings, and vampires at that, willing to help him rather than wanting to kill him or to kill for them.

Apparently, Lascaux understood what Jesse was feeling. An understanding light glowed in the obsidian depths of his eyes and he nodded. "Yes," he murmured, "Chris is for real." He gestured with a nod of his head to the men standing behind him, then turned, taking the dark-haired Russian by one arm. "Serge here has taught me the meaning of the word *love*. For my entire captivity, over six hundred years, he waited for an opportunity to free me." He released Serge with a rub of his hand on the other vampire's sleeve.

Lascaux pointed to the blond. "And this is Philippe. He's a hybrid vamp like Chris. He, too, knows what it means to love." Philippe and Serge each shook Jesse's hand before stepping back at Lascaux's sides.

Lascaux's gaze went to Chris, who, Jesse realized in that moment, had come to stand close at Jesse's side. "Christian, do you have the mold?"

Chris nodded and Jesse sensed his sheepishness, remembering Jesse's introduction to the fake head. "I'll bring it down."

"Yes, along with some clothing for your friend. We'll leave momentarily. We can make our plan en route."

Chris bowed his head, the gesture emanating respect for his sire, and then left without another word.

"Please…sit." Jesse finally found his voice and indicated the sofa facing the one he'd sat on with Chris.

"Thank you." Lascaux seated himself along with Serge and Philippe. Jesse watched them, noticing the reverent gaze which Serge kept on him. Philippe, he noted, watched Serge in the same manner.

Hmm. The three vampires seemed to form a complex love triangle of some sort.

Only moments later, Chris reappeared bearing the tray with the dreaded model on it and some clothing hanging over his arm. He set the tray down on the stone coffee table between the two sofas and sank onto the cushions beside Jesse.

"Go ahead," Lascaux urged. "Unveil the thing."

Chris leaned forward and slid the cloth away, revealing the likeness to his own head.

In spite of the fact Jesse now knew it was a fake, he still flinched. He couldn't help glancing at Lascaux to see his reaction.

The magnificent vampire stared at the model, his obsidian gaze taking it in appraisingly. Slowly he nodded. "You do amazing work, Chris. I daresay even Noiret, that piece of shit, will be fooled."

Lascaux must have registered Jesse's surprise, for the raven-hued irises lit on his face and the vampire's swarthy face creased in a smile. "Perhaps you're noticing that your vampire kith are as varied in temperament and nature as anyone else."

The subtle reprimand was not lost on Jesse. Of course, even though Lascaux didn't judge him for the past, as Chris's sire and protector, he would be compelled to convey some small measure of defense.

Jesse bowed his head and nodded. "Yes, I'm seeing that."

In the next moment, he felt Chris's hand, warm and comforting, slide across his back and rest there.

"*Alors*," Lascaux continued, "Jesse here will present this model to Noiret and then? Knowing that bastard, we must pray that he hasn't already killed Jesse's sister."

Jesse's gaze shot up to the vampire, blood coursing suddenly icy through his veins. "Hannah is alive!" *Aren't you?* He focused inwardly, as hard as he ever had done, calling his sister.

I'm here, Jesse. When are you coming?

Jesse breathed a heavy sigh of relief. *Today.*

Please hurry.

Hannah, hang on. We're coming.

We?

I'll explain later.

Please, Jess, hurry!

Jesse looked at Lascaux. "She's alive. She's begging me to hurry."

Lascaux nodded and looked down. The air in the room grew still with his seeming concentration.

What's he doing? Jesse asked Chris through their mind link.

Chris's hand pressed comfortingly against his back. *Probably accessing his mind link to Noiret.*

Jesse nearly jumped from the seat. *He has a mind link with Noiret?*

Chris looked at him and nodded. *He sired him.*

Lascaux cleared his throat, the sound compelling Jesse to look up at him. "So far, he hasn't moved her. He doesn't know we're coming. We'll leave as soon as you get dressed."

Jesse continued to stare at Lascaux.

To his surprise, a pained look crossed the vampire's features. "Yes, I sired Noiret. Another of my many grievous mistakes. Finally I'm getting a chance to undo it." He looked at Chris. "Second chances happen quite often to me, it seems, whether I deserve them or not."

Chris looked at his sire, his gaze full of admiration. "They're second chances because you take them."

Lascaux studied Chris's face a moment before a sad smile crossed his face. "Come on. Let's go."

"Jesse, here." Chris handed Jesse a shirt and trousers. "They'll no doubt be a bit big so I've included a belt."

Jesse accepted the clothing, wishing this were all over and Hannah were rescued so that he and Chris could just curl up together in bed and make love day and night. "Thank you."

Chris reached to his pocket and pulled something out, holding it to him. Jesse glimpsed the glint of the firelight off the blade of a knife. His slaying knife.

Chris's handsome face darkened. "You'll need it, no doubt."

Jesse nodded, wordlessly accepting the weapon from his lover. The irony of the moment was not lost on him. "Thank you," he managed to say, feeling the gazes of the other three vampires on him.

Chris looked down at him, his blue eyes radiating affection. Never before had Jesse been the object of such a gaze and he had to fight down the urge to lean forward and press his cheek to his lover's chest and stay there. Had Lascaux and his entourage not been standing a few feet away, he would have done just that.

"There's a bathroom right off the hallway," Chris murmured.

Jesse nodded and went quickly out, avoiding the other gazes on him. He dressed in a few seconds and sheathed his knife in the belt at his back.

When he went out into the hallway, the four vampires stood by the front door, waiting. He approached them, his eyes on Chris.

"Come on," he said, "Let's get my sister."

Chapter Ten

Lascaux's private jet had them in New York in under an hour. Another thirty-minute cab ride brought Jesse and the vampires to Noiret's club and left them off a block away.

The street was dark, the buildings lining the sidewalks factories closed for the night. Bass-driven music from Noiret's rave-style warehouse club vibrated in the ground beneath them and in the freezing cold, people were going in and out of the front entrance.

Jesse's heart pounded. His hand tightened on the sack containing the model of Chris's head. Chris's hand rested on his arm as they walked, pressing harder through the shearling coat he'd given Jesse to wear. Chris and Philippe were to find Hannah and free her in the event that Noiret went back on the deal after obtaining the head.

Around the corner from the club entrance, they stopped. Chris turned to him, his handsome face creased with a serious expression.

We're going to do this, Jesse. Chris's voice through their mind link echoed pleasantly through Jesse's body. *But whatever happens, I love you.*

Jesse fought back a rising tide of panic. *I love you too.*

Chris squeezed his arm and then at Lascaux's gesture, released him. Jesse watched him and Philippe turn and glide into the air, up to the roof of the building.

"They'll find her. Don't worry."

Lascaux's voice made Jesse turn. The vampire was watching him. "Serge and I will be close behind you and will join you as soon as we take care of Noiret's entourage. That's a promise."

Jesse nodded, one last spike of guilt catching him in the gut. "Thank you," he murmured, then turned and headed toward the entrance of the club. He bypassed the line of people at the door, his gaze roving absently over the spiked hair, nose rings, kinky leather, and tattoos as he approached the mohawked, six-foot-five bouncer.

The bouncer looked down at him past his multiple nose rings. "Wait in line, like everyone else."

The door opened and a blast of techno music wafted out, dying down again with the closing of the door.

Jesse gave him a hard look. "I'm here to see Noiret."

"What's your name?"

"Jesse Harmon."

Recognition lit the meaty man's face. Apparently, Noiret had already given instructions about him. Without another word, the bouncer stood aside, pulling the door open again.

Jesse tossed a glance to the line, seeing Lascaux waiting with Serge, as if they were regular guests of the club, then went in, immediately enveloped in music, cigarette smoke and writhing bodies. Lights flashed through the huge dance area, but Jesse ignored the dancers around him, making his way to the corner Noiret always inhabited.

Noiret was there, a new woman fawning over him, whispering something in his ear. God only knew what Noiret had done to the blonde from two days ago.

The vampire must have sensed Jesse's approach for he looked up, a moment of surprise slithering across his pale features.

In the next moment, a grin curled his lips and he gestured toward the back of the club.

Sudden fierce anger pounded through Jesse and he closed the short distance to the table, leaning over in a threatening manner. "I brought what you wanted and I'm here days early, you bastard. You get nothing until I see her."

Noiret rose slowly, his gaze piercing Jesse's. "Yes, I see. You decided on a Christmas present rather than a New Year's offering." He paused and took a sip of blood before looking back up. "You'll see her when *I* see that you actually do have what I want."

Jesse gritted his teeth, ready to pull out his knife and finish Noiret himself. And if Hannah hadn't been Noiret's prisoner, he would have. He turned and threaded his way through the writhing throng of dancers toward Noiret's office.

Noiret followed him in with two of his goons and closed the door behind them. He perched on the edge of his desk, lighting a cigarette, his two guards behind his chair. He blew a puff of smoke in Jesse's direction. "Let's see it."

Jesse came forward, pulling the string on the bag as he did so.

Noiret raised his flaxen eyebrows. "What, no silver platter?"

Jesse ignored him and reached in the bag, burying his fingers into what was once his lover's silken gold hair. He tugged the bag down and lifted the head, raising it up for Noiret to inspect.

Noiret hissed. For the first time since Jesse had interacted with Noiret, the vampire showed an emotion other than sadistic smugness. Jesse suppressed the sensations of horror roiling his gut. Why it was so difficult to remember that the head was a model and not actually Chris's?

Noiret drew closer, his cold gray eyes inspecting the flawlessly reproduced likeness. Jesse's heart pounded fiercely and his hand threatened to shake. The vampire hissed again. "Finally."

With a jerking motion, Jesse stuffed the head back into the bag. He then turned on Noiret. "All right, I gave you what you wanted. Now give me my sister."

Noiret's fascination faded, replaced by his customary shit-eating grin. "Very well. I'll show her to you and then you can go retrieve her." There was a sound in his voice that chilled Jesse's very blood.

Noiret went to his desk, picked up a remote control and pressed a button. A panel above his desk slid aside, revealing a television screen. The vampire pressed another button on the remote and a picture came onto the screen.

Jesse froze.

Hannah was there, her lean willowy form bound to a table. Her long raven hair hung over the edges of the table, above a strap across her forehead, holding her head down. Looking closer, he noticed the bounds were formed of hemp, a substance that obviously weakened her. She was utterly defenseless.

"It seems your sister has a weakness for hemp." Noiret's voice slithered like insects inside Jesse's body. "Oh, don't worry; I haven't sullied her purity, the dear. Although it wouldn't have mattered, the places she was going. Virginal women don't frequent gambling dens. But she has made good feeding these last few days."

Jesse dropped the bag with the fake head, his hand going for his knife. Red hot rage coursed through him. "You fucking bastard!"

Jesse reached under his coat, sliding the knife out. He charged, knife in hand, his only desire to kill Noiret, but the vampire was too fast and too strong for him. In one swift motion, Noiret had Jesse by the throat and slammed him up against the wall.

Jesse choked as Noiret lifted him, his feet leaving the ground. Noiret's eyes glowed with bloodlust and anger. He pushed hard against Jesse's throat, cutting off his air almost completely.

"That was a really stupid thing to do, immortal. You're lucky I don't order her beheaded this instant. If she weren't so fucking delicious, I would." He leaned in closer, giving Jesse a potent whiff of stale cigarettes mixed with death. "Perhaps you'd like to witness the service she's so generously been providing." He nodded to his goons.

Jesse tried to struggle, but Noiret had superior physical strength. Jesse's glance went to his slaying knife, which had clattered to the floor when Noiret grabbed him.

"Put him down this instant or I'll kill you where you stand."

Relief sliced through Jesse at the sound of Lascaux's voice.

Jesse moved his eyes, seeing Lascaux and Serge standing in the doorway. The music outside the door had been so loud, it drowned out their entrance.

Noiret turned his head, not easing his grip on Jesse's throat. "Where are my men? What have you done to them?"

The corner of Lascaux's lips curled and a gleam came into his eye. "They're enthralled with me."

"You fucker," Noiret hissed. He turned to his goons who also stood in the stillness of thrall.

Lascaux's grin faded. "You seem to forget I'm more powerful than you are. Now let the immortal go."

Noiret's grip loosened a hair then tightened again. "Big deal. The thrall will wear off. You should have killed them. But you wouldn't, would you? You've gone soft, getting yourself imprisoned for centuries over a piece of pussy. And all the while that priestess bitch was getting it from every angle by her guardians, not *you*."

Jesse saw Lascaux's expression pain before he visibly gathered himself, not giving in to the baiting.

Lascaux's black eyes glittered, the glow of blood lust rising in them. "Let him go now or I'll kill you. I'm still your sire."

Noiret squeezed harder. Jesse choked.

Lascaux and Serge flew across the space dividing them and Lascaux ripped Noiret off Jesse.

Jesse grabbed his throat as he slid to the floor. He was unable to move even to retrieve his knife and could only rub his throat while Lascaux grappled with Noiret.

The two goon vampires, their thrall obviously broken, charged Serge. The small office filled with the sounds of hissing and crashes as fighting escalated. Lascaux grabbed Noiret and threw him across the room into the opposite wall.

Jesse's wind came back enough for him to inch forward and grab his knife. He looked up at the screen and sighed in relief. Chris and Philippe were bent over Hannah, removing her bonds.

Jesse, help! More vampires are attacking me!

It's all right, Hannah. They're with me. They're rescuing you. I promise.

On the screen he saw Chris help Hannah sit up. She was looking at him, her expression less frightened. She was going to be okay.

He turned to see what was happening in the fight around him.

Serge had felled one of his attackers. The vampire lay on the floor, lifeless, his head half off.

Nausea churned Jesse's gut but he struggled to his feet. Lascaux and Noiret still fought ferociously, cuts open on their faces, healing quickly before they delivered more blows. The furniture in the room was in shards, so much broken, Jesse couldn't even see the bag with the head in it on the floor.

Noiret recovered from one of Lascaux's tackles and rushed his sire, pushing Lascaux onto his back across the rubble of what had once been an office. Noiret's eyes glowed fiercely and his fangs were bared, displaying his obvious hunger to end Lascaux's existence. Jesse watched the silent struggle of wills, realizing that even now, Lascaux wanted to end the fight without ending his protégé's life.

Yes, the oldest vampire *had* gone a bit soft. But softer...Jesse knew now, was better. Noiret represented everything wrong with the world.

Anger surged hot and fierce in Jesse's blood. He raised his knife and charged, his old slaying instincts and skills resurging at full force.

In one strike, he took Noiret's head clean off. There was not even a second for Noiret to look astonished as his head tumbled off his neck to the rubble.

The hands loosened their grip on Lascaux and the body slid off him, landing next to the head.

Jesse stared at Lascaux, his heart still pounding, his chest heaving from the effort of slicing through Noiret. "Are you all right?" He extended a hand to the vampire.

Lascaux reached out and accepted his help just as Serge came to their sides, having finished off his other attacker.

"I'm fine." He sat up slowly and looked at Jesse, a sorrowful expression creasing his handsome features.

Sudden shame and guilt flooded Jesse. "I'm...I'm sorry, Lascaux. I didn't have any --"

Lascaux cut him off. "Stop. You couldn't have done differently." He sighed deeply and turned his dark gaze onto

Serge. Affection softened his eyes. "Not everyone can be saved, no matter how much you care about them."

Serge leaned over, gently taking Lascaux's hand and helping him off the rubble of broken furniture, to his feet. When Lascaux was standing, Serge pulled Lascaux gently into his embrace, his love for Lascaux filling the space around them.

Lascaux stared down at his dead protégé for another moment before looking back up at Jesse. "Come, now. Let's go to your sister. Chris and Philippe should have her back to the car by now."

Jesse nodded, aching to see Hannah again and to feel Chris in his arms. He stepped away from the rubble where Noiret's body lay strewn next to his head. Jesse almost threw his knife down too, but changed his mind at the last second. The world was still full of creatures like Noiret, and he wanted to be able to defend those he loved. "What about the goons outside?"

"Don't worry about them," Lascaux answered as they picked their way through the rubble. "The thrall will take them again as we pass. When it's over, they won't know who's done this to Noiret."

Jesse sighed. He wiped his knife and tucked it back under his belt, following Serge and Lascaux from the office, thinking only of Chris and of the life he hoped to be spending with him, making love endlessly. Starting in the next few hours, too, with any luck.

As they made their way through the enthralled crowd, Jesse realized he did have loved ones now to defend. And he would defend them.

Chapter Eleven

Jesse sat between Hannah and Chris on Lascaux's jet. Hannah was in shock, both from having been a prisoner and from having been fed on excessively by Noiret and his goons. She clung to her brother, falling asleep with her head against his shoulder.

Apparently, Noiret had been able to penetrate her mind link with Jesse and so she kept as much as possible from her brother, protecting him, while she waited for rescue.

Chris held Jesse's hand through the entire flight, squeezing Jesse's fingers comfortingly every so often. Jesse's heart brimmed with love and gratitude to Chris and everything he'd done for him. Chris and Philippe had found Hannah easily and were able to fight off the vampires guarding her. Because Chris wasn't completely a CE, he had gone against his vow not to kill, making an exception for Jesse and Hannah's sakes.

Jesse looked up at him. *Chris.* He spoke through their mind link so as not to disturb Hannah.

Chris returned his gaze, a questioning look on his face. *What is it,* mon amour?

Jesse glanced away briefly, preparing himself to speak his heart, something that had always been difficult for him. *You don't know what it means to me, your helping me this way.*

Chris leaned over and kissed Jesse's mouth softly. He lingered there, lips parting slightly, silently urging Jesse to return the kiss.

Jesse took the invitation to taste him more deeply, sliding his tongue along Chris's upper lip and then slipping inside to dance it against Chris's tongue.

With rising heat, Chris pressed more firmly, closing his lips together, tugging sensually on Jesse's lips before ending the kiss. His blue eyes smoldered down into Jesse's, full of erotic promise. *Stop thinking you're the only sinner on the planet, Jesse.* And with that, Chris turned forward in his seat again, squeezing Jesse's hand where it rested in his on the armrest.

They remained that way for the rest of the flight and then again, in the limousine that brought them from the airport to Chris's door.

Chris caught a glance of the Christmas tree lights blinking through his living room window. Finally, coming home was not a lonely prospect. He smiled as he helped Jesse bring his exhausted, traumatized sister up the front steps, with Lascaux and his lovers behind them. For the first time in centuries, Chris felt a bit of holiday warmth and spirit and was glad he'd succumbed once again to the temptation to put up a tree.

Once inside the house, Jesse scooped up his sister and carried her to the bedroom Chris directed him to. He watched Jesse pull back the covers and lower his sister down, taking time only to remove her boots. Chris had given her a sedative that would help her sleep well through the night to the next morning. Even though she'd survived her ordeal, immortals were subject to many of the same slings and arrows as their mortal human counterparts and she needed rest.

Chris felt Jesse's affection for his sister practically swirling in the air around them. She was obviously Jesse's twin, judging by her ebony hair, olive skin and Roman beauty. Chris was moved by the gentle, protective way her brother handled her. Watching Jesse's hands as he pulled up the covers up over her, tucking them under her chin, Chris was struck with the sudden intense longing to have those same hands all over his own body.

Jesse left his sister sleeping peacefully and joined Chris. The other three vampires stood out in the hall, enquiring after her.

"She'll be fine after she's rested." Jesse looked at Valmont. "I'll never be able to repay all of you for what you've done." Jesse bowed his head.

Lascaux patted Jesse's dark hair. "If you want to repay us, just take good care of Chris here."

Jesse looked up, lips parted in obvious surprise. Slowly, he smiled and looked at Chris. "I can do that."

Chris stood in front of his sire, his ethereal heart overwhelmed with affection for him. "Valmont, I can never thank you enough for this."

Lascaux reached out, his hands coming to rest on Chris's shoulders. "You're welcome and all that is required of you in return is a room for the night." A grin spread across his dark features and he nodded, indicating his two companions. "One with a *very* large bed."

* * *

Finally, alone again with Chris.

Jesse stood by the edge of the huge bed, watching Chris rekindle the fire in the hearth and drop a branch of something scented into the flames. In moments, the scent of sandalwood permeated the air, making his body grow languorous. His mouth watered in anticipation of dragging his tongue down the center of Chris's hard stomach, moving closer to the delicious bulge waiting for his mouth…

Chris stood up and approached him. His large blue eyes reflected the glow of the fire, the light gently dancing off his pale skin and soft dusky lips.

All Jesse wanted to do was pleasure Chris, to shower on him the same bliss he'd given Jesse earlier, loving him and nursing him back to health in spite of the circumstances that had brought them together.

Rising up slightly on his toes, Jesse bridged the gap in their heights, his hands coming up to touch Chris's rugged, yet smooth cheeks. On his back, he felt the press of Chris's large hands, gently pulling him closer, closing the space between their bodies. And mouths.

Jesse closed his eyes, slanting his lips over Chris's. Mmm, so soft, yet so hard. Chris's musky scent blended with the spices wafting in the air, urging a primal rhythm in Jesse's heart that traveled down the length of his body to his rising cock.

With rising hunger, he slipped his tongue between Chris's lips. Chris answered with the slide of his tongue over Jesse's, tasting his teeth, sensuously tickling the roof of his mouth. The moist hot dance of their tongues urged Jesse to pull Chris closer, to slide his palms around Chris's head, the shorn hair silky against his palms.

Fuck. Chris tasted so incredible, his scent and flavor filling Jesse completely. One hand slipped down the back of Chris's head to the strong column of his neck, the tiny muscles shifting and flexing as they kissed.

Jesse's erection pushed to full hardness, straining against the jeans Chris had given him to wear. His hands slipped down to Chris's shirt, working the buttons open with frantic fingers. He didn't stop until he could slide his palms against that broad chest, the muscles warm and hard against his skin, the dusky nipples smooth and flat, tightening when he brushed them with his fingertips.

Jesse cupped both hillocks of muscles, squeezing them, delighting in the light rasp of hair, the quivering of the hard strength. He paused. Something was pulsing under his hand, deep inside Chris's chest. Was that...? Could it be?

He pulled his mouth away from Chris's and looked into the deep blue eyes, half hidden under his lids, the golden lashes like soft fans.

"What is it, *mon amour?*" Chris's smooth voice rasped slightly from arousal.

Jesse swallowed, uncertain as to whether he should venture to tell his lover what he felt under his hand. "Heartbeat," he whispered after several moments.

Chris tensed under his hands. "What did you say?"

Jesse gazed up at him, concerned at the surprise in his lover's face. "I feel your heart beating."

Chris's lips parted slightly and he turned, sinking onto the bed. His hands slid down Jesse's arms and grasped Jesse's hands, holding them lightly. "By the gods," he murmured, his eyes still appearing as if he'd just witnessed a miracle...or something of that nature. "Darelle told me once that this could happen." He lifted his gaze to Jesse. "I didn't believe her."

"What did she tell you could happen?"

Chris hesitated another moment, his blue gaze liquid in the soft glow of firelight. "She told me once, centuries ago, that there would be one being on this earth who would be able to feel my heart beat." He shook his head. "I thought it was a romantic fancy of hers. Not something real."

Jesse's own heart thumped. He remembered the first time he'd touched Chris's chest, searching for that heart and hadn't found it. "I didn't feel it before."

Chris nodded. "I know. But...you didn't love me in that moment. You do now, don't you?"

Jesse reached out and cupped his lover's cheek, brushing his thumb across the smooth pale skin. "Yes. I do." With one knee, he nudged Chris's legs apart and stepped between them, sliding his hands over the bulging muscle in Chris's back. He leaned over and pressed a kiss onto Chris's hair, at the same time reaching down to tug Chris's shirt off the rest of the way.

They might have eternity to make love, but he wasn't going to waste another second.

With gentle fingertips on Chris's jaw, he tilted the vampire's head gently back and kissed his lips, tasting them for what seemed a long time while his hands roamed over the warm muscles of Chris's back and shoulders, alive and hard. Enjoying every caress, he worked his way down, pulling away from their kiss so he could kneel and concentrate on working Chris's jeans open.

Chris leaned back, giving Jesse space to work down the zipper and pull the fabric aside, allowing that thick, glorious cock to spring free. It was already hard, the head full and taut, a drop of clear seed seeping from the tip.

The sight of the reddish veined shaft made Jesse's mouth water and he leaned over, taking it into his mouth in one hungry gulp.

A long groan filled his ears as he began to suck, taking Chris's cock deep inside, his tongue sliding over Chris's satiny skin. He slid his lips almost to the base and drew back, the tip of his tongue lapping up the droplets of seed at the tiny opening.

He grasped Chris's jeans, urging him to lift his ass so he could slide them the rest of the way off. He tugged them down Chris's legs and over his feet, his mouth hesitating on the delicious shaft just a moment until he was free to concentrate.

He moved Chris's legs wider apart, giving him access to the rest of his jewels. He lifted his mouth away and pushed Chris gently onto his back. "Stay like that," he ordered in a husky voice.

Chris rose on his elbows, his face flushed. A tiny grin teased at his lips. "Whatever you say, *mon amour.*"

Jesse returned his smile and leaned into him again, taking Chris's shaft in his palm and pumping it while he caressed the heavy sac underneath with his eager tongue. The wetness of his mouth caused his tongue to glide across the tender, musky skin. He feathered the tip of his tongue in quick circles, and then in larger ones, over each lobe of Chris's balls and down to the perineum, each movement pulling a groan of enjoyment from his lover.

Jesse closed his eyes, drinking in the scents and flavors of Chris's muscular body, loving the sound of his moans, enjoyment that *he* was giving Chris. His own body quivered and tensed, his bottom aching for the pounding hardness of his lover's cock inside him.

Quickly Jesse stood and stripped off his own clothes, climbing onto the bed, straddling Chris before the vampire had a chance to move. He looked down at Chris's face, the rugged lines of his cheeks and jaw, the soft curves of his lips, and for one brief moment, his heart ached mercilessly that he had once contemplated killing this glorious, beautiful being. His soul mate.

Chris's look darkened and Jesse felt his concern. "What's the matter, Jesse?"

Not wanting to ruin the bliss they were sharing, he cast away the guilt. No doubt it would return, but for the moment, they had each other. He smiled. "Nothing's the matter. I was just thinking how badly I want you to fuck me."

Chris's look darkened further, taking on a feral glow. "I'd love nothing more."

Jesse wet his hand with spit and rubbed his bottom and then slicked his hand over Chris's cock, straining and hard.

He pumped it several times with his hand and then rose up, guiding the swollen head to his tight hole. Maneuvering his bottom until the smooth head poked in, he hissed in pleasure and then pushed, impaling himself on Chris's delicious cock in one smooth glide.

Jesse gasped from the sharp pleasure-pain, his vision blurring as their bodies met. Chris groaned and bucked his hips.

Jesse righted himself, finding his balance, which was difficult from the weakening effect of pleasure. He could feel Chris deep inside him, that gorgeous thick cock rubbing all the right spots.

In slow even strokes, he found a rhythm, riding his lover's shaft and pumping his own cock with one hand. Chris's large hands held his hips, keeping him astride, his strong arms adding more lift to his movements.

Jesse's eyes fluttered closed and his head tilted back, the pleasure building hard and fast, overwhelming him.

"That's right, *mon amour*." Chris's voice slid like silk around him, deepening the sparks of pleasure bursting through him. "You fuck me so good."

His lover's words urged him harder and faster, the grinding of Chris's cock deep in his tight passage and the pumping motions of his own hand bringing him faster and faster to the edge.

In the next breath he spilled over, his seed pulsing out in milky streaks, anointing Chris's chest and stomach.

Chris groaned and lifted his hips, his cock twitching deep inside Jesse with his release.

Jesse slumped over, his hands bridging Chris's wide body, his hands sinking deep into the mattress. He leaned down and pressed his lips to Chris's, still panting. They rested like that, Chris's large hands moving in lazy circles over Jesse's hips and ass.

When he'd caught his breath, Jesse rolled over, letting his lover's partially erect cock slide out of him. If he hadn't known there was an eternity to feel that cock inside him again, the sensation of sudden emptiness would have been unbearable.

As it was, he planned to impale himself on Chris's cock again soon. And again. And again.

He rolled over, snuggling against Chris's side. Chris turned over, his hand sliding over Jesse's back, ignoring the warm puddle of cum that coated his skin. He smiled at Jesse.

Jesse returned the smile, his hand wandering lazily down to Chris's chest, seeking out the heartbeat that only he, in the entire world, could feel. The beat pulsed strongly under his hand and Jesse could have sworn it beat now only for him.

"Hey," he said to Chris in a soft whisper.

Chris looked at him, his lips curving in a smile. "Hey what?"

Jesse grinned. "Merry Christmas."

~ * ~

Sedonia Guillone

Sedonia Guillone lives on the water in Florida in winter and on the rocky coast of Maine in summers with a Renaissance man who paints, writes poetry and tells her she's the sweetest nymph he's ever met. When she's not writing erotic romance, she loves watching spaghetti westerns, cuddling, and eating chocolate.

Visit Sedonia on the Web at www.sedoniaguillone.com.

* * *

THE MASTER'S GIFT

Kit Tunstall

Chapter One

Hugh Klein lived in a huge house on the highest hilltop in the small town neighboring the nearest university, where Chris Hanna was a senior. Chris gazed at the outside with wide-eyed awe as he stepped out of the passenger side of the BMW Emory had driven to convey him to the meeting with Mr. Klein. "Dude, this place is awesome."

Emory nodded, looking distractedly at the brick and wood façade. "Inside's even better." He glanced at the gold watch on his wrist. "Hurry up, man. Mr. Klein's expecting us in two minutes, and he isn't someone you keep waiting."

Chris nodded, falling into step with his frat brother and close friend. Emory was off to a coveted position on Wall Street in a few days, and if Mr. Klein approved of him, Chris would be taking over the assistant job his friend was leaving behind. He was nervous, but hopeful that he could meet all of Mr. Klein's expectations. It would solve all of his problems -- an income for his final year of college, along with a place to live. The position even came with a car for his personal use. He cast a glance back at the BMW, imagining how the car might turn the head of Vanessa Shaye. Maybe she would finally notice he was a man and stop treating him with brotherly affection when all he wanted from her was passionate devotion.

Thinking of Ness made him sad. No doubt, she was on a date this Saturday night, while he interviewed for a job. The slightly spoiled daughter of a wealthy man, Ness had never worked, and probably never would. Her pursuit of a degree was merely something to fill her time. She had admitted that herself many times, accompanied by that tinkling laugh that made his insides ache whenever he heard it.

"Chris, c'mon." Emory elbowed him in the ribs to get him moving.

Chris shook off his melancholy thoughts and proceeded through the entryway. His eyes took in the priceless *objet d'art* surrounding him as they walked through the house, but he didn't allow his feet to stop. If things went as planned, he would have ample time to study the pictures, sculptures, and collectibles between assisting Mr. Klein and his college courses.

With a frown, he once again tried to imagine what being the other man's assistant entailed. Emory had been vague, saying simply that he did, "Whatever Mr. Klein asks." Chris imagined it would be a job filled with errand running, phone answering, and the requisite bowing and scraping a man like Mr. Klein would expect. He wasn't looking forward to the duties, but the perks should make up for the sheer boredom he would no doubt endure.

An unexpected rumble of nerves quaked in his stomach as he followed Emory into a somber study. The room smelled of leather and learning, with bookshelves to the ceiling, stacked neatly full of leather-bound volumes. The patina on the teak desk indicated it was an antique, and the surface was free of clutter. Only a blotter, laptop, and trays for paperwork occupied the area.

He turned his attention to his prospective employer when the man's leather chair squeaked as he leaned forward. Austere was the word that came to mind. Hugh Klein was blond, with fair coloring, and strange gray eyes that seemed to penetrate to Chris's core, reading the most intimate details about him. Imposing in a black turtleneck, the other man seemed to swallow up all the space behind the desk, though in reality he had an average build, with compact musculature. The light from the presidential-style lamp on the wall behind him illuminated his hair, picking out silvery highlights. His gaze scrutinized Chris from head to toe, making him shiver. To his shock and embarrassment, Chris's cock swelled with arousal when Mr. Klein met his eyes. In an attempt to cover his reaction, he practically leapt into one of the chairs facing the desk, sliding low and pressing his thighs together.

Somehow, he managed to sound normal when he accepted the hand Mr. Klein extended and said, "Pleased to meet you, sir."

Emory took the other seat, and Chris was conscious of his friend fidgeting as Mr. Klein asked him some general questions. He answered as thoroughly as possible, and then settled back into the seat when the other man fell quiet. An air of expectancy hung in the room, and he waited with bated breath, sensing something else was going to happen, but not sure what.

The preternatural sense of impending epiphany faded when Mr. Klein turned to Emory. "You trust Mr. Hanna implicitly, Emory?"

Emory nodded his dark head. "Yes, Hugh. I've known him since he was in seventh grade, and I was in eighth. We met when he defended me from the class bully, though he was barely bigger than I was at the time. Chris is a good man, and he'll guard your secrets."

Chris lifted a brow at the exchange, feeling his curiosity stir to life. He inferred from their conversation that secrets referred to more than financial statements or typical confidentiality.

Mr. Klein made a non-committal sound before focusing on Chris again. "You're active in some campus clubs, I see. Politics, speech, and the university chapter of the VCLU." His eyes narrowed. "How did you become a member of the Vampire Civil Liberties Union?"

Chris shrugged. "My folks are both members. My dad's always said there's no reason to discriminate against vampires. They have more laws in place than we do to protect humans. It's our own fear..." He trailed off, not wanting to launch into a passionate diatribe and risk alienating the man who might be hiring him. He was a proud member of VCLU, and he spoke out regularly for vampires' rights, but he couldn't afford to lose the job opportunity because of personal views.

Mr. Klein nodded. "That's excellent. Tell me, Chris, do you know any vampires?"

Chris tilted his head. "I don't know, sir. There might be some in the group, and there are probably some at the rallies and fundraisers, but I've never had one come out to me."

A smile of amusement crinkled Mr. Klein's lips, making him look years younger, and exposing a glimpse of a lighter personality than he had thus far displayed. "'Coming out.' What a charming way to phrase it. I suppose it can be likened to homosexuality. Both are feared and sometimes hidden. Thankfully, gays and lesbians no longer have to fear criminal persecution for being who they are."

Chris breathed a sigh of relief. Mr. Klein appeared reasonable and liberally minded, so it was unlikely they would clash over ideals regarding the treatment of vampires. "I hope it will someday be that way for vampires too, Mr. Klein."

"So do I. You have no idea how much I long for that." He parted his lips in a wider smile, revealing fangs slowly descending.

Chris gasped, and despite his views, a frisson of fear scrabbled into his gut. He'd never knowingly been so close to a vampire before, and his first thought was to guard his neck. He glanced at Emory from the corner of his eye, finding his friend was unsurprised by Mr. Klein's revelation. Seeing Emory's calm demeanor allowed Chris to regain control and keep from making an ass of himself. Well, much of one. "Does it hurt when they come down?"

Mr. Klein shook his head. "No. It's a natural process." He steepled his fingers together on the desk. "I'm satisfied you'll do as Emory's replacement, if you can work for a vampire."

Chris hesitated for an instant before nodding. "Yes, sir."

"I'll expect complete discretion."

"Of course, sir."

"Call me Hugh." Hugh shared a look with Emory before continuing. "Much of the job is straightforward. I'll need you to run errands for me throughout the daytime, answer phones, make appointments, and handle some clients or paperwork yourself."

"What do you do, Hugh?"

"I'm an antiquities expert, and my consulting services are always in demand."

Chris nodded. "I've taken business courses. I'm sure I can handle all that."

"There's one more aspect to the job, and it's better you see it now, so you can decide if you can perform this duty." Hugh gestured to Emory, who rose to his feet and walked around the desk.

Chris watched with puzzled interest as Emory got to his knees. His confusion cleared up when his friend undid Hugh's snap and zipper of his pants. A flash of white briefs shielded Hugh's cock from view for a moment, until Emory freed it from the underwear. It sprang into sight, erect and proud. The shaft was thick, about seven inches long, and straight as an arrow. Scarlet painted the head in its arousal, and a single drop of fluid hovered on the tip of his penis, slowly sliding downward. It almost disappeared from sight, but Emory caught the droplet on his tongue at the last second, before taking the other man's cock into his mouth.

It was difficult to breathe as Chris watched his friend fellate Hugh Klein. A whirlwind of emotions swarmed through him -- discomfort, envy, and longing. It felt wrong to watch the men together, but at the same time, Chris wished he were the one taking the thick shaft inside his mouth. Until that moment, he'd never doubted he was anything except straight, but all he could think about was touching and tasting Hugh's cock, and then having the other man touch him. Chris's erection jumped at the thought, as if to spring eagerly from his Dockers. He folded his hands on his lap to hide his reaction. It was strange enough to find the scene arousing in light of his sexual orientation. Having the other two aware of his conflicted emotions would be too embarrassing. Chris couldn't help feeling somewhat ashamed of his excitement, though he was not the least bit homophobic. Enjoying such an experience just wasn't part of his accepted self-image.

Hugh watched him with a strange impassivity as Emory sucked his cock. A fine sheen of sweat dotted his brow, and he seemed physically aroused, but his eyes were almost blank, as if Emory couldn't touch him emotionally. "As you probably know, vampires need blood for sustenance. Sexual pleasure, coupled with blood, reduces the amount we need."

"What about cloned blood?" How was it possible that he was having a nearly normal conversation while a member of his fraternity sucked the cock of the man about to hire him?

Hugh nodded. "I see you're up-to-date on science. Yes, I drink cloned blood, but you must be aware of its drawbacks."

"Only fresh blood has the necessary adrenaline and endorphins to fully replenish a vampire."

Hugh smiled. "Excellent. So, I drink cloned blood nightly, but I must have a fresh feeding every few days. When coupled with sex, that sustains me quite well. Hunting is dangerous and impractical, so this is my solution."

"It makes sense." Chris frowned, trying to think of a delicate way to phrase the question he wanted to ask. Carefully, he picked his words. "Are men your preference?"

Hugh shrugged. "Sex is sex, Chris. I've had women assistants in the past, but I find they often want more than I am willing to give. They give in to romantic ideas of love and marriage, forgetting ours is a business arrangement. I've yet to have that situation arise with a male assistant, so I tend to pick men. If that makes me gay, so be it. I am beyond labeling sexuality."

Chris nodded, not sure how to respond. It was all so businesslike and efficient. That suited him for a regular job, but it seemed a cold way to approach the more intimate aspects of the position. Still, it was for the best. He could understand Hugh not wanting emotional entanglements. He wasn't going to want more than an employer-employee relationship from Hugh. The situation could work out lucratively for both, as long as he could get past his squeamishness at the idea of sex with another man.

A vampire, actually. Sex and blood-drinking. Chris quivered at the thought, not certain if he was repulsed or excited by the prospect. Regardless of his mixed feelings, the opportunity to work for Hugh Klein was too good to pass up. "I will do whatever you ask of me."

"Excellent." Hugh broke off, a paroxysm of pleasure crossing his face as he came. His breathing was slightly ragged when he spoke again. "Emory is leaving me on Friday morning. You'll start then."

Chris held out his hand to seal the verbal contract. When their fingers touched, electricity seemed to spark between them. He pulled back, clasping his hand into a fist. Was it his imagination, or was Hugh equally unsettled by their brief touch? He cleared his throat, trying to buy time to erase his confusion. "I won't let you down." He hoped he spoke the truth, that he could really give Hugh what he needed. The physical reaction of his body told him he was more than up to the task.

Chapter Two

Chris moved in Friday morning and spent the next few days occupied with mundane business tasks. The master vampire was sometimes awake by early afternoon, but he rarely ventured from his room before nightfall. In his years as a vampire, Hugh had mastered many things, but did not yet have immunity to sunlight. Always, he remained on edge, wondering when Hugh would call on him to perform sexually, but his apprehension grew with each hour that brought him closer to nightfall. He had grown almost impatient with waiting when the other man finally summoned him. His homework sat on the desk, unfinished, as he left his room to hurry to Hugh's study. His stomach was a bundle of nerves, kinked into a knot, when he knocked on the door and awaited permission to enter.

"Come in." Hugh sounded as remote as ever. He could have been paging Chris to fax documents for all the emotion in his voice. But Chris knew it had to be for something else -- after all, the master vampire hadn't fed, or had sex, since Chris moved in. Unless he had found sustenance from elsewhere. Why did that possibility give him a strange pang in his chest?

Chris entered the room, walking over to the desk to stand before his employer. "You sent for me, sir?"

Hugh waved him over. With a hint of trepidation in his step, he walked around the desk, stopping a few inches from Hugh.

Hugh smiled. "I can hear your heart thudding around in your chest about a mile a minute." His amused expression revealed a hint of fangs. "Try to relax."

Chris nodded, his dry mouth making it impossible to speak.

"I'd say I won't bite, but we both know that's not true." Hugh reached out to grasp Chris's wrist, bringing him closer. He retained his hold even when Chris was standing as close as he could get. "But first…"

Chris nodded. He tried to act as though he went down on men every day as he started to kneel. Hugh's hand on his shoulder made him halt in the process, and he looked at him with curiosity. "Did I do something wrong?"

Hugh shook his head. "Not at all. I don't want you to do that yet."

His brow wrinkled in a frown. "But I thought --" Tingles of electricity arced up Chris's arm as Hugh began to caress his wrist.

"When I drink from you, I need you to be aroused. It's unlikely your first time giving oral sex to a man will be pleasurable. So, I will pleasure you."

A new attack of nerves plagued Chris when he pictured the man in front of him on his knees, his mouth around his cock. He shivered, excited at the prospect.

"Why don't you sit on the desk, Chris?"

He perched on the edge of the desk, hands balled at his sides. Every nerve in his body hummed with anticipation as he waited to see what Hugh would do next. A ragged exhalation shattered the silence when the other man unzipped his jeans and parted the opening in one smooth motion. Chris's cock sprang to life to meet Hugh's hand when he maneuvered the white briefs under his testicles.

Hugh smiled. "Your cock pleases me. Your size is generous, without being outlandish." He held the shaft in his hand, squeezing gently. "I like your pubic hair too. It's just a shade darker than your brown hair, but not shaggy or unkempt. Perfect."

"Thanks." He barely choked out a response to his master's praise. His penis jutted forward, swaying slightly with each minute movement of Hugh's hand. When he began sliding his cupped hand up and down his cock, Chris moaned. Women had given him hand jobs before, but this was different. He was accustomed to soft hands, tipped with a slight sting of nails extending from feminine fingers. Hugh's hand was solid and muscular, with roughened skin. He also worked Chris's erection with a sense of surety none of his female partners had possessed.

"That's it. Give in to the sensation." Hugh pumped his fist again, alternating the pressure he applied, using more at the base than the tip. "Let yourself come, Chris. Don't be ashamed of your pleasure."

Chris had tipped back his head, but he jerked it up again at Hugh's words. He met the other man's eyes, losing himself in the shadowy gray pools. The master vampire had been correct. He was holding back, embarrassed to find the other man's touch so enjoyable. It was as though the other man's words freed his inhibitions. With a moan that might have been a word if Chris weren't so lost in sensations, he gave in to the pleasure Hugh incited. Spasms rippled through his cock, and hot spurts of semen shot from the head, splashing across the other man's hand. He thrust against the velvet fist enclosing his member until the last drop of arousal flowed from him.

Panting, Chris slumped forward. He was vaguely aware of Hugh releasing his semi-flaccid cock and standing up. It wasn't until the other man's lips brushed against his neck that he realized Hugh was about to feed. An iota of self-preservation almost made him jerk away from the questing mouth, but Chris forced himself to remain still. He had agreed to see to all Hugh's needs.

"Relax." Hugh's statement was a wash of warm air against the bend of his neck that left Chris shaking with renewed desire. A second later, the hot sting of his teeth sliding through Chris's skin made him gasp. A flash of pain accompanied the moment, but quickly faded. The low sounds of Hugh delicately feeding from his lifeblood filled the study, but it was a soothing melody. All Chris's fear and uncertainty drained away, and he surrendered to his master's ministrations, feeling the urge to give Hugh everything.

It seemed much too soon that Hugh had finished. He lifted his head, wiping his mouth discreetly with the back of his hand. His half-smile seemed to make Chris the center of his world, as did the gleam of approval in his eyes. "Very pleasing, Chris."

"Uh, thanks, sir."

"Hugh, remember?"

Chris nodded, too dazed by what had transpired to tell the other man he couldn't think of him as anything so mundane as Hugh. "Yes, sir."

Hugh chuckled, a deep sound that made the touch receptors in Chris's skin vibrate. He patted his cheek. "I think you'll do nicely as my assistant."

"I only want to please you."

His eyes darkened to smoky intensity. "So you have, Chris." His lips were soft and moist against Chris's when he brushed them against his mouth. Hugh seemed as surprised as Chris by the tender gesture when he lifted his head. "I'm sure you will continue to please me."

Chris spoke from his heart, shocked at the words flowing from him. "I'll do anything you want me to, sir." Right then, he wanted to drop to his knees and take Hugh's cock into his mouth, to worship the other man's shaft and try to give him the same degree of pleasure the other man had gifted to him.

Hugh squeezed his shoulder. "I'm happy to hear that. Now, finish your homework and leave me to my paperwork. Sunrise will be here before I know it."

With a nod, Chris left him. Disappointment weighed heavily on him as he closed the door behind himself. He touched his fingertips to the warm wood, feeling bereft. It wouldn't have taken any amount of persuasion on Hugh's part for Chris to continue the sensual exploration of sex with the other man. He briefly wondered if he was now gay, but found he didn't care if he was. There was more to Hugh than he had ever imagined, and Chris couldn't wait to find out everything about the vampire that he could. There were so many ways to make that happen, it made Chris tremble at the possibilities.

Chapter Three

Hugh held off sending for the young man as long as he could, until hunger and desire had worn a hole in his insides that ached for fulfillment. Never before had he denied himself the need for sex or blood. His assistants had always provided a service, and they were interchangeable. Until now. What made Chris so different from the other men, and the few women, who had aided Hugh throughout his long years?

Driven by need and frustration, he used the intercom to page Chris three days after their first encounter. He hadn't yet determined why he was experiencing such tumultuous emotions around the young man, but knew he couldn't wait any longer for sustenance while trying to figure it out. It was disconcerting the way his heart raced the minute the other man tapped on the door of his bedroom. Hugh made his voice gruff to hide his confusing emotions. "Come in." He remained sitting on the huge bed, wearing nothing but a silk robe he had shrugged on after his shower, when Chris entered..

Chris walked forward with eagerness he seemed to want to hide from Hugh. With a smile, Hugh briefly entertaining the thought of telling him he could hear the thunderous rush of Chris's heartbeat, could smell the nervousness and excitement pouring off him. He decided against saying anything, because he had no right to strip bare the other man, to rob him of his protective illusions.

Hugh held out his hand, pleased when Chris took it without a hint of hesitation. Chris knelt on the floor before him, and Hugh's cock twitched with anticipation, as his stomach growled with hunger. The roast beef he'd had for dinner couldn't satisfy his hunger, not in the way sex and blood could.

Chris arched his neck, his lips parted. Hugh turned his head when he realized the man was trying to kiss him. "No." Seeing the hurt confusion cross his face, Hugh softened his tone. He put his hand on Chris's shoulder. "That's too personal. It leads to emotions that I don't want to have to deal with. Do you understand?" At Chris's nod, he cupped his cheek. "I don't want to hurt you."

"I know, sir. I just thought...well, it seemed like the thing to do."

Hugh nodded, knowing he was responsible for the young man's confusion. After all, he had given Chris a spontaneous, if brief, kiss at their last encounter. He still didn't know why he'd done it, so couldn't offer an explanation of his contradictory behavior to the man before him. "It would be if we were in a relationship. Ours is one of business. All I need from you is arousal and blood. It's a simple exchange." He stroked his cheek again. "I can smell your arousal. Does this excite you?"

Chris dropped his head. "Yes, sir. I didn't think it would, but --"

"It's okay to be aroused by what we're doing." As he spoke, Hugh smoothed his hands down Chris's arms.

"I know. It's just, well, there's a woman I'm into. I didn't expect to enjoy this."

Hugh smiled. "It's rare to find work we enjoy." With a gentle motion, he cupped the back of Chris's head to guide it down to his cock. The other man pushed aside the robe to free his erection seconds before sliding his mouth around it. Hugh sighed when Chris's moist mouth took in all of him. His first few bobs were clumsy, but still enjoyable. Hugh tightened his hand in Chris's hair and showed him a steady motion, which he settled into easily. "That feels good. Suck me."

Chris applied suction as he moved his head up and down, finding a pleasing rhythm that made Hugh arch his hips. When Chris swirled his tongue around the head of his cock, Hugh's body tightened as his orgasm started to wash over him. He lifted the hand Chris had braced on his thigh, bringing the wrist to his mouth. As his cock convulsed, releasing spurts of satisfaction, Hugh slid his teeth into the vein. Chris sucked in a long breath around his cock, his body stiffening at the intrusion before relaxing. The change in breathing prolonged Hugh's orgasm, causing him to suck more forcefully than he might have otherwise. Only Chris breaking away from his erection, his face a mask of pleasure and pain, made Hugh aware of what he was doing. He pushed away Chris's wrist roughly. Disconcerted by his loss of control, he reacted badly. "Leave me."

Chris rocked back on his heels. "What? Have I done something wrong?"

"Get out," Hugh snarled, baring his fangs. Regret mingled with satisfaction when he saw Chris's fear as the other man scrambled to his feet and raced from the room. It was only after his lover left that he collapsed against the bed, tears burning in the back of his eyes, with an unsatisfied ache filling his stomach. He tried to tell himself the void was only hunger, but couldn't ignore the telltale emotions swirling through his mind that made the conclusion a lie.

A combination of emotions drove Hugh from his bed in the middle of the night to seek out Chris -- hunger, desire, and remorse. The scent of Chris's body reached his nostrils as soon as he cracked open the door to the guest room where Chris had taken up residence. The mix of musk and heat emanating from his assistant made his mouth water, and the rumble in his stomach increased in intensity.

Hugh glided to the bed, laying the tube of lubricant he'd brought with him on the nightstand as he watched Chris sleep. His motions were tender when he pushed back the covers and slipped in beside Chris. The younger man stirred in his sleep, emitting a soft sigh as he snuggled against him. He smoothed his hands through the fine brown hair covering Chris's head, his long fingers catching in the waves at the nape of his neck. When Chris opened startled brown eyes, Hugh placed a finger against his lips to muffle the cry of surprise.

"Sir?" Chris asked against his finger, his breath a wash of hot air that made Hugh's skin tingle in reaction.

"I need you." As he spoke the words, Hugh acknowledged the deep truth in the statement. Not since his wife's murder during the *Necro sapien* Containment Agency's Paris Raids in 1934 had he felt anything like the need consuming him. It displeased him on one level, to have to deal with the unwanted connection, but on another, it was a happy event. During his time alone, he had become convinced he had burned out on emotion and would never truly feel again. That it should be the young man curled against him inspiring his rediscovery of emotions was surprising. He smiled, trying to ease Chris's apprehension. "Don't be frightened."

He turned his head from Hugh's hand. "I'm not. I'm only confused about why you're in my room."

"As I said, I need you."

"You didn't take enough earlier?" There was anger in his tone, but an underlying note of hurt.

"No." Hugh startled Chris by darting forward to touch his lips to Chris's. The other man stiffened at the intrusion, but his resistance faded quickly. With a moan, Chris relaxed against him, parting his lips to give Hugh access to the inner depths. He swept his tongue inside, exploring the moist recesses. Chris met his tongue thrust for thrust, his enthusiasm for the kiss evident in every move he made.

Hugh's own enthusiasm was almost shocking. By no means had he been celibate since Lynne's death, but there was a vast difference between mechanical sex acts used to induce desire he could feed on and having a meaningful encounter with a partner.

He chuckled, his reverie disrupted, when Chris pushed him into the mattress to climb on top of him. He straddled Hugh, and his grunts of pleasure were more satisfying than any blood meal Hugh had ingested in recent memory.

With clumsy, but energetic, motions, Chris smoothed his hands down Hugh's chest to caress his stomach. His mouth devoured Hugh's, this time with him taking the lead. The experience was so unfamiliar that Hugh didn't think to protest. He relaxed under the other man's passionate onslaught. It was only when Chris caught his tongue on one of Hugh's fangs, and rich blood bloomed in his mouth, that Hugh lost his ability to stay relaxed.

With more haste than finesse, he stripped Chris of his utilitarian white briefs, leaving him naked. He cupped Chris's buttocks, rubbing the other man's cock against his thigh. Ribbons of arousal leaked from the tip, painting Hugh's thigh. His own penis twitched in reaction, swelling fully against Chris's flesh.

"That feels so good, Hugh."

Chris's voice was little more than a rasp, and he had clenched his teeth, giving an appearance of pleasure bordering on torture, as he tried to stay in control. It was the use of Hugh's name for the first time that really caught his attention. A new wave of tenderness washed over him, and he released Chris's buttocks to cup his face, bringing him close enough for another deep kiss.

It was Hugh's turn to groan with pleasure when Chris took his cock into his hand, pumping Hugh from base to tip. Though he'd thought he had attained full arousal, his erection swelled further still when Chris shifted slightly, bringing his penis against Hugh's. It was strange, but exciting, to have a cock rubbing against his, their fluids of arousal mixing together. He thrust his hips without thought, dislodging Chris from his precarious perch.

Chris fell sideways, with Hugh directing his landing. Hugh curled against him, spooning his back. His cock nestled against Chris's buttocks, and he couldn't stop himself from entering him slightly. Only Chris's gasp of mingled pain and ecstasy made him stop and withdraw. He had never made love to another man, having limited previous sexual interactions to hand jobs and oral sex, but inexperience wasn't an excuse to forget lubrication and end up hurting his lover.

Hugh reached for the lube on the nightstand, applying a large glob on his hand. He rubbed it up and down his cock to ensure he was slick enough to penetrate his lover. Then he put his cock against Chris's crack again, pausing. "Do you want me to do this?"

"Yes, please." Chris sounded on the verge of sobbing. If Hugh hadn't heard his heart racing with excitement, hadn't smelled his arousal in the air, he wouldn't have continued. But his own senses reassured him it was okay to move forward. Slowly, with infinite care, Hugh penetrated Chris's ass, holding open his cheeks with one hand, while guiding his cock with the other. The tight bud of his anus tried to resist, but Hugh stretched him inch by hard-won inch, ensuring Chris was moaning only with satisfaction along the way.

Finally, he settled to the hilt inside Chris's ass. The passage was so narrow that Hugh felt nearly too constricted, but he didn't want the feeling the end. It was almost physically painful to withdraw from Chris enough to plunge back inside him. Only when he was fully embedded inside his lover did he feel whole.

Hugh wanted the moment to last forever, but biology overcame his intentions. His rapid thrusts soon brought him to a precipice from which there was no retreat, and he surrendered to his orgasm with a shout of gratification. Liquid burst from the head of his cock, filling Chris's anus with each spasm, eliciting cries from the other man too. Chris hadn't orgasmed, but he seemed close to doing so. As Hugh withdrew completely, he resolved his next action would be to give Chris the same intense release he'd just had.

He scooted backward and turned Chris onto his back. Their gazes locked and held. The awe in Chris's eyes pleased Hugh, and he rolled on top of his lover, kissing him on the mouth before speaking. "Thank you."

A blush suffused the other man's cheeks. "I...you're welcome," he stammered, clearly at a loss.

"You have made me feel things I didn't think I could feel again. After NCA agents killed my wife in the Paris Raids, I thought I had experienced my last tender emotions."

Chris's eyes widened. "I didn't know you were married. I'm sorry about your wife."

"Thank you." Hugh leaned back, finding he wanted to change the subject from Lynne. Thinking of her inevitably brought a hollow ache to the pit of his stomach, and tonight, he wanted to experience happiness, not dwell on sad thoughts.

With that in mind, he slid down Chris's body, until he knelt between his parted legs. His head was perfectly aligned with the other man's cock, and he lowered his head slowly. A mild sense of unease accompanied his initiation into the world of giving instead of receiving, but the desire to please Chris the way he had been pleasured spurred him on. Hugh took the other man's member into his mouth, finding he tasted like salt and sweetness at the same time. Chris's blood roared in his veins, and the steady thump of his pulse through his erection made Hugh groan. Sweat beaded his forehead as he fought back the compulsion to do more than suck on his cock. He wanted to penetrate the delicate flesh and drink from his lover again, but knew it would be a one-sided satisfaction. It was important to satisfy Chris too, so he restrained his vampiric urges. Focused on sucking, he bobbed his head in the same rhythm he had taught several assistants preceding Chris. It was so different to be in this position, but surprisingly enjoyable. It wouldn't make him come to give head to Chris, but his cock was stiffening again.

Chris's manhood throbbed in his mouth in concert with each dip of Hugh's head. The younger man's hips moved like a piston, shooting him forward to meet each caress of Hugh's mouth. His body trembled, and he cried out repeatedly as Hugh sucked him to a fever pitch. With a hard twitch, the first jets of gratification left Chris, and Hugh swallowed them as best he could, milking his lover for every last drop, until Chris was a sobbing heap on the bed.

Gradually, the harsh sound of Chris's breathing faded to a more normal pitch, and his body relaxed. Hugh left his lover long enough to shower and brush his teeth. By the time he returned, Chris had gone to sleep. He stood over him, his heart a warm pool in his chest, watching the other man sleep. Hugh had thought if he ever started to feel again, it would be a sensation akin to the tingling when one's circulation returned to a foot that had fallen asleep. Instead, it was a pleasant warmth that suffused his entire body, giving him a depth of satiation he hadn't experienced at any time in recent memory. It was even enough to blot out the remnants of his hunger for blood.

Eventually, Hugh left Chris to his slumber, knowing he would have to wake in just a few hours for his classes. Not just consideration for the young man had him leaving the bed. He wasn't quite ready to spend the entire night with him. It was one thing to have emotions for the young man, but something entirely different to let those feelings consume him. He wasn't ready for that; after the traumatic way he'd lost Lynne, he didn't know if he would ever be ready for a long-term commitment again, even if Chris wanted one.

Chapter Four

Chris found himself oddly shy around Hugh during the next few days. He answered whenever the other man summoned him, but otherwise, stayed out of his way. He thought he saw hurt reflected in Hugh's eyes more than once, but couldn't be certain. All he knew was the intensity of what he was feeling was freaking him out. He hadn't felt so strongly about anyone before, except maybe Ness. To feel this way about Hugh, another man *and* a vampire, was discomfiting.

Late in the week, he realized he had been avoiding everyone, not just Hugh, when Ness cornered him after physics. She was still as beautiful as ever, with a peaches-and-cream complexion that perfectly complemented her golden hair, but he didn't get the same ache in his stomach that normally assaulted him whenever she looked at him.

"Are you avoiding me?"

Chris shook his head. "No, of course not." She touched his arm, making his heart race, and reassuring him that his feelings for her hadn't faded. "I've just been busy with my new job."

She nodded, the harsh fluorescent light somehow giving her an angelic aura. "You haven't forgotten we're going to study this weekend, have you? Finals in sociology are Monday."

"Of course not." He tried to keep his expression neutral to hide the fact he had forgotten. The situation with Hugh had so consumed his thoughts that he hadn't had time to think of anything else.

"Is it okay if I come to your place? My roommate's boyfriend is visiting this Friday through Sunday." Ness rolled her eyes. "They'll be going at it like bunnies the whole time. I don't think we'll be able to concentrate with that going on."

"Uh…" Chris cleared his throat, managing to nod. "Sure. I'm sure that's fine."

"Great." She squeezed his bicep. "Email me directions, 'kay? I have to get to class."

"Sure," he said again, to her departing back. Her scent lingered, and he breathed in deeply to savor it. The heady aroma of magnolias usually triggered erotic thoughts of rolling with her in white cotton sheets bearing the same scent. This time, his brain conjured up the scent of Hugh's cologne in comparison, and he once again recalled with vivid clarity how good it felt to make love with the other man. He didn't want Ness any less than he had before meeting Hugh, but things had changed in a way he couldn't clearly define.

It wasn't going at all as he'd planned. Chris gnashed his teeth to keep in the angry words wanting to fly out of his mouth as he watched Hugh fawn over Ness. Their study session was supposed to start with pizza in his room, along with subtly dimmed lighting. They were going to transition from books to the bed at some point, at least in Chris's mental script he had created of the evening.

Instead, it had begun with Hugh unexpectedly being home. He usually went out on Saturday nights, so Chris hadn't thought about him being there. He had escorted Ness inside the house, and they had run right into Hugh in the living room. Chris still burned remembering the intense way Hugh had gazed at Ness for half a minute. An uncomfortable silence had grown, and she shifted from foot to foot. Then Hugh seemed to collect himself. He had taken her hand and kissed it in a noble gesture as Chris introduced them.

Somehow, Ness had ended up with her hand tucked into the crook of Hugh's arm, chatting away with him as if they were old friends, while Chris watched in brooding silence. When Hugh invited them to join him for dinner, she had accepted before he could refuse. That was how they ended up in the dining room, once again with Chris silently observing their flirtations. He jumped in surprise when Hugh stood up, placing his folded napkin on the table.

"Well, I must leave you. I know you have studying to do."

Ness leaned toward him, her body language an open invitation. "No, please don't. I'd love to talk more with you."

Hugh hesitated, but shook his head. "I really can't, dear. I have a lot of work to do, and I don't want you to fail your final."

She gave him a pouty look. "I don't care about failing."

He smiled. "Come back next Friday. We'll have the Christmas tree up by then, and the house decorated. It will be an early celebration."

Ness's eyes gleamed with eagerness, and she nodded enthusiastically. As she gushed over the invitation, Chris couldn't help a spark of angry amusement. If she could see her own behavior, he was certain she would be embarrassed. She prided herself on being a young sophisticate, but right now, she was acting like an awestruck ingénue.

Finally, Hugh left them, and he managed to get Ness into his room to study. His mood, already soured, turned dourer yet when she turned up the lights. Chris had left out a stack of slow music that should have put her in a romantic mood. She eyed the CDs with a grimace. "Snoozeville. Don't you have anything lively?"

He struggled to hide his displeasure. "Yeah, in the case." When she selected an *Outkast* CD and loaded it into the stereo, his dwindling hopes for seducing her died. He wanted to believe he would have another chance next week, but it seemed unlikely with the way she and Hugh were all over each other. He was seething with jealously, but the worst part for him was trying to figure out of whom he was jealous. Was he angry with Hugh for capturing Ness's attention, or was he angry with Ness for turning Hugh's head and taking the other man's focus from him? The fact that he had no idea plagued him almost as badly as the ugliness of the envy itself.

When Hugh sent for Chris the next afternoon, he went into the study expecting to provide blood and sex. Instead, Hugh set him to work on a huge stack of filing, which he tackled without enthusiasm. Resentment burned in him still, and he'd been anticipating showing Hugh a measure of his hurt by not responding to his sexual overtures. Now that the other man had failed to make any, his anger flamed hotter, with no outlet. He slammed drawers and tossed around the files with careless disregard for fifteen minutes until Hugh finally spoke.

"Is something wrong, Chris?" he asked in a gentle tone.

"No," said Chris shortly, shoving a file into the drawer with an exaggerated motion.

"Hmm." Hugh fell silent for a long moment before speaking again. "This reminds me of many arguments I had with Lynne. I knew I had done something to displease her, but she would never tell me what."

"Fascinating."

Hugh stood up, walking around the desk to stand beside Chris. He removed the file he had been holding, laying it on the stack. When he took his hand, Chris tried to tug it away, but Hugh held him firmly. "I have obviously angered you. I can't fix the problem until you tell me what I've done wrong."

Looking into his lover's eyes, Chris realized just how petulantly he was behaving. His shoulders sagged, and the tension left his body. "Never mind. It really isn't important."

Hugh squeezed his hand. "If it upsets you, it's important. Tell me what's going on. Please?"

Chris nodded, trying to phrase what he wanted to say. "I was jealous of how you were with Ness."

Hugh put his arm around Chris's shoulders. "I'm sorry. I did not think of your emotions. She is the young woman you mentioned you have feelings for?"

Chris nodded. "But it wasn't just --"

Before he could finish, Hugh took his hand to lead him down the hallway. "I have something to show you."

He held his hand, following without trying to speak again. Curiosity kept him beside Hugh until they reached the other man's bedroom. "What did you want to show me?" It seemed unlikely that Hugh had seduction in mind in light of what they had been discussing, so he didn't understand why they were entering his bedroom.

Hugh released his hand to walk to the armoire. He opened the teak doors to reveal it wasn't an armoire at all. Rather, it was an elaborate case for a full-length oil painting. "Do you see?"

Chris's mouth gaped open. "Ness," he whispered. But it couldn't be. For one thing, the woman in the painting wore a lilac dress reminiscent of sometime in the Victorian era. He walked closer to get a better look. Now he could see differences between the women. The one in the painting had a rounder face, with lower cheekbones. Her lips were fuller than Ness's, and her eyes were a lighter shade of blue. But the noses were practically the same, down to the dusting of freckles across the bridge, and the hair color was almost an exact match, though Ness wore hers layered and straight, while the woman in the picture sported fat ringlets under the lilac and lace hat.

He reached out to touch the painting, but thought better of it. With hand extended in midair, he turned his head to look at Hugh. "Who is she?"

"My wife."

Chris closed his eyes, feeling a pang shoot through him. It made him feel terrible that the twinge was his own pain, not empathy for Hugh. If Hugh wanted Ness because she reminded him of his wife, Chris would never win her. She was clearly enamored with the older man. He felt as though he had already lost her, despite the fact he had never really had her.

"I was...startled by her resemblance. Do you understand, Chris?"

He nodded, gritting his teeth.

Hugh's tone gentled. "No, I don't think you do. I wanted to know your young lady, because for a few moments, I saw the chance to have my wife again. However, it didn't take more than five minutes to realize that couldn't happen."

"Why not?" asked Chris with a frown.

The smile on his face reflected his melancholy. "I can't recapture what is lost, because there is no other woman like my wife, even Ness. She is not Lynne, not even fully in appearance. Your Ness is much different in personality and temperament than my Lynne."

"She's not my Ness." Chris couldn't hide the pain when he added, "She'd like to be yours, though."

Hugh closed the armoire before taking the hand Chris had forgotten he was holding outward. "She was attracted to me, but she is attracted to you too, Chris. If she is what you want, I will do my best to help you win her heart."

Chris dropped his head. "I don't know what I want," he said with a growl of frustration. "I want her...but I also want you. More than I ever expected." He lifted his head finally, losing himself in the silvery pools of his lover's eyes. "I think I'm falling in love with you, Hugh."

Hugh's eyes widened. "I thought I had done something to frighten you. You have been distant when we make love."

He stepped closer, putting his hands on Hugh's shoulders. "I'm so confused. I don't know what to do. This was supposed to be just a job."

"I feel the same." Hugh rubbed his cheek against Chris's hand. "I have never felt anything like this for my other assistants. Only one other time have I experienced such strong emotions, and that was for Lynne." He lifted a hand to cup Chris's cheek. "When I was with her, knew I loved her, I knew I wanted to spend eternity with her. When she offered me immortality to be with her, I had no hesitation." Silence stretched as Hugh seemed to search for words. "After she died, I locked away my heart, because it was safer. I didn't expect you to touch it, Chris. Had I known I would feel something for you, I probably would have sent you away."

That hurt. The words and the thought of never having known Hugh. In an attempt to evade the pain, he reeled away from Hugh, turning his back to hide the shine of moisture in his eyes. He jumped when Hugh put a hand on his shoulder.

"That would have been a mistake," said the other man in a soft whisper. "What I am discovering with you is reawakening me. You are transforming me, even more so than when Lynne transmitted the vampire virus to me." His voice sounded laden with hurt when he continued. "That's why it breaks my heart to think of you leaving me, but I want you to be happy. If your lady will make you happy, then you should pursue her until she is won."

Chris turned, taking the other man into his embrace. "I want...I don't know what I want, except this, right now." He kissed Hugh, probing the other man's mouth with his tongue. He deliberately pierced his tongue on one of Hugh's fangs to dribble blood into his mouth. Hugh's groan rewarded him for the small pain, as did the way the other man's arms enfolded him.

They held each other tightly for a long time, lost in the shared kiss. It varied between gentle and rough, demanding and giving, as the tempo changed. One moment, Hugh led, and the next, Chris was taking charge.

Somehow, they migrated to the bed without Chris being fully conscious of the steps that led them there. All he knew was one minute, he stood with Hugh in his arms, and the next, they were pressed together on the bed, tearing at each other's clothes in a passionate frenzy.

Chris was the first to bare his lover from the waist up, and he took advantage of it by raking his fingers across Hugh's nipples, making him moan. The crisp hair on his chest caught Chris's fingers, as if trying to keep him from ever letting go. He smoothed them gently, before once again scratching lightly over his nipples.

"What are you doing to me?" asked Hugh through gnashing teeth. Perspiration dotted his forehead, trailing down.

"I hope I'm driving you wild." Chris darted forward to catch the drops of sweat before they could reach Hugh's eye. He licked them away prior to moving his mouth lower, to press gentle kisses to his eyelids.

"You are." Hugh removed his polo shirt and tossed it without looking. "Shall I do the same?"

"You already do just by being here." Chris kissed his cheek, moving his mouth toward the other man's ear. Upon reaching his target, he took the lobe into his mouth to suck gently, offsetting the tenderness with a nip that made Hugh jump.

It was Chris's turn to jump when Hugh put his hand into his pants, tearing away the heavy denim as if it were nothing more than the thinnest gossamer. His briefs followed, and the ripping motion Hugh used caused a lingering sting to remain where the elastic had been. Hugh seemed to know, because his hands soothed over the sensitive spots until the pain was gone.

As Hugh caressed him, Chris's cock hardened upward, seeking out his lover's touch. He was moaning and arching astride Hugh. In the back of his mind, he knew he should be reciprocating, but couldn't focus on anything but the feel of Hugh's hand, especially when he engulfed his erection in his palm. Chris bucked his hips in time with Hugh's pumping hand, digging his fingers into the other man's chest hair to anchor himself. Spasms of fluid leaked from his penis as he grew closer to coming, and they splashed onto Hugh's stomach. Chris redoubled his thrusts until hot streams of ejaculate shot from him. "Hugh, oh, Hugh…" There was so much he wanted to say, but didn't have the coherence to voice his thoughts at the moment.

Trembling with the force of his release, Chris forgot to brace his weight and collapsed atop Hugh. The other man held him tenderly, patting his back in small circles as Chris struggled to regain his breath. Finally, the haze of passion faded from his eyes, and he pressed his cheek to Hugh's. "Thank you."

"You're welcome, my love."

Chris started to withdraw, but Hugh tightened his grip. He lifted his head to meet the other man's gaze. "Don't you want to penetrate me?"

With a smile, Hugh shook his head. "Later. For now, I am content to simply hold you."

Chris smoothed his hands over Hugh's chest and stomach. "Are you sure? Don't you need to...eat?"

"Eventually."

Chris tilted his head to offer his neck, but Hugh only placed a gentle kiss to the spot he normally bit before rolling them onto their sides. He lay against his lover, disconcerted by the turn of events. Hugh was by no means a selfish lover, but their encounters had never focused solely on Chris without a blood exchange. Being in Hugh's embrace made him feel loved and protected. At that moment, he never wanted to leave his arms, though part of him still ached for Ness. He still didn't know what to do. He would have to ask Hugh, but it seemed as though the other man was offering him more than their current relationship, maybe even forever together. Did he want to spend the rest of his life...maybe the rest of eternity...with Hugh? Or did he want to pursue Ness at the expense of Hugh's heart?

Torn between his choices, Chris somehow eventually fell asleep. Dreams of the two people in his life whom he loved most followed him.

Chapter Five

The Christmas tree and decorators arrived early the next morning. It was Chris's duty to oversee them while Hugh slept. Chris was used to handling his daily business, but overseeing a design firm as they transformed the elegant home to a resplendent paragon of the approaching holidays was a new experience. He had begun the task without much enthusiasm, but found the decorations had dragged him into a holiday mood by the time the workers left late that afternoon. With the emotional matters weighing on his mind, celebrating Christmas hadn't been a priority, but now he turned his thoughts to presents -- specifically, what would he give Hugh, a man who had everything?

Though he spent the rest of the day thinking about it, Chris didn't come up with a good gift idea for Hugh. By the time his lover joined him in the sitting room where the decorators had erected a twelve-foot fresh pine tree, he decided it was time to stop thinking about it for the time being. Chris greeted Hugh with a kiss, feeling freer than he had in a long time after their talk yesterday. He hadn't yet figured out what he wanted, but knowing Hugh wanted him allowed him to express feelings he'd been keeping inside since their affair began.

"It looks great in here," said Hugh, accepting a cup of hot cider Chris offered from the tray he had prepared a few moments before. "This year's color scheme is surprisingly harmonious. I had doubts when Anne first proposed teal and maroon, but the silver accents really bring it all together."

Chris nodded. When he first saw the decorations going up, he'd been surprised. They weren't the traditional colors he was accustomed to seeing around the holidays, but they were still pleasing, and somehow captured the festiveness of the season.

After sipping the cider, Hugh set it on a coaster on the glass-topped table. One of the decorating staff had strung silver ribbon all around the edge. "Speaking of Christmas reminds me that I haven't asked what your holiday plans are."

Chris shrugged. "What do you mean?"

"Would you like time off?" A small smile creased his lips. "That sounds strange. We hardly have an employee-employer relationship anymore. I guess I should ask if you'll be going away, or if you already have plans?"

He shook his head. "No, nothing. My frat usually throws a party, but I'm going to pass this year." Last year's had been the usual debauchery, but even then, it hadn't appealed to him. Mainly because he'd watched Ness hanging on one of his frat brothers all night, her current boyfriend at the time. With a shrug, he added, "I guess I've outgrown that."

Hugh nodded. "What about family? Won't you be seeing them?"

Chris waved a hand. "Nah. I don't usually bother." He winced. "That didn't sound right. I love my folks, but it's too difficult to visit around Christmas. My dad was in the Air Force, stationed in Germany during most of his term of service. After he retired, my parents stayed there. It's expensive to travel abroad this time of year, so we usually spend a few weeks together in the summer." He imagined introducing Hugh to his parents, but couldn't visualize the meeting properly. They were open-minded and liberal about equal rights for everyone, but he didn't know how they would feel if confronted with their son's involvement in a gay relationship with a vampire. If he decided to spend his life with Hugh, he knew it might take his parents a long time to accept his choice -- but he also knew they would eventually, because they loved him and wanted him to be happy.

"I know Ness is joining us Friday night for dinner, but would you like to invite others for Christmas day? Friends, perhaps?"

Chris shook his head, feeling a little shy. His tongue was thick when he said, "If it's okay with you, I think I'd rather have a quiet day here." The words resounded within him, and he was startled to realize just how at home he felt in Hugh's house, and in such a short time. Was it the warm charm of the house, or did it have more to do with the presence of the other man?

Hugh seemed pleased with the suggestion. "There are a few others I normally spend time with, but I'm certain they will understand me declining their invitation this year." He reached out to take Chris's hand. "I would prefer to spend a festive day with just you."

With a mischievous smile, Chris stepped forward, maneuvering Hugh to the left one step. "Look up?" As the other man tipped back his neck, he leaned forward to press a kiss to the column of his throat. "Mistletoe," he said against the skin.

A chuckle vibrated through his skin, tickling Chris's lips. "So it is." He tipped his head to the side so Chris could burrow into the bend of his neck and shoulder. He shivered when Chris nipped the flesh. He cupped his biceps, lifting his head to kiss Hugh on the mouth. Their nearly equal height served him well, allowing him to angle his hips against the other man's, so that their cocks pressed against each other. The denim of his jeans was a barrier he wanted to tear away, along with Hugh's wool slacks.

Hugh pulled at the hem of Chris's long-sleeve T-shirt, bunching it above his waist. His fingers were slightly cool, but a welcome presence, as he stroked them across his abs. Chris's stomach clenched with anticipation when Hugh's hand slid lower, and he hooked two fingers into the waistband of his jeans.

Determined not to let Hugh do all the seducing this time, Chris focused his attention equally between kissing his partner while simultaneously tugging at his black silk turtleneck to pull it from the slacks. Once it was loose, he let his hands roam freely underneath it, stroking and scratching lightly, enjoying the ripples of Hugh's flesh in response to his touch. He broke the kiss to pull the garment off Hugh, tossing it at the settee, but not bothering to ensure that's where it landed.

His own T-shirt followed quickly, with Hugh's assistance. Once bared from the waist up, he embraced Hugh, holding him in his arms, enjoying the skin-to-skin contact. It was nurturing and exciting at the same time. Hugh made him feel safe and protected, but also desired. It was a delicious confliction that had him wanting to be both rough and tender with his lover.

Following his instincts led Chris to lean forward and take Hugh's lower lip between his teeth. He nipped, applying pressure until Hugh's breath left him in a harsh exhalation. At that moment, he switched tactics, making his tongue an instrument of soothing, running it lightly over the shallow wound he had inflicted.

Hugh retaliated by grasping a handful of Chris's hair and dragging back his head to expose his throat. The wicked gleam in his eyes caused Chris's cock to flutter with a dark thrill of anticipation. A glimpse of fangs was all he caught before his lover's mouth descended. The tip of one fang grazed his throat, and a trickle of warm liquid accompanied the flash of pain. Again, his cock spasmed, and sticky pre-ejaculate spilled from the head, causing his underwear to stick uncomfortably.

He arched his hips, rubbing his cock against Hugh's. His lover couldn't hide his own excitement as evidenced by his raging hard-on pressing against Chris's. With a moan, he stopped teasing Chris with light rasps of his teeth and slid his fangs into the vein thundering under his mouth. Chris emitted a moan of his own, still shocked by how pleasurable it was to be bitten. The first flash of pain wasn't fun, but endorphins and adrenaline flooded his body, and they, along with his piqued desire, made the experience unfailingly erotic each time Hugh bit him.

Somehow, he managed to get his brain to work, albeit sluggishly. Chris fumbled with the leather belt blocking his path to Hugh's penis. When the buckle yielded, he pushed it aside impatiently to tug at the zipper and button. With more gusto than finesse, he dealt with those impediments, and the briefs underneath. Hugh's cock was hard and hot in his hand when he cupped it. He naturally matched the rhythm of Hugh's suckling mouth with his hand, pumping him in an expert fashion. Hot fluid leaked from his erection in steady streams, growing more prodigious as Hugh reached the point of climax. Chris held his breath when he sensed his lover was about to come, applying a scant bit more pressure to the sensitive head.

With a gasp, Hugh pushed him away, freeing his fangs from Chris's throat at the same time he disengaged his hand. "Not like that." His flushed cheeks indicated the blood he had imbued was flowing through his system rapidly, no doubt distributed more quickly than usual by his heightened state of arousal. "I want us to come together."

Chris nodded, wanting the same thing. He undid his jeans with more ease than he had displayed when dealing with Hugh's pants, as Hugh shed his garments, including shoes and socks. Chris matched his motions, until their clothes were an untidy pile of fabric spread across the ecru carpet. When Hugh held out his hand, he took it without hesitation, following him to the sofa.

"Lean forward, knees on the floor."

Chris complied, assuming the position while his stomach churned. His anus convulsed with anticipation, as if grasping for Hugh's cock. His own penis was a rigid shaft almost touching his stomach despite the fact gravity was trying to drag it downward. He couldn't resist stroking himself leisurely while he waited for Hugh to take position behind him. His ass ached for his lover's possession. He wouldn't have believed he could become so wanton so quickly, but here he was, about to be made love to by another man, and it was something he had come to love.

Or should he say loved to come, Chris thought, allowing a small smile to tweak his lips. Hugh was an expert at giving him satisfaction, and he was teaching Chris all he would ever need to know to keep his lover gratified. The idea of an eternity together was somewhat daunting, though he couldn't imagine they would ever become bored with each other physically.

He looked up at a sound, his eyes widening when he saw Hugh reentering the room. "What have you been up to? I didn't know you'd gone anywhere."

"I went for necessities." Hugh showed him a tube of lubricant before walking directly behind Chris, out of his line of sight.

Chris's muscles tensed with anticipation when he heard Hugh getting onto his knees, positioned behind him. The other man's body rubbed against his briefly, just enough to increase his need to a new intensity. His lazy self-pleasuring took on a new edge of need, and he stroked his cock more rapidly still when Hugh inserted the tip of the tube into his back passage to fill him with warm lube.

"None of that," Hugh said, sounding indulgent, as he took Chris's hand and placed it on the couch. "That's my job."

Chris was mildly resentful that he had been denied the added stimulation, but forgot about it when Hugh bent him forward at the waist, his hands positioning him. One remained at the small of his back, while the other parted Chris's buttocks to allow Hugh's erection to slide between them. He found the puckered bud longing for his possession unerringly, his head slowly stretching Chris until his ass parted enough to accept all of Hugh's length. It took a couple of moments for him to adapt, but soon, Hugh had his cock buried deep inside Chris's bowels, slowly fucking him in a rocking motion.

Hands balled into fists, Chris pressed his face into the settee cushion to keep from screaming. He wanted to tell Hugh to go faster, to fuck him hard, but held back -- only because he didn't want the moment to end yet.

The hand Hugh had used to guide his cock into Chris's crevice slipped under Chris, gently squeezing his testicles in an affectionate gesture before grasping his cock. Chris whimpered when Hugh began to pump his hand up and down his cock. The slightly rough skin of his palm exacerbated his arousal, while the soft stroking of his forefinger against the bundle of nerves at the V of his head brought him too close to orgasm too quickly. "No..." He trailed off, unable to verbalize wanted he wanted.

Hugh seemed cognizant of Chris's needs. He slowed his hand, and his cock began to slide deeper inside Chris and take longer to withdrawal. He groaned at the onslaught, tipping back his head, wanting to touch Hugh in every way he could. His lover responded by leaning forward to kiss Chris almost on the mouth. Their position didn't allow for a full kiss, but the contact was enough. In an instant, Chris's desire shifted again, and he began pushing back against Hugh's cock with renewed effort, wanting his lover to ride him hard.

Maybe Hugh was reading his mind. Chris thought he must have some way to sense what he wanted, unless he was just attuned to his body. It should have bothered him to think of the other man reading his thoughts, but he didn't care. In his heart, he knew Hugh would never hurt or betray him, would never use his thoughts against him in a moment of anger. If Hugh was scanning his mind, it was solely to give Chris pleasure.

When Hugh bent him forward even more, pressing his stomach into the settee, Chris turned his head so he could breathe. Wordless cries escaped him as Hugh began pounding into him, stretching his anus in a way that should have hurt, but instead felt only delicious. He didn't slack on massaging Chris's cock, his hand moving so quickly it would have been exhausting for a mortal man to keep the pace. When Hugh's cock quivered deep inside his back passage, Chris's manhood responded in kind, loosing the first spurts of satisfaction across Hugh's hand, against the linen upholstery. It was odd how their cocks spasmed in time with each other, their breathing synched; even their inhales and exhales corresponding. He had never experienced anything like it.

As Hugh gently withdrew from him before leaning forward to hold him, the two of them resting in the same position, Chris thought it was the most wonderful moment of his life. He couldn't imagine sex without this synchronicity now that he'd had it once. Did that mean he couldn't find satisfaction with anyone other than the man holding him? Or did it simply mean Hugh had shown him what making love should be, and he couldn't settle for anything less ever again?

Chapter Six

Despite how far he had come in the week toward making a decision, hovering as he was on the edge of committing to Hugh if the other man blatantly offered it, Chris still couldn't control his physical and emotional reaction when Ness took off the faux fur coat that Friday evening, seconds after he let her in. Black velvet pants encased her coltish legs, hugging them so tightly he could see the dimples in her knees, along with the perfect formation of her calves and shins, encased in leather boots. She had paired the sexy pants with an even sexier sweater. It was a tunic, flaring at her hips and ending mid-thigh. The red cashmere had a plunging neckline trimmed with white feathers, and it was so snug on her breasts he could immediately discern she wore a push-up bra. The sleeves, also fringed with white feathers, ended at her wrists, and when she pulled at the cuffs, the neckline inched down precariously, displaying even more of her generous cleavage.

He had never seen her dressed so blatantly sexual before, and it was obvious she had seduction in mind. Chris didn't try to fool himself into thinking he was the target of her manipulations. It was almost physically painful to smile at her, talk normally, and lead her into the dining room as though he had no cares in the world. Inside, he was a howling mass of anger and fear. He didn't want to lose her, and much as he hated to feel that way, he couldn't help a measure of resentment directed at Hugh for diverting Ness's attention from him. It had seemed like they were finally progressing from more than just friends until the other man came between them.

Chris tried to dismiss his thoughts, not wanting to be jealous of Hugh. He understood the other man's interest in Ness, and he also knew Hugh didn't want her the same way he did. Maybe he was physically attracted to her, but he didn't want an eternity with Vanessa Shaye. He wanted that with Chris, even though he hadn't yet acknowledged the open invitation or given Hugh any kind of firm response. That made him feel worse, and it was all he could do to sit at the table, trying to work up some enthusiasm for eating, after rolling out the serving table loaded with food Hugh's housekeeper had prepared earlier in the day.

The roast duck, pecan stuffing, and green beans almandine were excellent, but he could muster little appetite. Chris watched Ness flirting with Hugh, leaning forward to touch him, laughing in a high-pitched, sparkling tone that grated on his nerves. If it had been in response to something witty he had said, he didn't doubt it would have inspired a completely different reaction. His ability to make conversation seemed nonexistent -- perhaps the sodden lump of duck lodged firmly in his throat prevented the words' escape.

Ness turned her bright blue eyes to him, making Chris feel like he was choking even more. He took a long swallow of the wine as she said, "So, what do you do for Hugh?"

He tried to picture her reaction if he answered truthfully, but couldn't conjure how she would take it. Ness was a member of the VCLU, and she was a liberal, but that didn't mean she would be ready for the truth, especially considering she had her eye on Hugh. Instead, he shrugged. "Whatever needs doing. Anyone could do my job."

Hugh leaned across the table to put a hand on Chris's shoulder, giving a light squeeze before releasing him. "Do not be so modest, Chris. You're indispensable to me." His eyes spoke volumes that he left unvoiced as he turned to Ness. "I don't think I could get by without Chris."

Ness seemed unable to look away from Hugh's gaze. "Really? Does your wife...girlfriend feel the same way?" Her tone revealed it was a not-so-subtle question.

With a slight hesitation, Hugh shook his head. "No wife, and no girlfriend. Just me...and Chris. I depend upon him greatly."

Once again, she turned to Chris, flashing him a thousand-watt smile. "Chris is the dependable type."

He barely stifled a groan. No doubt, Ness meant it as a compliment, but it made him sound as interesting as aged tofu. It would have been better to hear her describe him as reckless or dangerous. Even excessively tardy would have been a better "accolade."

With a non-committal sound, Hugh stacked his dishes and rose to his feet to place them on the serving tray. Ness immediately followed suit, and Chris managed to pry himself from the chair and do the same. Without asking, he started pushing the tray back toward the kitchen, pausing when Hugh touched his arm.

"Bring coffee, if you don't mind. We'll have some in the sitting room. Perhaps with a snifter of cognac?"

Chris nodded, wondering what the mysterious gleam in his lover's eyes heralded as he did so. In the thoroughly modern kitchen, he brewed premium Columbian coffee and placed the silver coffee set on its salver. The coffee machine worked quickly, and he soon had the tray ready to take into the sitting room. His stomach fluttered with nerves as he approached the room. The flashing lights from the Christmas tree illuminated the hall, but made it difficult to see much in the otherwise unlit room when he stepped across the threshold.

Chris's hands shook, and he barely set down the coffee without spilling it when he saw Ness sitting on the cream settee where he and Hugh had made love the other night. The red of her sweater was a marked contrast to the linen upholstery, but that observation didn't hold his attention. Instead, he couldn't look away from the sight of Hugh bending over Ness, his mouth at her neck. He almost blurted out a warning to Ness that Hugh was about to bite her. A moment later, relief flooded him. Thank goodness he hadn't spoken. Hugh wasn't biting her. His lips were exploring her neck in a slow, sensual kiss.

It felt like someone had punched him in the gut, and it took all of his self-control not to launch into a tirade directed toward Hugh. How could the other man do this to him after everything he had said? Hugh had sworn he didn't see Ness as a replacement for Lynne, had even offered to help Chris capture her heart if that was what he wanted. It was suddenly clear just what Hugh's words were worth. Nothing. He'd probably lied about his feelings for Chris too, just to get more of a reaction from him so he didn't need as much blood.

A red haze had descended over his eyes, so it took Chris a moment to realize Ness was waving to him. He arched a brow. "Do you need something?" His voice was an arctic wind that should have served to cool their ardor, but Hugh never lifted his head, and Ness seemed just as into the experience as she had a moment ago.

She smiled, a slow, seductive stretching of her lips that revealed a marvel of orthodontia. "Come join us."

He blinked, certain he had misheard her. "What?"

Ness shook her head, dislodging Hugh. He remained bending over the back of the settee, but looked up at Chris. His gaze seemed to be conveying the same invitation Ness had issued. She spoke again, patting the cushion beside her. "Don't be obtuse, Chris. You must know what I want."

His feet started moving even though his brain seemed frozen. "I...no..."

She sighed, but seemed amused. "I learned something interesting in my last biology class. Did you know female sheep just stand in the middle of a field waiting for a male sheep to come by and fuck them?"

He shook his head, completely baffled by where she was going with the information.

"Sometimes, a ram gets confused and does the same thing. He just stands around waiting for the female to become the aggressor. If you get two animals of a like mind together, they'll both stand there all day, wasting time waiting for the other one to approach them. Not much happens, except they both get frustrated."

He was beginning to see where she was leading him, but still couldn't quite comprehend it. "That isn't possible. Why would you be waiting for me?"

Ness rolled her eyes, trading a look with Hugh that made her giggle. "Because I'm a silly sheep, sweetie. I knew you wanted me, so I kept waiting for you to make the first move. If it weren't for Hugh, I'd probably still be waiting on you."

Chris stopped before them, hovering just out of touching distance of either of them. "What does Hugh have to do with anything?"

"He's the one who persuaded me to tell you how I feel. Said you'd probably never tell me, because you thought I couldn't possibly want you." She shook her head. "Where'd you get an idea like that?"

His mouth seemed to work on autopilot. "I'm nothing like the men you've gone out with in the past."

"Precisely, which is one of the many reasons I want you."

It was his turn to shake his head. He would never understand how women thought. "If you want me, then why was he kissing you?"

Ness's stare centered on him, and she seemed to be trying to hide a streak of embarrassment. "I want him too. I want both of you...at the same time."

As she spoke, the words resonated within Chris. She had verbalized his own desires. In this scenario, there would be no choosing between Hugh and Ness. He could have them both. His cock hardened at the thought, and he found himself closing the distance between the three of them to take a seat beside Ness. Hugh placed a hand on each of their shoulders, and he looked up at the other man, trying to project all that he was feeling with just his gaze. Hugh responded by squeezing his shoulder, and the gesture conveyed more than Chris could have imagined.

He moved first, taking Ness's hand in his. The simple contact made his heart race, and when Hugh bent to kiss his neck, it pounded out a rapid staccato. Head tipped back, he watched Ness from the corner of his eye to see her reaction to Hugh touching him. She watched with wide eyes, her mouth agape. She seemed on the verge of saying something, but closed her mouth. Chris's nerves tightened, and he wondered if she would rebuff them. He knew instinctively that he would reject her if she reacted negatively or said anything to hurt Hugh.

After a hesitation, Ness leaned forward to kiss the other side of his neck. The tension faded, and he relaxed, eyes closed, as both of them nibbled and sucked lightly on his sensitive skin. At some point, Ness moved her mouth higher, sweeping up his neck to place her mouth against his. Her breath was sweet and smelled of cinnamon. He wondered how she had accomplished that in light of the dinner they had just eaten, but the thought fled when her plump red lips touched his. He molded his mouth to hers, letting her set the pace of the kiss.

While she tentatively explored his mouth with her tongue, Hugh was busy coming around the sofa to kneel in front of them. He began unbuttoning Chris's shirt, and when he had pushed it open, Ness put a hand on his chest. Chris tangled one of his hands in her hair, pulling her closer in order to deepen the kiss. His other hand settled on the back of Hugh's head to bring him close too. Hugh rested his head against Chris's chest, his tongue sweeping out to lathe one of his nipples. He caught his breath at the sensations overwhelming him, and she used the opportunity to slide against him, pushing her tongue deeply into his mouth. Chris responded to her brazen strokes with his own, meeting each parry and thrust of her tongue as she swept it around his mouth.

"Oh." He moaned when Hugh bit his nipple. Chris was aware of Hugh moving his hands lower, to unfasten his slacks, and he thrust his hips upward. Doing so dislodged Ness, sending her sprawling across his lap, with Hugh's hand trapped between them. "I can't believe this is happening."

Ness nodded, laying her head on his shoulder. "Me neither."

Hugh didn't speak; he just continued with his self-appointed task to undress Chris. Ness made no effort to move off his lap, seeming to enjoy the way Hugh lifted and pushed against her in his quest to remove Chris's pants. He made a soft sound of satisfaction when the slacks yielded to him, and he peeled them away. Once again, Chris lifted up so the pants and briefs would slide down his body. The linen felt cool and smooth against his buttocks when he sat down again.

Ness had turned her head to watch Hugh's progress, and she smiled when he dispensed with the shoes and socks quickly before fully removing Chris's garments, then his own. "You're good at that."

Hugh looked up, a half-smile twisting his lips. "I've had some practice."

She extended a long, shapely leg to him, wiggling the toe of her high-heeled leather boot. It was an unspoken invitation he accepted without hesitation. Chris watched as Hugh peeled off one boot before tackling the other. He held his breath, waiting to feel a dart of jealousy, or maybe a pang of envy, but none came. All he experienced was arousal and joy that he had both people who meant the most to him with him right then. Even when Hugh had dealt with the boots and brought his hands to the waistband of Ness's velvet pants to pull them down, he wasn't jealous. The pants fell by the wayside, revealing her red satin thong. It excited him to see Hugh's paler hands against Ness's tanned buttocks when he cupped them, kneading lightly.

She moaned, tossing her long hair while wiggling her hips. Hugh continued caressing her as he shifted her position on Chris's lap, until she was straddling him. Chris took advantage of the new angle to lift the hem of her sweater and pull it over her head. His cock twitched, encountering the smooth skin of her bare thigh, when he saw the satin bra underneath. The deep red color was both festive and a perfect match for her panties. His hands shook lightly when he put them on her back, searching for the hooks.

Ness giggled, writhing on his lap when Hugh slid a hand down her ass to caress her slit through the panties. Chris could feel his hand moving slowly, and he experienced a twinge of envy that Hugh was touching her, but it wasn't bitter. It would be his turn soon enough. "Look in front, love."

He brought his hands around her chest, cupping her breasts. He couldn't wait any longer to touch them, even just long enough to find the release to her bra. She whimpered when he thumbed her hard nipples through the satin. "That feels so good, Chris."

He jumped with surprise when Hugh grasped his cock in his hand, his thumb pointed up. "Ah, God." Chris's eyes widened when the other man began pumping his cock. Each thrust of his hand upward brought his thumb against Ness's clit, and she was soon squirming on his lap in a writhing heap, crying out both their names.

Chris tried to hold off his orgasm. In an attempt to distract himself from the delicious sensation of Hugh giving him a hand job while fingering Ness, he returned his focus to the bra. The clasp was tricky, and he was near cursing when he finally wrestled it open. Sweat from the exertion beaded his forehead, and he wiped it on his forearm before returning his hands to her breasts. They had been firm under the satin, but the fabric couldn't compare to the natural silkiness of her soft skin. Once again, he rubbed his thumbs against her nipples, making them harden even further. She sobbed when he scratched her lightly, as Hugh pushed against her clit.

Unable to stop himself, Chris lifted her off his lap, bending his head to taste one of her breasts. She tangled her hand in his hair when he licked her nipple, pushing his face against her skin. Chris took the bud into his mouth, sucking forcefully. His body spasmed in reaction to Hugh pumping his cock, and he climaxed without meaning to when she wriggled against his cock and Hugh's hand. Chris bit down without thought, making her cry out. In a panic, he withdrew, but the ecstasy contorting her expression revealed she had enjoyed it.

To his surprise, Chris maintained his erection. He looked up, over Ness's shoulder, when Hugh cupped his cock again, this time guiding him to the sweet heat of her pussy. His head hovered at the entrance of taking her, and he reached around Ness to take Hugh's hand, wanting the other man to be part of the moment completely. With a smile, Hugh broke the touch to caress Ness's hips. She was a willing participant when he slid her down Chris's cock, moans of pleasure escaping her.

"Baby." Even Chris wasn't sure which of his lovers he addressed with the endearment. The liquid heat of her pussy engulfed his cock, and when she rocked against him, he groaned. His shaft was already sensitive from the orgasm he'd just had, and each thrust of her slit against him seemed likely to drive him over the edge.

But he didn't want to go without Hugh. Chris grasped Hugh's arm, pulling him as close against Ness as he could get the man. She leaned back against him, continuing to ride Chris even when Hugh removed his hands from her hips to cup her breasts. Almost empathically, he shared in the pleasure each of his lovers received, and it fed his own. Before he could stop it, his cock convulsed deep inside Ness, and he came with their names on his lips.

Without missing a beat, Ness lifted herself off him, bracing her knees on the couch, and offering Hugh the opening Chris had just filled. As Hugh knelt slightly to align himself, Chris gripped his forearms, holding him tightly.

Ness cried out with pleasure when Hugh penetrated her, and Chris leaned back to allow them more room. Ness leaned against him, with Hugh following, glued to her back. The new position allowed Chris to wrap his arms around Hugh, and they embraced Ness between them. Hugh thrust into her forcefully, and she arched back to meet each plunge of his cock into her pussy. Chris held them both, alternating between kissing Ness's neck and holding Hugh's gaze. He could feel the tension building between both of them, and pulled them closer.

With a low groan, Ness shuddered on his lap, her body convulsing with her release. Hugh uttered a harsh moan of his own as he pushed deep inside her. While he hovered on the edge of coming, just before release, Chris stretched forward to place his mouth against Hugh's. He captured the hoarse cry of satisfaction his lover loosed when his body jerked with satisfaction, and then penetrated Hugh's lips with his tongue. Ness was still between them, her mouth buried against Chris's chest, while her tongue traced leisurely circles over his skin.

They remained in that position for what might have been hours. Chris had lost track of time. He was only aware of the proximity of his lovers, of their bare skin -- Ness's warm in contrast to Hugh's cooler flesh. At some point, Hugh withdrew from Ness, somehow shifting the three of them onto the floor, where they lay in a sprawled, tangled heap. Satiation made his body limp, and the trendy angel atop the tree was the last sight his fluttering eyes took in before they closed when he fell asleep.

Chapter Seven

"Now what?" he asked sometime later. They had shifted at some point so that he cradled Ness in his arms, and Hugh spooned him, his arm draped over his and Ness's hips.

She stretched, and a yawn partially distorted her answer. "I could go for a shower, a comfortable bed, and more loving...not necessarily in that order."

"That all sounds good, but it wasn't what I meant." He hesitated, wondering if it was too soon to be talking about the thoughts on his mind. "I was thinking beyond the moment."

"Oh." Ness shrugged. "Why worry about it now?"

He turned his head to look at Hugh as the other man sat upright to brace himself on his elbow. "I owe someone an answer." Chris frowned. "That is, if you were asking what I thought you were?"

He brushed a strand of hair off Chris's face. "Was I asking you to spend your life with me?" Hugh nodded. "I'd like nothing more, but you have to make the decision that's right for you." His fingers were soft as silk when he caressed Chris's cheek. "I only want you to be happy."

Ness shifted in his arms, rolling away so she could sit upright. Her expression mirrored her uncertainty. "What's he talking about, Chris?"

It was difficult to meet her eyes, even knowing she shared his attraction. After making love with her, he still had no idea how she really felt about him, other than she desired him. "Until I came to work for Hugh, you were the only person I thought about. You were on my mind all the time, and I went over and over how I could get you to feel the same way. I loved you so much it was killing me not to have you."

She frowned. "You talk like that's changed. Don't you still love me?"

He reached out, taking her hand. "Yeah, I do…but I love Hugh, too." Sighing, Hugh shook his head. "I don't know how I'm ever going to choose."

Hugh's arm around his shoulder was solid support. "You know how I feel, but it has to be about how you feel. Listen to your heart."

Chris shook his head again. "My heart's telling me something I can't have."

"What's that?" asked Hugh.

He looked up, first at Hugh, and then at Ness. "I want both of you."

A smile crossed Ness's full lips. "Who says you can't have what you want?" She leaned forward, getting onto her knees so she could scoot closer to him. Her arms settled over Hugh's around his neck. "Why can't you have us both?"

He inhaled her scent, closing his eyes to focus on his thoughts. "It's not that simple. I want both of you, but not just sexually. I want more than sex. I love you both."

Ness slid her fingers through the hair at his temple. He opened his eyes at the soft touch. "I love you too, Chris, and I think Hugh and I could have a special bond eventually. We both love you so much, and we're attracted to each other. Who says it can't work?"

"Nobody would understand. We'd have to hide our relationship."

Ness shook her head. "Who cares what people think? All that matters is we're all happy with the situation. I'm willing to try if you both are."

Eyes wide, Chris nodded. He couldn't believe she was so accepting of the situation. Could he really be so lucky as to have both of the people he loved with him forever?

Before he could get his hopes too high, Hugh spoke. "You have to know everything before you can commit to this idea, Ness."

Chris's stomach felt like it dropped into his ankles. How could he have forgotten his lover was a vampire, an immortal, and that making a life with him meant quite a bit more than it did to other couples committing to each other? He'd had a chance to get used to the idea, and it didn't frighten him to face becoming a vampire. It seemed unlikely that Ness would be so eager to make the decision she was suggesting once she knew everything.

"Chris?" Hugh nudged verbally.

He met the other man's eyes, nodding. It was with a sense of impending doom that he took Hugh's hand in one of his, and Ness's in the other. The revelation had to come from Hugh, and he held his breath while waiting for him to begin.

Ness looked confused and frightened, her gaze darting between the two of them. "What's going on? You two are freaking me out."

Chris squeezed Hugh's hand to offer silent support. However Ness reacted, he knew he couldn't bear to part from the man beside him. If he couldn't have both of them, he would stay with Hugh and still be happy.

"You know Chris and I met because he came to work for me as my assistant, yes, Ness?" At her nod, he continued. "He performs myriad duties for me, including sustenance."

She frowned. "What? I don't understand."

Hugh opened his mouth, and his fangs were clearly visible. "I am a vampire."

Chris's heart sank at the way she recoiled. "Ness --"

She pulled free of his hand. "He's a necro, and you knew it, Chris? Why didn't you tell me?"

"Don't use that word," he said more sharply than he intended.

Tears sparkled in her eye. "He could have hurt you, killed you, and I never would have known what happened to you. How could you be so reckless?"

"I can see how far your ideals extend." He shook his head, having trouble hiding his disgust. "Why are you a member of VCLU? You clearly don't believe in equality for vampires."

Her eyes widened, and her gaze cut to Hugh. Ness groaned. "Oh, I'm so sorry. I didn't mean --"

"Save it," snapped Chris. "You've already shown how you really feel. I think you should leave." He turned to Hugh when the other man placed a hand on his shoulder. "I'm sorry I brought her into your life, endangered you."

Hugh put a finger to his lips. "Shush, love. You are overreacting." He pressed more firmly when Chris tried to speak. "Her concern was for you. Did you not hear her? She is not rejecting me, Chris. She responded simply from the thoughts that came to her, regarding your safety, and how she would feel without you."

With a frown, Chris turned his head to look at Ness. She was huddled into a miserable ball, her head bent forward. "Tell me honestly how you feel now, Ness."

She lifted her head, confusion clear in her eyes. "I don't know. I want to be with you, but I'm frightened."

"I will never hurt you," said Hugh.

Ness hesitantly reached out to touch the back of his hand, still clasped in Chris's. "I know that. What I don't know is what you both expect from me. Where do I fit into the picture now?"

"Where you did before. You can be with us in whatever capacity you choose." Hugh withdrew his hand from Chris's, putting Ness's hand in its place. "We both love Chris. That doesn't mean we have to love each other. That might grow in time, if you choose to join with us." He shrugged. "Or maybe you and Chris will be together without me."

"No," said Chris. The answer came to his tongue without thought or hesitation. "I don't want to be without you."

Hugh smiled at him. "Does that mean you want to be like me?"

Before he could answer, Ness said, "A vampire? You're going to make him a vampire?" Fear showed in her eyes again, and she squeezed his hand. "You don't have to do this, Chris."

A spark of anger flared, but he pushed it down, knowing concern prompted her words. "I want to. I can't imagine being without Hugh now that I've found him. I feel the same way about you, and I want you with me, but I would never force you to do something you don't want to. You don't have to become a vampire to be with us."

Her body sagged with relief. "I...it's not that I won't someday...maybe...I, uh..." She trailed off, biting her lower lip.

Hugh reached out, pushing the hair out of her face. "When, or if, you are ready to become immortal, you will have that option."

She nodded. "Okay." Her glance shifted to Chris. "When are you going to do this?"

"Soon." His nerves jangled at the thought, but he was resolute in his decision. "Whenever Hugh is ready, so am I."

"I leave the decision to you."

Ness surprised Chris with her next question. "Can I be there? I've heard a new transformation requires a lot of blood."

Hugh seemed as surprised as Chris. "It is true he will need to feed within hours of the change. Are you offering your services?"

The way her body trembled betrayed her nervousness, but she nodded. Her expression was set. "Yes. I want to be there for him, however he needs me."

Hugh turned to Chris. "Are you ready?"

He blinked. "Now?"

With a shrug, Hugh asked, "Why not?"

Ness put her hand on his thigh. "Whatever you want, Chris."

After a hesitation, he nodded. "Yeah, I'm ready."

Hugh leaned back to sit on his calves. "It hurts some, but will be easier if you are aroused. Do you feel up to this?"

He nodded again, feeling confident in his decision.

"Come sit in front of me, facing toward Ness." Chris positioned himself in front of Hugh as requested. "Ness, come to Chris, facing toward him." She complied, and they were soon sitting together, the three of them in a formation that somehow gave the feeling they were preparing for a ritual.

Hugh leaned forward, embracing Chris. His mouth was close to his ear, and he whispered, "Touch her breasts, Chris. They are so beautiful."

Chris reached out to cup one of Ness's breasts, and she arched her back to allow him to hold more of her. Her nipple was hard and firm under his thumb when he pressed against it.

"Kiss her," said Hugh, and he leaned forward to touch his mouth to hers. Ness parted her lips, and he swept his tongue inside, thrusting in a gentle motion that mimicked the one Hugh initiated when he grasped his penis. Ness moaned when he flicked his fingernails across the sensitive bud, and her passion increased his own. His cock grew even harder in Hugh's hand, and he bucked his hips.

"Lay her down, Chris," said Hugh in his ear.

Chris leaned forward, taking Ness with him. Hugh released his erection to grasp his hips, keeping them up. "Kiss her breasts, Chris, and then taste her pussy."

It was erotic to have Hugh direct his actions, and he did as the other man suggested, taking the breast he had neglected into his mouth. Ness moaned, arching her hips, when he sucked the nipple forcefully. With his other hand, he continued to roll her nipple in his fingers.

He was vaguely aware of Hugh moving behind him, and when the other man put the head of his cock against his anus, Chris stretched backward to meet him. The shaft was slick, probably from the lube they had left in the sitting room last time, and he entered Chris slowly. It made every inch of his body tighten with pleasure, and he squeezed Ness's breast without thought. Her whimper of pain made him let go, and to make amends, he slid his mouth down her breast, across her stomach, and toward her pussy. Hugh kept pace with his movements, matching his new position seamlessly.

"Please." She grasped his hair to push his head down the last half-inch, forcing his mouth against her slit. Chris slipped his tongue inside her, licking her clit. She tasted salty, but sweet, and her heat almost burned his tongue. He circled the appendage around her clit, making her cry out. His questing tongue explored her slit fully, sliding into her slick opening as Hugh thrust in and out of him. Unconsciously, he mimicked Hugh's thrusts with his tongue, darting in and out of her. Her body shook, and she said his name around a sob of pleasure as he increased the tempo. Chris could feel her straining toward orgasm, and he shared her frustration. His body ached for release, but his cock received no stimulation.

Hugh suddenly put his hand against Chris's cheek, turning his mouth away from Ness's pussy. "Drink." When he pressed his wrist to Chris's mouth, tangy liquid flowed onto his tongue. It was hot and salty, like the taste of Ness, but with an underlying coppery taste and scent that identified it as blood. Queasy at the thought of consuming blood, he forced the reality from his mind, instead turning himself over to instinct and swallowed on autopilot.

Hugh pulled his wrist away, bringing his hand back to Chris's cock and began pumping it again as he thrust inside him. Chris turned his head back to Ness, once again focusing on bringing her to orgasm. He licked and sucked her clit before darting his tongue deep into her opening. As Hugh thrust into him, while working his cock in his palm, Chris moaned against her pussy, which made her whimper.

Everything seemed to happen at once. Hugh's erection swelled inside him and began spasming. At the same time, Ness's pussy convulsed, and she dug her fingers into his scalp while calling his name. Her frantic thrusts against his face told him she was coming as much as the rush of arousal she loosed onto his tongue.

Hugh withdrew from him, bending over him to put his mouth against Chris's neck. His teeth penetrated his skin, and the pleasure/pain made him jump. As his lover drank deeply from him, he continued to stroke his cock until Chris couldn't stand another moment. His stiff erection tightened further, and his hips arched against Hugh's hand. Finally, Chris let his own release wash over him, his shaft convulsing in Hugh's hand as he came.

The fangs leaving his skin left a little sting, but Chris barely noticed it. His head spun, and his vision was blurry. Blackness washed over him, and he slumped against Ness, his cheek pressed against her thigh. Hugh was saying something, but he couldn't make out the words. A floating sensation filled him, carrying him farther away from the voices. He hovered on the brink of a void, preparing to throw himself into it.

The sharp sound of Ness's voice brought him back. Chris blinked, and his eyes focused on Hugh, bent close to him, their faces inches apart. "Hugh?" His voice was a rusty rasp.

He seemed relieved. "I thought we had lost you for a moment. You need to drink now."

"What?"

"Drink," said Hugh with exaggerated pronunciation.

A weak laugh escaped him. "I heard you. I don't know what you want me to drink."

"Me," said Ness. She smoothed his hair with her hand before turning his head so that his mouth was against her thigh. "Drink some of my blood, love."

Weakness made him feel sluggish and weighed down, but his senses were still sharper than they had ever been before. He could hear Ness's blood thundering in her veins, making it easy for him to hone in on the one closest to his mouth. He traced it with his tongue, feeling her shiver in response. As he did so, his new fangs descended, cutting into his lower lip until he opened his mouth. Her skin was warm and sweet, and his teeth penetrated her flesh easily. He heard her groan, and it didn't have the same note of pleasure as he'd heard before. Knowing he was hurting her made him stop.

"Keep going," she said, sounding as though she spoke through gritted teeth.

"Don't stop yet, Chris. You're hurting her a little, but you need her blood. When you learn more, you'll know how to give her pleasure instead of pain."

With their encouragement, he drank from Ness, swallowing her blood as quickly as he could. The taste had changed, no longer having the sharp, coppery taste that Hugh's blood had. It was sweeter than ambrosia, richer than the best wine, and he understood how vampires could stand to consume it for an eternity. It took every ounce of self-control to pull away when Hugh told him to stop.

The weakness had fled, and he rolled over, sitting up in one smooth motion.

"How do you feel?" asked Ness as she discreetly pressed her hand to the wound he'd made in her thigh.

"Amazing...alive..." He trailed off, unable to articulate just how the transformation had changed him.

"Do you have regrets?" asked Hugh.

Chris paused. "Just one."

His lover's face crumpled. "What is it?"

He smiled, taking Hugh's hand. "I regret that I can never give you a gift as amazing as you've given me. Thanks to you, I have found the loves of my life, and that life will last forever. I can't ever do something as wonderful for you."

Hugh laughed, drawing Chris into his embrace, while Ness curled against him. "Don't be silly. You've given me your heart, Chris. What better gift is there than that?"

Chris silently agreed as he laid his head on Hugh's shoulder. He'd received so much to be thankful for this

Christmas. With his two lovers curled against him, he watched the twinkling lights on the tree, feeling a warm glow that had nothing to do with the decorations or impending holiday, and everything to do with Hugh and Ness. He couldn't imagine being happier than he was at that moment, and to know that happiness would last forever was overwhelming. He found himself unable to speak, to verbalize all that he was feeling, but it was unnecessary. They already knew.

~ * ~

Kit Tunstall

Kit Tunstall lives in Idaho with her husband, son and two spoiled dogs who think they are human. She started reading at the age of three and hasn't stopped since. Love of the written word, and a smart marriage to a supportive man, led her to a full-time career in writing. Romances have always intrigued her, and erotic romance is a natural extension because it more completely explores the emotions between the hero and heroine. That, and it sure is fun to write.

NOW AVAILABLE In Print from Loose Id®

HARD CANDY
Angela Knight, Morgan Hawke and Sheri Gilmore

HOWL
Jet Mykles, Raine Weaver, and Jeigh Lynn

DANGEROUS CRAVINGS
Evangeline Anderson

COURTESAN
Louisa Trent

LEASHED: MORE THAN A BARGAIN
Jet Mykles

ALPHA
Treva Harte

Publisher's Note: The print titles listed above were previously released in e-book format by Loose Id®.

NEW! Non-fiction from Loose Id®

PASSIONATE INK:
A GUIDE TO WRITING EROTIC ROMANCE
ANGELA KNIGHT

Printed in the United States
148069LV00002B/16/A

9 781596 325180